A Home for Friendless Women

KELLY E. HILL

A Home for Friendless Women

Kelly E. Hill has a PhD from the University of
Louisville and an MFA in fiction from Spalding
University. She lives in Louisville with her family.
A Home for Friendless Women is her first novel.

A Home
for Friendless
Women

KELLY E. HILL

Vintage Books
A Division of Penguin Random House LLC
New York

A VINTAGE BOOKS ORIGINAL EDITION,
MARCH 2024

Library of Congress Cataloging-in-Publication Data
Names: Hill, Kelly E., 1979– author.
Title: A home for friendless women: a novel / Kelly E. Hill.
Description: New York: Vintage Books, [2024] |
Identifiers: LCCN 2023019588 (print) |
LCCN 2023019589 (ebook) |
ISBN 9780593685815 (trade paperback) |
ISBN 9780593685822 (ebook)
Subjects: LCGFT: Novels.
Classification: LCC PS3608.I43453 H66 2024 (print) |
LCC PS3608.I43453 (ebook) | DDC 813/.6—dc23/eng/20230602
LC record available at https://lccn.loc.gov/2023019588
LC ebook record available at https://lccn.loc.gov/2023019589

**Vintage Books Trade Paperback ISBN: 978-0-593-68581-5
eBook ISBN: 978-0-593-68582-2**

Book design by Nicholas Alguire

vintagebooks.com

Printed in the United States of America

To the real-life women and children of the Home.
I think of you often.

Author's Note

A Home for Friendless Women is a historical novel based on a nineteenth-century institution by the same name that took in pregnant unmarried women and sought to "rehabilitate" them through hard work and Christianity. I learned about the Home while working as an intern at the Filson Historical Society in the spring of 2017. I had a chance to look through the Home's old record books, and the more I learned about it, the more fascinated I became, both by the women who ran the Home and the women who stayed there. The gap in the historical records about the Home was wide and deep. For example, the inmates were often nameless (unless they did something "bad," in which case they might be named), and the entries about the Home were intriguingly cryptic: "three gone to respectable homes to work"; "one left without permission"; and, my favorite, "two women have been sent to City Hospital, one to Insane Asylum, one expelled." Writing this book allowed me to give these nameless women backstories and lives outside the Home. It also allowed me to explore nineteenth-century ideas of motherhood, education, reproductive rights, and respectability, all of which were inextricably tied to social class and race. I've sought to reconstruct the lives of these women alongside primary sources that would have been relevant to their lives; I quote *The Louisville*

Courier-Journal extensively, and chapter headings, when not biblical, are borrowed from *The Essential Handbook of Victorian Etiquette* by Professor Thomas E. Hill. Many quotations have been adapted to suit the novel, in which cases that adaptation is noted in footnotes. While the Home for Friendless Women did exist, this novel should be read as a work of fiction.

PART I

Ruth

The Home for Friendless Women minute books
January 3, 1878

*Two women have been sent to City Hospital,
one to Insane Asylum, one expelled.*

Women, beware! Beware! You are on the brink of destruction. You have hitherto been engaged only in crushing your waists; now you are attempting to cultivate your minds! You have been merely dancing all night in the foul air of ball-rooms; now you are beginning to spend your mornings in study. You have been incessantly stimulating your emotions with concerts and operas, with French plays and French novels; now you are exerting your understanding to learn Greek and solve propositions in Euclid. Beware, oh beware! Science pronounces that the woman who *studies* is lost!*

---

* R. R. Coleman, MD, as quoted in *For Her Own Good: Two Centuries of Experts' Advice to Women.*

"Never make yourself the hero of your own story."

———————————

Some of us arrive at the Home of our own volition; others are brought here. I like to make wagers in my head about which girls will crumble under confinement and which will last the full eighteen months. The girl Cora, who arrived last night in the care of a doctor, I believe will stay. A girl's outward appearance is not a good indicator of her inner strength, although wrist size is. Those with delicate, birdlike wrists don't last long here. Maybe when men grow tired of measuring one another's skulls, they can test my hypothesis.

Take Louise, who arrived last month claiming to be a married woman of good standing. In her shimmering blue dress, her pale arms no bigger than a child's, Louise said she needed to stay in the Home during her pregnancy because her husband wouldn't leave her alone. Morning, night, and all the hours in between, she told Matron. She feared the constant intercourse would lead to miscarriage, as it had three times already. Even though Matron had her doubts, she brought Louise's case before the Board, who agreed she could stay.

On Louise's first full day in the Home, she complained morning, night, and all the hours in between. The size of her room (Where will I hang all my hats?), the food (Excuse me, I'm missing a celery dish), the gall of being assigned chores (Sew curtains?!). After twenty-four hours Louise decided to return to her husband.

I suppose he's better than no celery dish, I said to Matron as Louise stormed out.

The new girl Cora does not have small wrists, but she did forget to light the fire ahead of today's lecture, and the sitting room is bitterly cold. While bright, the fire is not yet hot enough to reach those of us by the drafty windows. As we shiver, Reverend Davidson sweats. Parallel tracks of perspiration begin at the crown of his head and race down his face. He swipes ineffectually at his eyes and cheeks with a handkerchief and surveys us, a motley group of women in hard-backed chairs. A captive audience. The reverend helped found the Home. Unlike the other benefactors who stop by for supper or tea, he prefers to deliver educational lectures on his visits.

Reverend Davidson's wife is the current president of the Board. The sitting room is named after her, and her portrait looms above her husband's sweating body. I think she was aiming for mysterious with her small half smile, but with her old-fashioned hairstyle and wide eyes, she looks more mystified than mysterious in the painting.

"Let us pray," Reverend Davidson says.

We bow our heads and recite along with him:

Bless the Lord, O my soul,
And forget not all his benefits,
Who forgives all your iniquity,
Who heals all your diseases,
Who redeems your life from the pit.

"Amen," Cora says loudly, and Mrs. Davidson frowns at her.

Reverend Davidson begins pacing in front of the fire, hands clasped behind his back. "Would the Egyptians have supported woman suffrage?"

Kate gives my hand a sympathetic squeeze. I have heard

three versions of this lecture in the five months I have been here. Would Galileo have demanded that women have the right to vote? Jane Austen? The esteemed George Washington? And now the Egyptians are eager to chime in.

"I do not claim to be an expert on ancient Egypt," Reverend Davidson says. "However, study and analysis of a culture's artifacts reveal much about their attitudes and beliefs. Which is why I have brought curiosities from the ancient world."

Mrs. Davidson passes him a small wooden box with a brass handle, which he makes a show of opening. Maggie stifles a yawn, Cora shifts in her seat and cranes her neck to see better, and Kate absently rubs a hand across her belly. Behind us, in a row by herself, sits Theresa. She hasn't spoken a word since her twin sister, Catherine, died last month. I don't know if she avoids us or if we avoid her and her palpable, frightening grief. Sometimes she will look at us with eyes so blank and wide, it's easy to think she is the one who died and we are the earthly voices calling out to her. If Matron did not remind her, I doubt she would remember to comb her hair or change her clothes. Theresa and Catherine shared the same blond hair and large brown eyes. Catherine was left-handed, though, which Maggie said was a sign of bad luck, and she's not surprised that the poor girl died the way she did, since she was clearly cursed. It was difficult to tell the sisters apart when Catherine was alive. I used to think of them as CatherineTheresa, a creature out of mythology with one body and two heads. The sisters arrived together from Ruby Sherwood's bagnio on Fourth Street. The things they have seen, the poor girls, Matron had said.

Impossible not to speculate if the same man impregnated them both. God, I hope not.

Reverend Davidson plunges his hand into the box and holds up a dingy piece of muslin, which he unfurls with no small amount of drama. "Any idea what this was used for?"

The limp cloth looks suspiciously like one of the bandages we keep in the upstairs hall closet, last wrapped around Catherine's arm after she burned herself in the laundry room.

"This was once wrapped around a dead body."

Cora gasps.

Catherine is dead, so he's not wrong.

"I was lucky enough to attend an unwrapping party years ago. Something I will never forget."

It's hard to picture the good reverend at a party, much less an Egyptian unwrapping party. Even less likely that he was such an interesting guest that the host gave him, as a parting gift, the very cloth that had been wrapped around a mummy. Imagine the stench of such a cloth! Though he's waving it about, I don't smell a thing—and these days, my stomach turns at the most innocuous of smells.

He rummages in the box again and this time emerges with a bloodred scarab pin, identical to one that Mrs. Davidson often wears on her visits. "The scarab beetle was an important symbol to the Egyptians, representing existence and growth. Sometimes they were wrapped up with a body, where they would be a stand-in for the heart."

He walks around the room and holds out his cupped hand for us to admire the pin. When he holds it before me, I see Mrs. Davidson's initials carved in tiny script on the beetle's hind legs. "How interesting," I murmur.

"May I touch it?" Cora whispers, extending a hand.

"This is priceless beyond measure, young lady."

Reverend Davidson returns to the front of the room, where he brandishes more items from his home: the bronze bust of a pharaoh he doesn't name—Ramses, I decide—and a smudged pencil sketch of a river he says is the Nile. With each item, we clap politely as if this is a real lecture.

Sometimes I wonder if his talks are as rambling as they strike me or if my brain is scrambled from the baby. Maybe the reason Mrs. Davidson looks so puzzled in her portrait is because she was forced to sit through one of these long-winded suffrage talks.

"Now what does any of this have to do with suffrage, you might be wondering?" He hands the box to Mrs. Davidson, who retreats to the far side of the room.

Mrs. Davidson sets the box on a nearby chair before quickly grabbing hold of it again. I overheard her tell Matron she mustn't be careless with her jewelry or valuables around girls of our class. They'll snatch the bonnet off your head if you don't watch them, she warned. This must be why she never removes her hat or gloves.

Who in Reverend Davidson's life has him so concerned about women voting? It must be his daughter, Minnie. She visited the Home a few weeks ago, and it was quite a shock to learn the Davidsons have a beautiful daughter. Minnie shares her mother's wide eyes, but they give her face an energetic rather than surprised look, and her reddish hair, the same color as her father's, was twisted up and away from her high forehead in a swirl of curls, rather than plastered to her face with sweat. She has quite small wrists; doubtful she'd last long as an inmate in this place. During her visit, Minnie peppered us with questions: Did we like living in the Home? Where did we live before? Were we still able to wear corsets in our conditions? Mrs. Davidson was so startled by that last question she dropped and broke her teacup, the one with the tiny rosebuds circling the inside rim. It was Matron's favorite. Still, she didn't say a word as she carefully swept up the pieces. When Minnie learned Kate's name, she recited a poem:

O Lady Kate, my cousin Kate,
You grew more fair than I:
He saw you at your father's gate,
Chose you, and cast me by.

He watched your steps along the lane,
Your sport among the rye;
He lifted you from mean estate
To sit with him on high.

"Do you know that one?" she asked, and Kate shook her head shyly. "It's by a woman poet. A poetess?" she wondered. "If that's not a word, it should be!"

After Minnie left, I found a small leather book, deep purple with an impossibly soft cover, in her chair. It was a diary of sorts, where she listed the parties she had attended and the parties she had hosted, along with food served (*To ensure I never repeat a dinner's menu!*). At the back of the book, there was a list of women's names on a page titled "Friends" and a list of men's names under the heading "Prospects," although some names were crossed out with *MARRIED* written beside them. I didn't plan on keeping the book, but the cover was so soft and we aren't allowed any books, and reading about Minnie's parties and menus was like being given a novel. When I feel guilty about hiding the book inside my pillow, I tell myself she likely hasn't even noticed its absence.

"In practice, woman suffrage works a positive moral injury on society," Reverend Davidson says now. "When we study the Egyptians, do we read the writing of an Egyptian Lucy Stone? Do we admire the artwork of those Egyptian women who wanted more than they had been given, when they had already been granted so much? Do we marvel at the statue of an Egyptian Amelia Bloomer who encouraged immodest dress in impressionable young Egyptian women?" Reverend Davidson looks mournfully at us, as if expecting one of us to blurt out the names of such bold women.

Queen Hatshepsut would surely not be impressed with today's lecture. I cross and recross my ankles, wishing my chair was closer to the fire. What I wouldn't give to be in bloomers instead of this godforsaken corset.

"Women have power, of course," he says. "Isn't that right, Eliza?"

Mrs. Davidson nods vigorously. "The moral authority a woman holds in her home is considerable."

"Yes!" he cries. "Because women have had power in every society, the kind of power they wanted and could handle. Here in America, men are badly besmirched by active participation in elections, and the women who attempt to purify the current election methods are apt to get mired in it themselves. Ask the poor women of the Wyoming Territory. They didn't ask for this doubtful privilege. In fact, most of them don't vote because they don't want any part of the sordidness. They are happy to leave voting—that necessary, but nasty, business—to their husbands and brothers, their fathers and sons. The women of Kentucky are wise and know what they can handle. They understand that the kinds of people they would meet on the streets would only lure them into a frightening and dangerous world. Follow the path laid out by Egyptian women," he urges, "and be content with all you have been given in this life, for even women such as yourselves can be redeemed from the pit."

He rests his hands on the table, bows his head. After a pointed glance from Matron, we clap.

I imagine the look on Matron's face if I were to point out the very obvious reason we don't study the writings and art of those Egyptian women—what husband or father or brother would record the words of such a quarrelsome woman?

"Reverend Davidson, thank you as always for enlightening us," Matron says. It is nearing Christmastime, when annual subscribers are asked to renew their pledge to support the Home so he could lecture on the joys of drowning kittens and we would be forced to listen attentively.

"We certainly won't look at a simple bandage the same way again, will we, girls?" Matron asks, and we dutifully nod our heads and smile, a pack of dumb cows.

Since Catherine's death, Matron has lost weight, her former roundness replaced with a sharp angularity. Her dresses hang loose on her, and even her hair is limp. But it's her eyes that are the most noticeable. They are too big for her face, loose-looking, as if one good squeeze would send them flying out of her face.

"Never appear to notice a scar,
deformity, or defect of anyone present."

Theresa cut her hair last night. The ends are jagged and barely skim her jaw. I have never seen a woman's hair so short; it's mesmerizing in its ugliness. Theresa's hair, as Catherine's did when she was alive, changes color depending on the light. At times her hair reminds me of the honey Matron adds to biscuits when it is someone's birthday. Now that it's winter and we are indoors most days, her hair is darker, like maple syrup. Catherine used to take great pains with her hair, but there has always been a carelessness to Theresa's beauty, as if she can't be bothered.

This morning, Maggie and Matron had spotted Theresa's hair at the same time.

Oh my God! Maggie set the pitcher of milk down on the table with an audible *thunk*.

Matron was forced to decide which sin was more grievous: the cutting of hair or the taking of the Lord's name in vain. Maggie, please.

Theresa calmly poured milk into her tea, buttered her toast.

Theresa, please. Matron's voice was pleading rather than scolding. She has been overly indulgent with Theresa since Catherine's death. I think she blames herself. What did you do? What will the Board members say?

Oh, they'll hate it, Maggie said. Especially Mrs. Davidson.

It's bad luck to cut your hair during pregnancy. Her baby will be born with all kinds of defects now. She'll catch a chill too, with her neck exposed like that.

Matron spent the morning curling and coaxing Theresa's hair into some semblance of a feminine style. Unfortunately the combs and pins only drew attention to her long, pale neck. Matron finally tied a flowered scarf around Theresa's head and sent her into the sitting room.

I did not used to spend the evening hours sewing curtains, but I have learned it's calming to sit and work mindlessly on things that don't belong to me. At least there is a comforting drudgery to life in the Home. When I'm sweeping the floors and helping Matron with the laundry and sewing curtains in the evening, I am able to forget, for a time at least, just where and why I am doing these very familiar chores.

It had been threatening rain all afternoon, the sky a bruised plum. The rain didn't wrench free of the clouds until after supper. The drops make a satisfying noise on the roof, providing a natural rhythm as I mend the curtains in my lap.

Maggie and I work on real lace curtains, which bring in an extra twenty-five cents. Theresa's stitches, neat and tidy, are better suited to lace than mine, but since her sister's death, I can't count on her to finish a set in time. Some evenings she simply stares at the curtains in her lap as if the whole idea of sewing is new to her, so now she mends Nottingham lace. Kate also works on Nottingham, not because she is a poor sewer but because she is afraid to work on real lace, in case she ruins it. When she was alive, Catherine was in charge of dividing up the sewing work, but it's my job now. I created a new system for the work closet recently, organizing the packages by date of arrival rather than last name of the client. It's more efficient this way, although I felt a twinge of guilt when I undid Catherine's method.

The curtains I'm mending this week are patterned with dragonflies and flowers. Aunt Janna used to say you could tell a lot about a woman from a glance at her curtains. After five months in the Home, and after mending countless curtains, I agree with her. Some curtains are frayed but clean, and it's easy to imagine them hanging in bright and cheerful rooms. I've also mended odorous curtains, greasy to the touch. They remind me of that saying about marriage: "If your husband smokes, be thankful he doesn't chew tobacco. If he smokes and chews, be thankful he doesn't drink. If he does all three, be thankful he won't be around long."

I hand Cora a pair of scratchy red curtains to mend. New girls always get the worst of the bunch; this particular set smells strongly of tobacco and is covered in brown stains. She'll have to give them a good scrubbing with egg yolk to remove all those spots. "Be sure to use a thread that closely matches as you mend." I point at the basket of sewing supplies over by the fireplace. I hope she doesn't balk at chores the way Louise did.

"Today's lecture was ghoulish," Maggie says. "I don't want to say it's bad luck in case that brings bad luck, but . . ."

I look over at Kate and shake my head.

"You can't be too careful, you know," Maggie says to Cora. "I once knew a woman whose husband kissed her, alcohol on his breath, and seven months later that baby was born with six fingers on his left hand. This same man swore in front of his wife, and guess what happened to that baby?" She doesn't wait for Cora to answer. "Deaf," she says triumphantly. "One good ear, and one ear completely missing." She runs a hand down her face and Cora stares. "The skin was perfectly smooth where the ear should have been. He couldn't hear a thing if you talked on that side. And here they let Reverend Davidson lecture on the most morbid topics to women in our condition."

Maggie loves to share stories about bad luck. Her parents

and her husband all died the same year. Died in his sleep, she said about her husband. I never imagined such a thing would happen to a man who was only twenty-three. It wasn't all that peaceful a death either. The look on his poor face.

After the funeral, she discovered he was in debt and she was pregnant.

Maggie has a thick puckered scar in the middle of her right cheek. When she first arrived at the Home, I had to make a real effort not to gawk at her face. Now I hardly notice the scar. How she got it is a mystery, since she tells a different story each time. From a dog, she told me. From an uncle, she told Kate. When it's just us in the Home, she doesn't hide her face, but when someone from the Board visits, she grows terribly self-conscious. Maggie has thin, light-colored hair, and no matter how she arranges it, the scar always shines through. When there are visitors, she hides in the kitchen or her room, claiming to be ill. She's like a cat who lived in our barn when I was younger, friendly as could be when we were alone, quick to flee at the sound of an unfamiliar voice.

Maggie is also convinced that the tree across the street from us, the one covered in misshapen lumps and bumps, is haunted. She claims to have seen women gathering around it at night. Witches, she whispered, so Matron wouldn't hear; Matron doesn't like that kind of talk.

From my bedroom, I have a clear view of the tree, and on nights I can't sleep, I stand at the window and study the view below. I've never lived in a city as big as Louisville, and I'm still amazed at all the activity on the street. Once I saw a man relieve himself on the tree. Another time I saw a man walk around it, rubbing his hands up and over the bumps, as if measuring it. Nothing with women or witches casting spells; men are the only ones walking around the neighborhood at night.

To be fair, I don't fault Maggie for seeing bad luck everywhere.

"The only bad luck that will come from the Egyptian lecture is if Reverend Davidson forgets to return the bandage to the hall closet," I say.

"Are there lectures every day?" Cora stabs tentatively at a curtain with a needle and no thread.

"Don't forget the thread," I remind her, and she crosses the room and returns with black thread.

"You'll want red."

"The thing is," she says, "I don't actually know how to sew."

I laugh out loud. "You can't be serious."

"No one taught me," she says defensively.

"Every woman knows how to sew," Maggie says.

"Not me."

"I've never heard of such a thing," Maggie says. "Surely you know how to crochet, then."

"Knit?" I ask.

"Embroider?" Maggie asks. "Quilt?"

Cora shakes her head.

"Nothing in this life will surprise me now," Maggie says. "I have seen it all. A woman who doesn't know how to do something in her very nature."

I think of the ledgers in Matron's office, all the money the Home is losing. "Sewing curtains is the main way we bring in money, and we're expected to sew every night in the hours before bedtime."

"You're very lucky to be here," Maggie says to Cora. "There aren't many homes like this. Other cities just leave their girls to die on the streets."

"Dr. Munro said that Matron is a wonderful person and that I would really enjoy my stay here. How is the food?"

Maggie frowns. "This isn't a hotel, Cora. The last girl who complained about chores is no longer here. Louise." She shakes her head. "A spoiled brat, and I'm not afraid to say it, turning up her nose at chores like she was the queen of Spain. You must do your fair share. I would offer to teach you, but Ruth and I are working on lace curtains, which bring in fifty cents each." She looks pointedly at Kate.

Kate puts away her curtains with a small sigh. "I'll teach you." She shows Cora how to thread the needle and hands her a piece of muslin to practice stitches. "The smaller the better."

"If you want to know about the Egyptians, Cora," Maggie says, "I mean really learn about them, ask Ruth. She went to college."

Cora laughs. "College! Is that true, Ruth?"

For some reason I think of the time my roommate, Sally, fainted after a geography lesson, how she lay on the ground twitching, her fists clenching and unclenching as she gasped for air. Were these the hysterical fits we'd been warned would strike without warning, the natural result of too much mental stimulation? Miss Voght had knelt down and loosened Sally's corset, and immediately she relaxed.

"I went to Oberlin. Lucy Stone graduated from there."

"I'd never heard of Lucy Stone before today," Kate whispers.

I try to hide the surprise on my face. "She was an abolitionist before the war. A famous suffragist too."

"I heard Dr. Munro say Lucy Stone has a very displeasing face," Cora says. "What happened to *your* face?" she asks Maggie.

"A rusty nail," Maggie says in a voice that discourages further questions. "I don't know why the suffragists are so angry all the time. All that shouting about unfair treatment and demanding the right to vote will age them. What does someone like me know about voting anyway? What right do I have to thrust my nose into matters that have nothing to do with me? I saw that woman's picture in the paper once." She jabs at the curtain before her as if it's Lucy Stone's face there in her lap. "She looks terribly old. Hideous, really."

"She is old," I say. "She's nearly sixty by now."

"She looks older because of all that anger she carries," Maggie says. "Frowning and shouting are not good for the complexion."

"I would be too frightened to vote," Kate says. "What if I did it wrong?"

"How could you be wrong if you voted with your conscience?" I ask.

"What if I canceled out my father's or brother's vote?"

"If you had a good reason to do so, maybe they would reconsider their own position."

"Of course she's angry," Theresa says suddenly, "and old-looking." This is the first time we've heard her voice in over a month. The words sound as if they are scraping her throat. Maybe all she needed to do to find her voice was cut off her hair. She keeps her head bent over the curtains in her lap as her right hand moves the needle in and out of the fabric. "She's tired of being told she doesn't know what she's talking about."

I wonder if she is talking about herself or Lucy Stone.

"Look!" Cora triumphantly holds up the fabric in her lap to reveal a trail of uneven red stitches. "Dr. Munro always said I was a quick learner."

THE LOUISVILLE COURIER-JOURNAL

JOY TO THE WORLD! WOMAN IS FREE!

Among the many modern discoveries looking to the happiness and amelioration of the human race, none is entitled to higher consideration than the renowned remedy—Dr. J. Bradfield's Female Regulator, Woman's Best Friend. By it woman is emancipated from numberless ills peculiar to her sex. Before its magic power all irregularities of the womb vanish. . . . It cures suppression on the menses. It removes uterine obstructions. It cures constipation and strengthens the system. It braces the nerves and purifies the blood. It never fails, as thousands of women will testify. This valuable medicine is prepared and sold by L. H. Bradfield, Druggist, Atlanta, GA. Price $1.50 per bottle. All respectable drug men keep it.*

---

* August 1876.

"A lady should have the escort
of a gentleman in the evening."

———————

The Home is the oldest on the street. Built in 1870, it's set back
from the road with a long, winding walk to the front door. The
neighbors walk quickly past the Home as if it were a graveyard
or an asylum; it's clear none of them are thrilled to live on the
same block as a bunch of friendless women and their bastard
children.

On the day I arrived, I noticed the Home's gray stone and
the red door, the flat roof and the tall, pointed windows. I
noticed the grass burned brown from the hot summer days.
Where were all the trees? I wondered. Later I learned the trees,
save the witches' tree, had been cleared to make way for the
houses. That day, I did not notice the fountain in the backyard, filled not with water but with a creeping plant. I did not
notice the twitching of curtains as the women inside watched
yet another girl with a round stomach climb out of a carriage
to take that long, torturous walk up to the house. The "walk
of shame," I call it now: eyes fixed straight ahead, chin up, the
only sign of distress the slight trembling in your legs as you set
down your suitcase and knock on the bloodred door. The day
I arrived my right hand trembled so badly I had to hold it up
with the left in order to bring it to the door.

I was here for a month before I discovered the gargoyle
perched above the porch, watching the street with narrowed
eyes and crossed arms. Maggie says we're lucky he's there to

keep bad spirits at bay, because who knows what kind of bad luck would befall us otherwise.

I don't know how far the house is from the river. I can smell it some days, a deep, dark smell that sneaks inside the Home and gets into our clothes. Maggie says that's not the river, merely the stench of the stockyards, where the Irish live. How strange to live by water and yet never see it.

In our rooms we are permitted a rug, a washstand, a mirror, and a rocking chair. We are not permitted books, writing materials, pets, plants, letter openers, or knitting needles. Mrs. Davidson recently complained to Matron about the mirrors, and Matron assured her that should she observe a sudden onset of vanity or immodesty, she would personally remove all mirrors from the Home.

I have a new nighttime ritual that Mrs. Davidson would surely see as confirmation of this immodesty. When the house is finally quiet, I shed my nightdress and stand before the mirror to study my naked body.

In seven months my breasts have nearly doubled in size and spill out of my palms. My stomach, also twice its normal size, does not ache in the same way, although I often feel the need to cup my hands underneath it, as if it's a too-ripe apple about to fall from a tree.

It isn't vanity that draws me to the mirror each night. The woman who stares back at me is a poor imitation of the woman I once was. The mirror woman is a fallen woman, a sinful woman, a magdalen. My first week at the Home, I woke to find my naturally straight hair had a new wave to it. Even my hair is unfamiliar.

If I were to leave the Home, walk out the door right now and head for the river, maybe all these things would fall away one by one. I would look into the river's glossy surface and find my hair to be straight once again, my stomach flat. Maybe to reverse this curse, I simply need to break the mirror in my room, dash it onto the floor, and the mirror woman would be destroyed as quickly as she was created.

Was I vain before? Maybe it is vanity to say no too quickly, to disavow that there was ever a time I took excessive pleasure in my appearance. It's true that in the past I spent very little time contemplating my looks, and now I spend quite a bit. Even the things that Aunt Janna used to complain about when it came to my body, my thick arms and unruly hair, never bothered me. My body was strong. I could walk for miles without tiring, I could carry an armful of books without a struggle, and wasn't that better than being beautiful?

My only vanity back then was the mistaken belief that my body was mine alone to control.

Last spring, my dresses grew uncomfortably tight across my chest. I knew then, but I couldn't make myself tell Miss Voght until the summer. When I finally told her, I was crying so hard she didn't understand. Once she finally did, she made me pennyroyal tea that smelled of mint and tasted like burnt bark. I drank every last drop. It didn't cause any bleeding, only made my legs cramp painfully that night.

There are other ways to remove an obstruction, Miss Voght said. If broken apart, the word *obstruction* can be easily reassembled. *Run. Suction. Root. Sob. Son. Soon.*

On my bed is the quilt Miss Voght gave me the day I left Oberlin. The blocks are different sizes and the lines are uneven and the colors are rather displeasing to the eye; she never was very good at the domestic part of our lessons.

I hope it keeps you warm, Miss Voght said when she gave it to me. Her eyes were full of tears and so were mine, but we both blinked them away. Chin up, Ruth, she said. This isn't the end for you. The quilt was the last thing I packed at Oberlin and the first thing I unpacked in my room at the Home. I have slept under this quilt every night for five months, and I will tell Miss Voght, if I ever see her again, that it has kept me warm and is the nicest gift I've ever received and that I will leave it behind when I leave the Home. A different woman will sleep under its simple block pattern, and I hope it keeps her warm when her tears fall and mix with mine.

I've had such peculiar dreams since arriving at the Home. Last night I dreamed I was a man taking a walk through the park. A cane announced my arrival. It was nighttime, but I was not scared of the shadows or the other men because they greeted me warmly, tipping their hats at me. They wanted to know where I was going and what I thought about the news of the world. In the dream I talked and talked until my mouth ached. It was nice to have a mouth hurt from talking.

Something is inside me, something I did not ask for and desperately don't want, and it grows a little every day without any effort from me. In the mirror, my stomach hardens and ripples as the obstruction moves.

Just because you don't want something doesn't mean you aren't occasionally amazed by it.

"Never will a gentleman allude to conquests which he may have made with ladies."

———————

Cora is struggling with her knitting lessons. Tonight she holds the needles as if they were small animals attempting to bite her. Kate is patient as she explains how to cast on, and she is patient when Cora asks for help every few minutes.

"Oh, I'll never learn!" Cora is on the verge of tears.

"You will," Kate says. "You have to practice, that's all." There's a reason Matron calls her Patient Kate.

Kate is nearing confinement, and her stomach is so large she needs help getting out of her chair. She's taken to sleeping upright in the rocking chair in her room because she said she can feel her supper sitting in her stomach. Like a stone shooting up flames into my throat, she said. She's embarrassed at how often she needs to use the bathroom.

"Theresa, you should show Cora how to knit," Maggie says. "She knits the most beautiful things. Such intricate patterns. You should see her lace scarves."

Theresa does not look up at the sound of her name and does not offer to show Cora her knitting prowess. Her face stays hidden behind her short, loose curls.

"If you practice every night, you might be skilled enough to make something for your baby before you reach confinement," Kate says.

"My *baby*?" Cora asks. "I don't have a baby, you silly girl."

Maggie once told us of a woman she knew whose stomach grew hard and round. When she said she wasn't pregnant, no one believed her. She died of cancer within the year; only in death was she finally credible. There's something almost obscene about the health radiating off Cora; everything about her is plump: her cheeks, her arms, even her lips are full and pink. Her belly is nearly as large as mine. I feel something tighten in my own stomach.

"I'm not here to have a baby like you girls," Cora says. "My stomach got a little fat, but that happens if a girl eats too much cherry pie. Dr. Munro brought me here because he and Mrs. Munro are going to visit her sister in New York for a few months and she—Mrs. Munro's sister, that is—doesn't have room in her house for me. Besides, New York is so cold! Better to stay here in Kentucky and rest while they are away. They'll come back for me, when the visit is over. They're so good to me."

It's been raining for two days now. An insistent rain. Are the people who live by the river fearful of the water swelling its banks, the inevitable breach onto land? I have not seen any men walking at night in this weather.

Maggie and Kate are still, their sewing forgotten. Even Theresa has paused in her sewing. The silence in the room grows and grows until it is almost unbearable. I hear the bells from the Catholic church by the park sounding their nightly call.

"Your stomach isn't fat from too much cherry pie," I say once the chiming has stopped. "We're all here for the same reason." I am suddenly angry with this girl. Furious. It's all I can do to stop from kicking her fat pink ankles.

"Not me!" Cora shakes a knitting needle in my direction. "What wickedness to suggest such a thing. I'm only fourteen years old."

☙❦❧

As a child, whenever I did something that displeased Aunt Janna, she would say, That's your mother in you, Ruth. According to Aunt Janna, her sister was a selfish woman obsessed with her own beauty and intelligence. Aunt Janna was a thick woman who saw little need for ornamentation or for reading anything but the Bible.

My father was a farmer and an artist. He liked to paint quaint country scenes: thatched cottages with colorful gardens, burbling brooks running behind a pretty farmhouse. I don't know where the ideas for these paintings came from. Outside my window I saw only fields, yellowed in the fall, green in the spring.

Rather than sell his work, my father preferred to give it away. According to Aunt Janna, this drove my mother crazy. I know this is true because I found my mother's diary in a trunk in the attic. On the first page she wrote, *I look outside the window of our house, at the changing light and the changing trees, and I compare this to the ridiculous rivers and cozy cottages he paints and gives away, and it makes me want to scream.* She pressed so hard with her pen on the word *scream* the ink is darker there.

Her diary was full of poems and sketches. Even as a young girl, I could tell the poems, random words with the occasional punctuation mark sprinkled in, were not very good.

> *Naked woman purple child!*
> *let us journey*
> *to the center storm*
> *the center of the storm?*
> *wait for me there.*

But her sketches! I reveled in the chance to see the world through her eyes. Her first drawings were of apples. Trembling silhouettes became confident borders; blemish-free apples later succumbed to decay and deformity, the forbidden fruit laid bare and stripped.

Later she graduated from sketching apples to painting with paper and brush borrowed (or were they stolen?) from her husband. All the colors he ignored in his own work, well, she would use them all. *Such a shock I received, as my brush slid across the paper that first time. I paint like a God,* she wrote.

I found a stack of her paintings in the attic, lovingly wrapped in an old blanket. They were all self-portraits. In some she was nude, and in others she was smiling. She painted herself outdoors and indoors. In one, she painted herself inside the frame, with a hand reaching out toward the viewer. In my favorite, her hair is a swirl of pink and green, her eyes two flat sapphires, her body a shadowy absence, a series of brushstrokes, there but not there. No timid trembling when she painted herself.

She finally showed her work to her husband. *He doesn't understand what I am trying to express. This is partly my fault, as the artist. Nevertheless, I refuse to take all the blame.*

I wish I had one of my mother's paintings to hang above my bed here, like I did back at Oberlin, although the Board doesn't think that art would serve girls of our class. I gifted Miss Voght my favorite painting of my mother before I left for the Home, and she said she would take good care of it until I came back to claim it. I have no intention of ever returning to Ohio, so it's hers to keep now. I wonder if Mrs. Davidson would find the painting or the mirror a more corrupting influence.

If she had lived, would my mother have chosen her family over her art? Or would she have found this idea that a woman can't have both as preposterous as the placid rivers her husband loved to paint? I wonder if she would have found a way to quiet the rage burbling inside her or if she always would have written the word *scream* with the same urgent desperation she did at twenty-four. She took herself, and her art, seriously. Even as a child I could see that.

Before I was born, my mother moved to New York for a year to study art. The months she was away, she wrote her husband a letter a week. Why he saved these letters, I don't know, but I found them in the trunk as well, bound with a piece of twine. At times she adopted a chatty, conversational tone, seeking his advice on how to keep her brushes clean, how to remove paint from the skin. Sometimes she teased him for being so conventional. *Tell me, my dear—are you still in love with the past? You never could resist those Italian artists so enamored with their own image.*

Other times she was critical, cruel even. When she learned he had sold a painting, she wrote, *I feel no pride in reading this news, for I know the painting you speak of and I pity the person drawn to purchase such blandness.* In that same letter, she asked him to send money.

Eventually she ran out of money. When my father refused to send more, she came back, walking inside their home as if she'd never left.

Just pranced her fancy self right back in, Aunt Janna said. No apology, no plea for forgiveness.

I was born nine months later. My mother complained about pain in her legs after delivery, and the doctor applied blistering poultices to them. He told her to rest in bed for a month. When she was given permission to get up, she pinned a flower in her hair and walked into the dining room, where my father was eating supper and I was napping in my cradle. Oh, what a pity, she said before collapsing. She was twenty-six, six years older than my current age. A week after her death, my father went into the woods with a shotgun to hunt for turkeys and did not return.

She killed him, Aunt Janna said, as surely as if she fired that shotgun herself.

Her face was unexpectedly tender when she spoke of my father.

As a young girl, when I would see girls with their mothers or their fathers, I would think that having parents seemed nice. It also seemed incompatible with my life, like waking up one day to discover I lived in a castle and spoke fluent Portuguese. I see now that my father's art bothered my mother not because it was quaint or old-fashioned. No, it was the safety of his subject matter and vision that infuriated her. If there were no limits to what you could do and who you could be, why would you choose serenity and harmony over exploring life's darkest depths? If you could crack the world open and break free, why would you stay safely ensconced in your cage?

I've imagined telling my mother about this baby, and she always looks up from a painting of herself to say, *Oh, what a pity,* before collapsing.

"Never read letters which you
find addressed to others."

———————————

Most days I spend the hours between breakfast and lunch in
Matron's office. Her desk is a mess and she's constantly losing
things. Also, her eyesight is failing, and she desperately needs
an assistant. Mrs. Davidson says there's no money for one. We
spend the first part of the morning searching for her green-
handled letter opener, her eyeglasses, and her teacup. I can't
find the letter opener, but I locate the cup beneath a stack of
papers by the window, and I point out that her eyeglasses are
tucked into the sleeve of her dress.

Sometimes I imagine this is my office, and instead of sam-
plers with Bible verses hanging on the wall and porcelain angels
and lace doilies lining the bookshelves, there are hundreds of
books, and on Saturdays I curl up on the sofa with one and
don't emerge until suppertime. Instead, I sit at the desk Matron
has set up in the corner by the window, and I look through the
newspaper for mentions of the Home. Matron has saved every
article, even the early ones before the Home officially opened
and neighbors wrote scathing editorials about sinful women
moving in next door to pious, hardworking Christians. Those
were trying times, Matron once said.

It's drafty by the window, but I have a clear view of the
street, and I would read through the newspaper and look out
the window all day if I could. Based on the way people walk

with heads bent low, hands thrust into mufflers or pockets, it must be cold out there. I think of the winters I spent at Oberlin, how I used to grumble with the other girls about the long walk across campus, the February wind worming its way under my thick woolen scarf, arriving to class with flushed cheeks and cheerful complaints about the cold. Sometimes I can't bear to remember all the things I took for granted back then. What a stupid, foolish girl I was.

Today is coal delivery day, and I keep an eye out for the wagon. Even though the coal is stored in the basement, delivery day means extra sweeping. That dust manages to travel upstairs and dance about the floors.

We are allowed outside once a week to attend church services. There has been talk of building a chapel in the Home so we don't have to leave the house at all. I hope the chapel is built after I leave, because I will take the staring and the whispering at church if it means we are allowed to breathe the outside air. The closer I get to confinement, the less I enjoy our Sunday outings. It's like being given a single bite of bread when you are starving to death; it only makes your hunger more acute.

Next to the window is a sampler that proclaims, BUT IF THE WICKED MAN TURNS FROM ALL HIS SINS WHICH HE HAS COMMITTED AND OBSERVES ALL MY STATUES AND PRACTICES JUSTICE AND RIGHTEOUSNESS, HE SHALL SURELY LIVE; HE SHALL NOT DIE. The girl who stitched this ran out of room toward the end so that the last four words—*he shall not die*—are crammed together as one. Surely she meant to embroider *statutes,* not *statues.* The first sampler I ever made was only twelve words long: THE WAGES OF THE RIGHTEOUS IS LIFE, / THE INCOME OF THE WICKED, PUNISHMENT. I was proud of that sampler, even if I didn't have a clue what it meant.

❧❧

I find two mentions of the Home in today's paper. The first is an annual report detailing expenses. When I see the budget in print, it is clear that even if we sewed curtains day and night, the Home would still be in serious financial trouble. Without more subscribers, it's doubtful the Home can keep going another year. The last sentence of the report reads: "In November, one woman died in childbirth. Catherine left a clear testimony that the Home had blessed her and changed her for the better."

The last thing Catherine said was: Don't let him do that to me! The unnamed him still haunted me. Was she talking about the doctor who couldn't stop the bleeding? The son who was the reason for the bleeding? Or the man responsible for the labor that lasted an entire day and a night? I cut out this article, along with one about the package reception scheduled for Christmas Eve, and I paste them into the book. I think about the girl who will help Matron find articles after I leave. Will she also run her hands along the cracked black leather covering? Will she drag out this task, painstakingly pasting the articles into the yellowed pages with a precision and patience she did not know she possessed? I wish I could leave a message for her to find, years from now.

Chin up, girl. This isn't the end for you.

Matron also keeps letters from people asking if the Home has room for someone they know. These are not in an official book. Instead they are hidden inside one of the many Bibles in her study. Maybe this is not a hiding place, although it must be, because Matron has never asked me to catalog and file these letters and she is very big on organization. I always tell myself I won't snoop and read letters that have nothing to do with me, but after a few weeks, I always lose my resolve.

"Coal's here," I announce when the wagon arrives. Once Matron is downstairs, I quickly find the Bible, third from the

left on the second shelf. I spot the new letter immediately,
cream-colored stationery with a pleasing thickness, the pen-
manship practiced and unhurried:

Dear Madam,

*I would like to express my admiration for the work you
have been doing with the fallen women of Louisville. The
good and restraining influences you model to girls of this
class, combined with a solid Christian education, will surely
yield women our country will be proud to claim. A young
woman under my care is in need of shelter and concealment.
Unfortunately, I have been unable to secure lodging for
her at our home for fallen women here in Nashville. I can
assure you that Cora is a good Christian girl and will
gladly embrace all opportunities for self-improvement. That
she should have fallen into sin is sadly a common occurrence
with young women these days, as I'm sure you have had
reason to discover. Unless I hear from you otherwise, I
will bring the girl next month and leave her in your
capable hands. As a small token of my appreciation for your
charitable Home, I will send a small sum of money which
might offset the burden of one more sinful woman and aid
in future endeavors of your esteemed Home.*

Yours sincerely,
Dr. William Munro

I think of Cora shaking her knitting needle at me: I'm not here
to have a baby! I try to picture Dr. Munro, but in my mind he
becomes the doctor who delivered Catherine's dead son. Old
and balding with a sharp smell, as if he had recently bathed in
vinegar. Before Matron returns, I slip the letter into my pocket.
I did not used to be the kind of woman who took letters and

engagement books. It's amazing how quickly you can become someone you don't recognize.

Matron is worried the dreary chill of winter will turn even the best subscribers into misers. She wants to send a letter in advance of Christmas, when generosity and goodwill are still abundant. I am very good at writing these letters. Since I started helping with the letters, we have had three additional subscribers. My secret? I imagine I am writing a letter to the Aunt Jannas of the world, women whose sympathy for fallen girls extends to their purses but never their homes. I read aloud a paragraph to Matron: "'I have had countless pitiable magdalens enter the Home with heartrending sobs and streaming eyes to ask, "Will not those who profess to be Christians help us to leave the dens of sin, shame, and misery into which we have been driven by men who by false promises accomplished our ruin?" Any money sent to us would be thankfully received and acknowledged by these respectable friends.'"

Matron listens with closed eyes. "We can send that to male subscribers," she says. "For the women's groups, add more about repentance."

As she talks, her glasses slip down her nose. They do little to counteract the cloudiness that skims across her eyes. I wonder if she will ever gain back the weight she lost after Catherine's death.

"Tell me, how do you think Cora is doing? She has a very cheerful disposition, although she needs quite a bit of instruction with her chores."

A *sinful woman,* Dr. Munro wrote about the fourteen-year-old girl in his care.

"Most girls her age are cheerful," I say.

"I suppose she was quite spoiled before."

"I'm worried Cora doesn't understand why she's here."

Matron takes off her glasses, rubs her face. "She understands."

"She claims she's fat from eating too much cherry pie."

"Girls aren't sent here for eating too much pie. She simply doesn't want to own up to her part in this."

"When I was her age, I too might have been confused about why my body was changing. No one explained these things to me."

I think of my old barn cat, how one day she ran into the woods behind our house, and when she returned a few weeks later, her belly was swollen and she crawled under our porch to deliver six kittens. For a long time after that, I thought that if I ventured too far into the woods, I too could end up with a bellyful of babies.

"According to Mrs. Munro, Cora was acutely aware of the part she played in her downfall."

"Cora is barely aware of how to hold knitting needles."

"Ruth." Matron's voice is a warning I don't heed.

"Surely Cora is not the first girl Dr. Munro has sent to a home like ours."

"That's enough, Ruth."

"And now she will have a baby while practically a baby herself. Why is it that we are the ones sent away, and nothing happens to them? Tell me, where is the fairness or justice in that? When will they receive punishment for their wicked actions?"

Rage sloshes inside me, liquid hot. It threatens to leak out as tears.

There is a long silence. When Matron finally speaks, her eyes are somber. "Are you truly repentant, Ruth?"

I swallow hard, clench and unclench my hands behind me.

"No one is too far gone for salvation. This is a lesson I learned myself many years ago. You will be granted forgiveness," she says, "but you must acknowledge your sins."

From *salvation: stain, last, vast, nails, Satan, salvo.*

I wonder, not for the first time, why Matron spends her days worrying about the finances of a home like ours. I try to picture Matron as a young, friendless woman, but it's difficult. Even if she were once in my shoes, she is far above me now, gazing down in pity from the land of respectability. If I ran this home, I would never forget a woman does not fall on her own, that it takes a mighty push from someone more powerful.

"The world will not bend to your will, Ruth," Matron says as if she can read my thoughts. "Your stubborn attitude will not serve you."

"I don't know how to be someone I am not."

From the window I watch two men walk down the street. They walk in unison in a way that makes my throat ache. What I would give to be outside, to exercise, to walk. The smell of freedom would bring me to my knees.

Matron follows my gaze. "We had a problem with the first group," she says, in answer to my silent question. "Girls leaving without permission, trying to go home or, worse, back to their sinful ways. It's why the Board requires a full eighteen months."

"I would not return to sinful ways if I were allowed outside," I say to the window. This would have been my fourth and final year at Oberlin. Maybe I would be fretting about my impending graduation. Or maybe I would be anxious to graduate, eagerly planning a move. Would I have moved out west to Wyoming? East to Philadelphia? Stayed in Ohio? All the books I didn't get to read, all the papers I didn't get to write, all the friends I left behind. Everything was taken from me, and somehow I'm expected to accept both the loss of my former life and the suffocating label of "sinful." "I was *not* a sinful woman before," I say, still facing the window, "and I am *not* a sinful woman now."

"You are here for the same reason as the other girls, Ruth."

"Then none of us are sinful. We are merely the unfortunate recipients of someone else's sin."

"Pride will only hinder your effort at true repentance," Matron says. "Now, you have chores to finish."

I am smart enough to hear the dismissal in her words. Even Matron has a limit when it comes to girls of our class.

Later, when I am alone in my room, I pull out Minnie's book and transcribe all the words used to describe us: we are *respectable friends, victims of misfortune, pitiable magdalens.* How strange to be all these things at once. After a moment, I add one more of my own. *Liars.*

I write this word with the same angry hand my mother wrote *scream* in her own diary.

"Ladies should not allow courtship
to be conducted at unseasonable hours."

———————

Kate told me a riddle when she first arrived at the Home: her
mother had eight children but was pregnant only four times.
I guessed four sets of twins. The correct answer was two sets
of twins, one set of triplets, and Kate. Kate keeps a drawing of
her family in the top drawer of her dresser; she and her mother
have the same curly dark hair, and her brothers and father all
share dark eyes and darker hair.

Since Catherine's death, Kate often comes to my room on
the nights she can't sleep. Her room overlooks the back garden,
and she said the only shape she can make out in the dark is
the diseased ash tree. Maggie would claim it's bad luck to stare
at a diseased tree in our current condition. It's impossible to
hear someone constantly mention bad luck and not believe the
occasional story, Kate said.

Kate climbs into bed with me. We lie back to back, our
stomachs jutting out on either side like the wings of a strange
animal. I used to sleep on my back. Now my stomach looms
above me and I can't breathe, as if my own body wants to crush
me. I adjust the quilt so it covers us both.

"Do you ever think about Catherine's son?" she asks.

I sometimes picture his stillness, the cord wrapped around
his neck like a noose. I can still see Matron struggling to cut
the cord, how she had to bear down with the scissors. I think

of Theresa sitting in the rocking chair in her sister's room, cradling her dead nephew while crying silently. "No."

"He wasn't baptized," Kate says. "I pray for him every day because I don't know where he went." I can tell she is crying from the way her shoulders shake.

The nearer Kate gets to confinement, the more she worries about this baby, specifically his soul. I tell her that Catherine's son was blameless, that he will not be punished for his mother's sins. I say this even as I think, *What do I know about these things?* I say this even though it contradicts everything we are told here in the Home about penance and who is worthy of life everlasting.

During labor Catherine screamed until she was hoarse, her eyes wild. Even at the end Theresa could not calm her sister. Am I being ripped apart? Or in half? she kept asking.

Bear down one more time, Beatrice, the doctor said.

Her name's not Beatrice, Theresa said, but her words were swallowed up by Catherine's screams and the rush of blood, and I sometimes worry, the way Kate worries about her baby, that Catherine left this world as Beatrice, and what happens to a person if she leaves as someone else?

The baby inside me shifts suddenly, and I rest my hands on my stomach. I think of the time a white crow flew into the library at Oberlin, how it flapped about in panic by the windows, seeking a way out. Such a strange purgatory, the constant threat of death hanging over us, the constant reminder of life moving within us.

"Do you ever worry about dying, Ruth?"

"Yes."

"I wish I were more like you. You hide your fear well."

"Matron says I am prideful, and my aunt used to say I was too stubborn for my own good," I say. "Best not to copy me."

I imagine I can hear Kate smiling in the dark. "Did you have a friendship album when you were a young girl?"

"Of course."

"I was very good at drawing pictures. Dogs, boats, castles. I bet you wrote limericks."

"Poems mostly."

"About marriage?"

"About death," I say. For some reason this strikes us both as funny, and the bed shakes with our silent laughter.

"Tell me one," Kate says when she catches her breath.

I'm only half joking when I say, "Don't tell Maggie."

When I am dead, my dearest,
Sing no sad songs for me;
Plant thou no roses at my head,
*Nor shady cypress tree.**

"How morbid!" she cries.

"Aren't all young girls?"

"Oh no, not me," Kate says.

I believe her. As a young girl, Kate was exactly like she is now: patient, kind, forgiving.

"What would you write in my friendship album?" I ask.

"I would draw you a picture."

"Not a picture of Reverend Davidson lecturing about suffrage, I hope. How difficult to capture all the sweat."

We collapse into giggles again.

"Silly girl, I would draw a picture of the house you'll live in when you leave here. The house for you and your baby."

Kate believes that as soon as the baby is born I will change my mind, that my love for this baby will pierce me like a thorn. She says there are lots of men who will marry me, that I can assure people I was once a sinful woman but am now a penitent Christian. She sounds exactly like Matron when she says these things.

---

* Christina Rossetti, "When I am dead, my dearest."

I can't imagine these words—*sinful woman* and *penitent Christian*—leaving my mouth. Surely I'd be struck dead for uttering such blasphemy.

"I hope you'll let me visit you and the baby," Kate says. "I hope you won't forget me once you leave here."

"I won't forget you." I don't add that I don't want to visit anyone from the Home after I leave, nor do I want them to visit me. Instead, I want my time here to have never happened. I can't imagine any life in which I become this baby's mother.

"If I have a daughter," Kate says, "I hope she is as strong as you, Ruth."

"I hope you have a son then." But I am flattered.

"It will be hard to return to the farm after this," Kate says with a sigh. "After living in a house with a parlor and a dining room table that seats twelve and a mirror in every room. William might think I'm too fancy for him."

Kate said that on the drive to the Home, her fiancé, William, cried and cried, while she sat beside him, dry-eyed. She said if I had seen his face and looked into his eyes, I would know how sorry he was for her condition, and this is how she knows that he is back home saving money so he can marry her and provide a home for their family. She said that she hoped that someday her family, and especially William, would forgive her.

When I asked why she was the one who needed forgiveness, she said it was her fault they sinned, that she should never have allowed him to call on her when she knew her parents would be in town for hours.

He should not have called on you when he discovered they were away, I countered.

What is it like to be Kate, so patient and soft-spoken? She believes everything she is told here; she accepts the judgment and drudgery of the Home without question. Recently I have started to think that this life seeks to destroy both the meek and the strong alike. God help us if the meek like Kate inherit the earth—they won't know what to do with it.

"I have a request," Kate whispers now, "if I die."

"You won't die."

"Catherine did."

I think of the daily retching I heard from her room, even after the point of quickening. "Catherine was sick every day of her pregnancy, and her baby came too early."

"If I die, will you make sure they baptize the baby?"

"You aren't going to die."

She rolls over so we are facing each other. Her hands find mine, and they grip with surprising strength. "Promise me, Ruth."

"I promise."

She relaxes onto her back. "What would you write in my friendship album?"

"A poem, of course."

I think of the poem Minnie recited on her visit, how she left off the part where poor Kate is put in her place by her cousin, the fallen woman.

> *Yet I've a gift you have not got,*
> *And seem not like to get:*
> *For all your clothes and wedding-ring*
> *I've little doubt you fret.*
> *My fair-haired son, my shame, my pride,*
> *Cling closer, closer yet:*
> *Your father would give lands for one*
> *To wear his coronet.*

I do not want a son, fair-haired or otherwise. I do not want him to be my shame or my pride. Wanted or not, a baby should not be asked to carry such a burden.

The last time I did laundry at Oberlin, I laid out my dresses to dry with the arms thrust upward. From a distance, they resembled Christ on the cross, and when I returned for the wind-warmed clothes, I was as tender as Mary, gathering her son one last time into her arms.

I am 223 days removed from the incident at Oberlin, and I have not changed my mind about this baby. There is a world where the baby and I live in a nice home and Kate and her family visit us, but I suspect that is the make-believe world of friendship albums.

"A true lady will go quietly and unobtrusively about her business when on the street."

———————

Sunday morning we walk the short distance to the Second Presbyterian Church. We waddle behind Matron, two by two, like fattened ducks. The cold air burns, and I gulp greedily at the smells: trees, smoke, leaves, horses. They are the smells of an active and busy world, not the smell of women and endless piles of curtains and laundry. If Matron would allow it, I would sleep outside. I imagine her face if I were to ask such a thing, and I laugh aloud as I walk. Even with my stomach jutting before me, there is a lightness to my body.

We pass by the tree Maggie claims is haunted and the statue of the man on horseback at the entrance to the park. He gazes past us at a spot in the distance. My first week in the Home, I dreamed that I walked over and laid my hand on the statue and the horse became alive under my palm, and when I looked up the man was gone, and I knew, in the way of dreams, that this was my horse now and he would take me wherever I wanted. When I woke in my bed at the Home, I cried like I was back in Oberlin telling Miss Voght about the baby.

Matron likes us to read our Bibles as we wait for the service to begin. I suspect this rule is as much for us as it is for the other churchgoers, so they will see us as pious and humbled. The girl who had the Bible before me must have been fond of the Psalms, because my book naturally opens to 25. I have read these words enough times that they feel like a message she specifically left for me.

> *Remember your mercy, O Lord, and your steadfast love,*
> *for they have been from of old.*
> *Remember not the sins of my youth or my transgressions;*
> *according to your steadfast love remember me*
> *for the sake of your goodness, O Lord!*

"As long as God is our Father," Reverend Davidson says, "we are never orphans."

It's cold enough in the church that even he is bundled up and not sweating. Sitting next to Kate and Maggie, I am comfortably, drowsily warm from the heat of their bodies.

Worry, Reverend Davidson reminds us, is the work of the devil and will not help us in this life or in the one that follows. Surely it's not possible to go through this life without worry. But I'm thankful to be spared a message about the evils of suffrage today. I spot Mrs. Davidson and Minnie in the front row. Minnie stifles a yawn and looks around the church, while Mrs. Davidson listens intently, leaning forward as if to catch every word. After one of his interminable lectures about suffrage, I saw the reverend place his hand on the small of Mrs. Davidson's back. You are a great comfort to me, Eliza, he had said. And the smile she gave him was so open and trusting, she was briefly as beautiful as their daughter.

This is my body, given up for you, we sing, and then we are released.

The sun darts in and out of the clouds on the walk home, and the air smells of snow. "We should all be careful today," Maggie says. "Abrupt changes in weather are bad luck for women in our condition."

Kate is walking slowly today, even though she's normally not one to dawdle and draw out our final moments of freedom. She doesn't answer when I ask if she feels all right. When we reach our street, she suddenly grabs my hand, squeezing so hard I gasp. Her normally small eyes are wide and frightened.

On the walk up to the Home's front door, Kate stops. "Oh." She holds her hands beneath her stomach and looks down at the puddle forming beneath her skirts.

∞

"Please, no doctor," Kate begs once we're in her room. I help her strip off her wet garments and change into one of the nightgowns reserved for birth days. I braid her long hair to prevent tangles. "My mother never had a doctor present, and she delivered healthy babies every time."

There is a tally in the kitchen of how many babies have been born in the Home. The specter of Catherine's son, baby thirteen, hangs over us now.

I kneel beside Kate and give her fingers a reassuring squeeze. I hope she doesn't notice how mine shake.

"You have until sewing time," Matron says finally. "After that I will call a doctor whether you wish it or not."

A slushy rain begins falling around lunchtime. At one point Kate climbs out of bed to rock back and forth on her hands and knees. Her moaning and the sleet on the roof blend together into an eerily beautiful sound.

Maggie relieves me in the afternoon, and I sit at the dining room table and eat bread with cheese and fruit even though I'm not hungry. The food is as dry as paper in my mouth. Even from downstairs I can hear Kate's cries.

On birth days I am reminded that my own body will crack open to release what's inside. I'm no stranger to pain, yet I have seen that the pain of childbirth is different, that your body becomes a train speeding through a dark tunnel and you cannot stop it, you can only surrender and hope you make it through alive. Until Catherine's labor, I did not know that pain could distort a woman's face until she is unrecognizable. My choices are to either die during labor or soon thereafter, like Catherine and my mother, or survive and end up with a baby I never asked for and don't want. On birth days, I am reminded of how helpless I am, how little control I have over what my body ultimately chooses to do.

After Catherine's death, Matron asked the Board for chloroform to help with prolonged labors. Mrs. Davidson refused: How will these girls earn humility and self-improvement if you make even the curse of Eve manageable?

I wonder what happened to Mrs. Davidson to make her so hard that when given the chance to alleviate pain in a fellow woman, she chooses not to. How does a woman, how does a mother, become such a monster?

With the approach of evening, the sleet turns to snow and falls silently. I am not one to normally pray, yet I say a prayer that Kate will deliver her baby without a doctor.

When I return to Kate's side, the room smells of iron, and Matron is kneeling between Kate's legs. Catherine's doctor was so old that we had to help him into the chair we had placed at the foot of the bed. He refused to look between her legs and instead blindly groped under the sheet while staring at a spot on her forehead. His fingernails were ragged and dirty. As I helped Theresa wash Catherine's body to prepare her for burial, I thought that I would not want that doctor's filthy nails scratching at me. I would not want the world's oldest man to deliver my baby, and I would not want his face to be the last one I saw before I left this world for the next.

"You're doing just fine," Matron says to Kate now, and she lowers the sheet back over her legs. A white ring of dried sweat circles Kate's forehead like a halo. Kate stares past us; she is here and not here. I wonder if during labor, I too will find a way to be present in body only.

Kate suddenly sits up in bed and rests her weight on her elbows. The bearing down pains are much closer together and last longer. She claws at the sheet until she rips a small hole. When I try to wipe her forehead with a cool cloth, she violently shakes her head and moves out of reach. She takes a deep breath, as if about to plunge underwater, and this time when she bears down, there is a sound of something breaking loose, or breaking free. Blood too, the right amount, I hope, and the baby's head briefly appears.

"Two good pushes," I tell her, and amazingly the baby slides out after her second push. Matron snips the cord, wraps it in a piece of linen before securing the cord to the baby's belly. I wipe the boy's eyes with a cheesecloth and hold him up for Kate to see. In my arms, he is warm and smells like the inside of a barn.

"Ten fingers, ten toes," I tell her.

I wash the boy as Matron delivers the afterbirth. During his bath, he opens his eyes and then quickly closes them, as if unsure of this new place in which he finds himself.

"You would make a fine nurse, Ruth," Matron says approvingly as I swaddle him with a blanket warmed from the fire downstairs. Kate is fine and her baby is fine, and tears of relief fill my eyes.

Kate suddenly cries out again. She looks at me with terrified eyes, and I am afraid she will start convulsing like Catherine did. "There's another one," she pants, and then she groans as she once again grabs for the sheet.

The second baby does not come out with two pushes because the baby's left shoulder gets stuck. Matron slowly turns the baby until finally the shoulder is out too. This turning and twisting is not painless for Kate; at one point she passes out. Likely it is not painless for the baby either, because she emerges screaming. She screams as Matron cuts the cord, screams as I wipe her eyes, and screams during bath time, as if the water were scalding rather than cleaning her. Only when she is swaddled and lying beside her brother does she grow quiet. The two babies curl against each other and offer identical, shuddering yawns. The girl is nearly bald, only a few blond wisps, but the boy has dark hair that sticks straight up in the air.

"Twins," Kate says. There are tears in her voice.

"Your mother had twins," Matron tells her with a smile. "This is not uncharted territory for you."

While Matron strips the soiled linens from the bed, I help Kate with her bath. The water flashes red, then murky brown. Afterward, I help her into a clean gown and pile blankets onto her legs to keep her warm. She falls into an exhausted sleep almost immediately.

Before bedtime, Maggie and Theresa visit. "Look at that hair," Maggie says about the boy. Theresa is silent, her expression unreadable, as she stands over the twins. Whatever she is thinking, she does not feel the need to share.

I have scrubbed the floor and the soiled sheets are downstairs in the laundry room, but Cora refuses to come inside Kate's room. "It smells," she whispers, wrinkling her nose. Even though she is standing in the hallway, her stomach is so large it is in the room with us. I wonder what she tells herself to explain how her belly continues to swell day by day, even in the absence of cherry pie. I think of what Kate just went through, of what awaits this girl, and if Dr. Munro were standing before me now, I would not hesitate to wrap my hands around his neck and squeeze. I wouldn't stop until he admitted he was the sinful one.

"Are you in pain?" Cora asks Kate when she wakes.

"Oh yes," Kate says.

"Do not be afraid of being an 'old maid,'
for the term has lost its disgrace."

In the spring and summer at Oberlin, we girls were required to be in our rooms by eight, half past seven during the colder months. The boys did not have a curfew. We were permitted to visit the library between six and ten on Saturday mornings, while the boys did their outdoor chores. Interactions with male students were discouraged.

> *Never speak to a man through an open window.*
> *Never walk to class with a male student.*
> *Never ever, under any circumstances, visit a man in his room.*

Based on the number of engagements published in the *Oberlin Review* each spring, quite a few students broke at least some of these rules.

Most of the girls at Oberlin wanted to find a husband before graduation. Contrary to what Aunt Janna said, I was not opposed to the idea of a husband. My first year I simply found it easier to avoid all the romantic entanglements that everyone else found so intoxicating. This seemed especially prescient on my part after my roommate, Sally, was expelled for what the *Oberlin Review* called "moonlight wanderings" with two unnamed male students.

All Oberlin girls were on the literary track. We jokingly called ourselves the "Ladies Department." Instead of Latin and

Greek, we studied French, poetry, modern literature, and religion. Every semester we took a class called Household Economy with Miss Voght. No one knew how old she was. Thirty? Forty? She did not wear a wedding ring, and rumors swirled viciously around her: that her husband had left her for someone else, that her fiancé had died in the war, that her husband was royalty and lived abroad. Most of the girls thought her strange. They didn't understand her plain dresses and scuffed shoes or how she could be content teaching us, instead of raising her own family. I didn't find her strange at all; I thought she was wonderful.

"You are here for a useful education," Miss Voght said on our first day. "You are also here to be a restraining influence on the male students, to model superior manners for those young men who will go on to become ministers." Nine girls anxiously stared back at her. "That is a tall order. You can be sure the male students are not being lectured about the need to control your unbridled passions." A few of us blushed; some laughed nervously.

"How many of you know how to sew?" she asked that day. "Cook? Garden?"

All hands rose.

"What about physics? Chemistry?" Hands swiftly returned to our laps.

"There's a way to study both the domestic and the sciences," Miss Voght said. "Should anyone back home inquire about your classes, be sure to focus on the former."

Our studies were interrupted on Mondays so we could wash and repair the men's clothing, on Tuesdays so we could attend the men's debate meetings, and on Wednesdays so we could clean the dining hall and other buildings on campus. My favorite room to clean was the museum in the science hall. It wasn't technically a museum, but it was well stocked with botanical specimens and ten microscopes. FOR USE BY MALE STUDENTS

ONLY! read the sign above the microscopes. I often wondered, as I cleaned and organized that room, what ideas the teachers feared would fester within us girls if we were to look through the eyepiece of a microscope, what else we might ask to see for ourselves.

On cleaning days, I always requested the museum. Other girls disliked the smell of the drying skins in the taxidermy room next door. Not me. I dragged out this chore so I could say aloud the names of the plants as I cleaned their glass cases. The poisonous ones sounded especially beautiful. *Mandragora officinarum. Conium maculatum.* Before coming to Oberlin, I had known to avoid these poisonous plants by their shape alone, and I was seeing now that there was a whole world hidden beneath the one I had known. It was like being handed the keys to a secret kingdom. What if I graduated before I looked at all the plants in the glass cases, before I read all the books in the library, before I crammed myself full of knowledge? While in school, we girls were indulged. But after graduation, we were expected to leave it all behind, so our real lives as wives and mothers could begin.

I feared I would be Lot's wife, unable to avoid the temptation to look back for one final glimpse. So many ways a woman can turn to salt.

THE LOUISVILLE COURIER-JOURNAL

FRANKFORT GOSSIP:
WOMAN AS OFFICE-HOLDER

Before and since the election of State Librarian, the subject of woman as office-holder has been exhaustively discussed. Mrs. Cornelia Bush is the first and only lady who has held an elective office in the State, a special set having been passed in the Legislature two years ago, opening that office to the admittance of women. It is admitted by all that Mrs. Bush has fulfilled every duty of the office efficiently and to entire satisfaction. I have heard more than one gentleman testify to the agreeable changes that have transpired since she has taken charge of the Library rooms. The neatness and entire order prevailing where was wont to be confusion and dust—every book in its place, the added grace and coziness which her taste and untiring care confer upon a room. Therefore the question is not now as to woman's ability to fill the office but merely one of taste and feeling. "I do not like to see a woman mixed up in politics," said one of the most intelligent members, "electioneering among all sorts of men, as she must do to obtain the office."[*]

---

[*] January 1878.

"Do not indulge in satire—no doubt
you are witty . . . but it matters little."

My second year at Oberlin, I became friends with a boy, Daniel, whom I met after a debate meeting. He had not been very good in the debate, short on facts, even shorter on quick rebuttals, but he had a friendly face and was gracious in defeat, and I surprised myself afterward by telling him he had done well.

"All these silly classes they make us take," he complained as we left the library. "What use will I have for solid geometry and Cicero when I'm a minister?" *Sigh-cero*, he said.

"*Cic-ero,*" I instantly regretted saying. No one liked to be corrected, much less by a woman.

He surprised me by laughing. "Maybe I should pay more attention in class."

Daniel hadn't wanted to attend college, but his mother had insisted, a fact I added to my list of amazing things mothers did. He, like some of the more adventurous male students, planned to move to Wyoming Territory after graduation. Daniel had a romantic idea of the West, all the people out there he could save with his eloquent sermons. I hoped his sermons were more eloquent than his debate rebuttals. Clearly he would need a wife to write his sermons for him. It certainly never crossed my mind that I would be that wife. For starters, I wanted a husband who knew how to correctly pronounce Cicero. Luckily, Daniel was not interested in me either; he was in love with a girl named Adelaide who lived down the hall from me that year. Adelaide was a quiet girl who blushed easily and whose dresses were always neat and clean.

After the debate meeting, Daniel would often stop by the museum while I was cleaning. Sometimes I would help him with his French homework, but mostly we just talked. It was nice to talk to someone, to have someone seek me out. I realized I had been a little lonely since Sally was expelled.

"I saw Adelaide today, and she said, 'Hello, Ernest,'" Daniel glumly reported one afternoon.

"I hate to tell you this," I said to him, "but the Adelaides of the world are not likely to move to Wyoming Territory, which is a shame because women can vote there. Not just in school board elections either. And the teachers, men and women, are all paid the same."

"You should move out there after graduation," Daniel said.

"Maybe I will," I said. "If you don't have a wife at that point, you'll need my help writing your sermons."

"You know what's nice about you, Ruth?" Daniel said. "I believe you actually want to be noticed for the things you think rather than your appearance."

"It's safer to be noticed for how you look instead of what you think," I said. "That's what Miss Voght says."

"I heard two brothers had a duel over the right to marry her and they both died, and she swore she'd never marry."

"I haven't heard that one before." I stopped in front of the microscopes. "Don't you think it odd, that we can be trusted to clean the microscopes but not use them?"

"Using the microscopes doesn't strike me as a grand privilege," Daniel said. "I see no reason why you should be denied the boredom of Linnaean taxonomy."

"I would love botany!" I cried. "You don't know how lucky you are."

"Botany seems like a science women would excel at," Daniel said. "There's no killing, no dissecting, nothing that would overwhelm the sensibilities. In fact, it's not so different from flower arranging and flower painting."

I made a mental note to discuss with Miss Voght the possibility of a botany lesson snuck into Household Economy.

Once when I was running behind in my chores, I held out a rag to Daniel. "Help me clean the cases?" The boys had outdoor chores only once a week, to avoid disruption to their studies.

I suppose I was testing him. He looked surprised, and he did not take the rag from me.

A friendly reminder that Oberlin was not Wyoming.

"Never should a lady accept gifts
from a gentleman not related or engaged to her."

At the end of my third year, I was returning slides to their proper drawers since someone had failed to do so, when I looked up to find a male student standing in the doorway, watching me. I was so startled I nearly dropped the slides. Earlier, I had flagrantly broken the rules by peering into the microscopes.

He looked around at the gleaming glass cases. "I've never been in here. All my chores are outside, with the animals." He did not look like he spent a lot of time outdoors, with those shiny black boots on his feet. Later I tried to remember other things about him, such as his hair or his eyes, but I couldn't. Or maybe my mind wouldn't let me. But I do remember those shiny black boots.

He rested his hands directly on one of the cases and peered down at the plants inside. "What's so special about them?"

"Some are poisonous," I said. When he lifted his hands, I could clearly see the outlines of his fingers on the glass.

His eyes took in my dress and face with bored indifference. Later I would think that he remembered next to nothing of my appearance, much like I wouldn't remember his. "They wouldn't let girls clean the cases if there were poisonous plants inside."

Something in his voice made me instantly wary. "I must have been mistaken."

"I've seen you before," he said, "with that boy, Daniel. Is he your beau?" He said *beau* in a teasing voice, but his smile did not extend to his eyes.

I worked to make my face as blank and smooth as possible, a trick I mastered as a child. Only later did I learn that this blankness only raises the ire of some people; they seek to transform your disinterest into something they understand, a match for their own roiling feelings.

"You were friends with that girl, Sally, who was expelled a few years ago. Expelled for"—here he tapped his greasy fingers against the case—"'moonlight wanderings,' correct?"

I suddenly knew, as clearly as if he had said the words aloud, that he was one of the unnamed male students who had been with her that night. I'd often wondered what, if anything, had happened to the boys.

"It's a shame," he said with a shake of his head, a gesture that looked more rehearsed than spontaneous. "Girls of her class don't know better."

Sally had been a tall, friendly girl with thick red hair. She had an extensive collection of hair ribbons that she kept organized by color, and she was absolutely brilliant in mathematics. In fact she was so far ahead of the rest of us girls that she was permitted to join the male students in their class, although she had to sit in the back of the room, and if she had a question, she was supposed to submit it in writing after the lesson. I was jealous of her for this privilege, I'll admit. The night before my first geometry exam, she sat beside me on my bed, where I was frantically cramming theorems and formulas into my overtaxed brain. She carefully brushed my hair and then tied it up with old rags so it would be curly in the morning, and she told me that if I got nervous during the exam, I should twist a curl around my finger until my breathing calmed enough for me to remember the formula. No one had ever styled my hair for me. No one had ever told me it was all right to feel nervous. The next morning Sally tied a pink ribbon in my curls (Knock 'em dead, Ruth), and when I got my test back later that week, we spun around the room, loudly cheering my A, until the girl next door banged on the adjoining wall for us to quiet down.

In February of our first year, someone claimed they saw Sally out past curfew walking with two male students. I came back from class one day to find her half of the room empty. On our dresser she'd left me one of her lockets. *Wear this and think of me,* read her note. The locket was in the shape of a fan and covered in delicate reeds and butterflies, and I'd often admired it. I instinctively touched it now, hanging from my neck.

Girls of her class, the boy had said, and I saw in that moment, with the kind of clarity that arrives only in moments of true fright, that he believed that girls of any class were his for the taking.

I was not finished cleaning the museum, but I could not bear to be in the room with him one minute longer. "Excuse me," I said. "I have to get to class."

When I went to walk past him, his hand shot out and gripped my wrist.

Aunt Janna used to lament my big bones: How will we ever find dresses to flatter those thick arms? In his hand, my wrist looked like any woman's wrist, delicate and breakable. I had not noticed, as he was slouched against the glass cases, how very tall he was. "Let go. Please." I was embarrassed at the tears in my voice. "I want to leave." I did not feel strong in that moment, as I tried to twist my arm away.

"I won't tell anyone."

He pushed me against the table and several slides fell to the floor. One hand clamped over my mouth and the other fumbled under my skirts. *This is what it feels like to drown,* I thought, and then there was a sharp, searing pain, like I was being ripped apart, or in half, and the broken slides on the floor swam in and out of focus, the way objects do in dreams.

When he was finished, he threw his handkerchief at me. His shiny black boots avoided the broken glass on the floor as he walked out. I waited on the floor until I couldn't hear his footsteps anymore, and then I closed the door. I wasn't ready to leave the museum yet, to be outside this room, to see all the familiar faces and sights of campus. I stayed in the museum, locking the door from the inside, and I cleaned the cases again and again, until they were so clean they squeaked, until my hands stopped shaking, until the pain between my legs was a dull ache.

It was a nice spring day, cool but sunny, when I finally emerged from the museum. I felt as if I were seeing the grounds for the first time. There were the tulips planted by the first-year girls last fall. Garish flowers of red, yellow, and pink. I walked past the library, which I visited every Saturday when the boys were busy with their chores. Daniel often teased me that he rarely saw me without a book. "Reading Ruth," he called me sometimes.

I had been told to want a husband and a family, and I did. I didn't want to live alone like Miss Voght. I also wanted to make my own way in the world.

Behind the library was the farm where the boys worked. Whatever they had to do there took up only four hours, one day a week. THE MORE YOU ACT LIKE A LADY, THE MORE HE'LL ACT LIKE A GENTLEMAN, proclaimed a sign in the dining room. All the things I would be and do if I were not held responsible for the behavior of others.

Aunt Janna had not understood my desire to attend college. She said it would lead to ruin, but it was my life to ruin. I saw, as if a piece of muslin had been suddenly lifted from my eyes, that she had wanted something different for me. She had not understood me, and she had not particularly liked me. For some reason she had stayed after my mother and father died and had found the money for my schooling. What would she say if she knew what had just happened?

She would blame me, of course. As would the other students and teachers. They would say I had encouraged him, tempted him. *Why did you have the door open? What were you wearing? What did you say to him?* Because if he had not behaved like a gentleman, it was because I had failed to act like a proper lady.

I passed a group of boys on their way to class. They were dressed similarly, same haircuts even, one indistinguishable from the next. It wasn't their fault they saw us Oberlin girls as interchangeable; no one had ever told them we weren't.

Back in my room, I climbed into bed with my boots on. I was still bleeding, but I did not get a rag. I had already decided I would never wear this dress again.

The next morning I found his handkerchief on the floor of my room. I had no memory of bringing it back with me. I stared at it for a long, long time. I would not be surprised if someone told me I stared at that handkerchief for a full hour. Sally's locket was warm against my bare skin. I should have tried harder to find Sally. The only time I asked after her, Miss Voght said that Sally had moved back home, and her tone of voice made clear that I should not ask again.

The look on his face as he threw the handkerchief at me, as if I were a speck of dirt on his boot, something to be stepped over and forgotten. His look said, *The scales of justice will always tilt in my favor.*

I won't tell anyone, he said.

But I didn't have to remain silent. I snatched up the handkerchief from the floor and slid it into my trunk.

"Never make noise with the mouth or throat [while eating]."

The morning of the Christmas Eve package reception, we wake to find the dining room overrun with flies. "Don't tell me this isn't bad luck," Maggie says. The flies are larger than any I've ever seen, and even I feel uneasy as I watch them traverse the room in lazy circles.

Matron instructs us to hang an elder bush in the doorway and leave vinegar-soaked cloths of cucumber peelings in the corners. Cora and Theresa stand in the middle of the room and swat at the flies with brooms. The sight of them, their bellies swaying as they chase the flies, sends me into a fit of laughter. Cora and I chase each other with the brooms, and when we breathlessly collapse into the dining room chairs, we could be mistaken for any two women indulging in silliness before a party.

The afternoon is spent transforming the house for Christmas. The reverend delivers a tree to the Home, and we decorate it with strings of popcorn and cranberries. Matron sends us into the back garden for ivy to hang on the banister and mantel. I hum a Christmas carol as I gather greenery in my arms, the pure pleasure of being outside and feeling the sun on my face. The cold air smells of evergreen and woodsmoke.

Cora and Theresa bake cookies, and Maggie and I glaze the angels and gingerbread men with colored sugar. When Matron isn't looking, we all sneak a cookie. "I love Christmas," Cora says, biting off the wings of an angel.

Maggie taps Cora's stomach. "As do babies."

I laugh aloud at the surprised look on Cora's face, although later I'd wonder why I found that so funny.

An hour before the party is set to start, the flies begin dying in earnest. Their bodies accumulate on the dining room table until it looks as if it were covered in black ink. We take down the elder bush, throw out the cucumber peelings. We sweep and sweep and sweep. "These flies will be the end of me," Matron says grimly. Out the dining room window, I watch a vulture swoop in and out of the trees across the street. Luckily Maggie doesn't see the bird.

⚬⚬⚬

Kate has one more week of confinement before she will go work for Mrs. Kesselman, the secretary of the Board. After a year of honest work, she will be given money to travel home with her babies. I find Kate sitting in bed feeding Sophia, who snuffles and flails her arms about as she sucks with loud smacking noises. William lies patiently in the cradle awaiting his turn.

I help her change the babies into clean gowns, and I surprise myself when I run a hand across Sophia's head. Such softness. I know I shouldn't play favorites, but I can't help but prefer her feistiness to William's docility. It's easy for him to be placid—isn't the world designed to meet his needs? It's Sophia who will be forced to bend her will to others, time and again.

Matron has said Kate can attend the party for an hour, as long as she doesn't exert herself. We find a pink dress with green flowers that another girl left behind, and I tie a green velvet ribbon around her neck to make it more festive. She shows me the corset she has modified so she can feed the twins, the slits she added above and below the bust, which can be raised and lowered as needed. "Brilliant," I tell her.

"My mother taught me," she says. "I'll help you make one when it's your time."

In her flowered dress, with her hair braided atop her head, Kate looks like the mother in a children's book. I turn her to face the babies. "Doesn't your mother look beautiful?" From the bed, Sophia squawks and caws, while William lies there, silently gazing at the ceiling. She, a songbird; he, a hawk.

ജ

With the impending prospect of guests in the house, Maggie becomes agitated. She fusses with her hair, fretfully smoothing it down across her cheek. I think of my old barn cat, the one who didn't like visitors.

"I should lie down. I feel very unwell."

"Did you eat too many cookies?" Cora asks.

"Maybe the baby is coming." She is pale, sweating.

"You have another month, silly girl." Mrs. Davidson would not approve of the way Matron indulges Maggie. "Go lie down, and I'll check on you later."

Maggie scurries away.

"Ruth, you greet the guests at the door. Cora and Theresa, you'll help me in the kitchen. Kate, go sit down with the babies so you don't get overtired. And, girls? Don't speak unless you are spoken to."

Mrs. Kesselman is the first to arrive. A large widow with a loud but perpetually hoarse voice, she has a series of moles running amok on her face. There's a large one beneath her nose, an even larger one stuck to her chin, thick clusters on her cheeks. The one on her chin sometimes has a long white hair growing from it. Tonight the chin mole is hairless, thank goodness.

"Good evening, girl," she booms when I open the door. She

hands me her coat and a pile of presents adorned with colorful ribbons made of yarn and gives my stomach a friendly pat as she walks into the sitting room.

Mrs. Davidson and Minnie arrive next. Minnie is splendid in a purple velvet dress. Mrs. Davidson, in bile green, appears ill by comparison. The red beetle pin by her throat resembles a blob of blood. Minnie carries a large package that she insists on lugging into the house herself. Based on the way she staggers as she carries it inside, it's rather heavy. Mrs. Davidson hands me a small, thin package wrapped in brown paper and tied with twine. "For Matron's eyes only."

I am relieved when Mrs. Norris the Board treasurer arrives alone. Her husband has called me Roseanne, Rosie, and Rachel, and his inability to learn my name has never prevented him from finding a way to squeeze my behind.

Mrs. Norris has a daughter named Ruth. Because of this, she once told me she says an extra prayer every night for me. But don't tell the others, she had said. I don't want to encourage rivalries. This other Ruth can't seem to stay pregnant—all her pregnancies this year have ended in miscarriage. My envy of this other Ruth is boundless.

Tonight Mrs. Norris squeezes my hands between her small cold ones. Her wrists are the size of a child's. It's a wonder she was able to have a child herself with those slim hips. "Merry Christmas, Ruth dear."

"Do not intersperse your language
with foreign words and high-sounding terms."

———————————

We sing carols by the piano and eat cookies. Cora plays "The First Noel" and "God Rest Ye Merry, Gentlemen." Her voice is high and sweet. All day I have seesawed between extreme emotions: joyful one minute, sorrowful the next.

"Is it time for presents yet?" Minnie asks when there is a lull. She doesn't wait for an answer before retrieving the package she carried in earlier. "I made it myself." She leans the present against the end of the couch and stands with her hands on her hips. She looks as pleased as a child waiting for praise. "I thought it might brighten up the sitting room."

"How thoughtful of you, Miss Davidson," Matron says.

"I have no idea what she painted," Mrs. Davidson says to Mrs. Kesselman and Mrs. Norris. "She wouldn't let me see it."

"She wanted it to be a surprise for you too. Isn't that lovely," Mrs. Norris says.

"That's one way to see it," Mrs. Davidson says.

"Mrs. Whitehead, would you do the honors?" Minnie asks Matron, who nods and begins carefully removing the paper. "Go on," Minnie urges. "Rip it right off."

"Oh my," Matron says. She squints at the painting and tilts her head. "I've never seen anything quite like this." She turns it around so we can see it.

Kate coughs politely into her hand.

"What *is* it?" Cora asks.

Minnie beams at us. "I was inspired by a painting Monet did of a poppy field."

It's as if someone taught Minnie to paint trees and people, but she forgot the specifics and instead decided to paint the idea of them. Yellow and green dots signify leaves, and two blurry figures in hats stroll on a path. A red lamppost stands among the trees, and behind that is a gray building that I immediately know is the Home.

"It's marvelous." It's the most honest thing I have said in months.

"It's my first attempt at impressionism. It's all the rage in Paris. Wouldn't it look charming over there?" Minnie points to the spot beside Mrs. Davidson's portrait, and her mother's frown deepens.

"We've spent close to a small fortune on art lessons over the years," Mrs. Davidson says. "She used to paint the most beautiful landscapes."

"What did she call it?" Mrs. Kesselman asks. "Infantilism?"

"Impressionism. The artists paint outdoors. *En plein air*," Minnie says with a French accent that would have been the envy of all the girls at Oberlin. "It helps them capture sunlight. I thought Mother would object if I tried to paint outside."

"She leaves for Paris in two days to study art," Mrs. Davidson says. "She'll be studying under the director-general of the Louvre."

Excitement practically radiates off Minnie, even as she attempts to look modest. How different my life would be if I were Minnie Davidson. Expensive art lessons and trips to Paris, doting and indulgent parents. I think of my mother's trip to New York, cut short because of money, and of the paintings she made and the ones she never got to make, and I wonder why some are handed their dreams with a bow on top, and others of us are forced to fight for every crumb of dignity.

We open the remaining packages to less fanfare. Mrs. Norris gives us lavender soap and new hair combs, and Mrs. Kesselman gifts us white-and-yellow-striped booties. "Nothing worse than a baby with cold feet," she shouts. When Kate slips them onto William, he wiggles his feet and we all laugh.

Mrs. Davidson presents Matron with a new prayer book for the Home, as well as a check. "That should tide you over for a few weeks at least."

Since Matron doesn't have her glasses on, I suspect she doesn't know the actual amount. Still, she exclaims over Mrs. Davidson's generosity and says we will use the prayer book daily.

"Of course these girls still need to help with expenses," Mrs. Davidson says. "Sewing curtains is not enough. They should be mending garments and quilts as well, especially now that there are twins."

"No harm in having a second," Mrs. Kesselman says, taking her fifth cookie. She licks at the green sugar glaze coating her bottom lip. "I've always found twins to be rather frightening. Although admittedly these two appear rather even-tempered."

"She can't take care of both babies, of course," Mrs. Davidson says.

Kate blushes. "My mother had twins. Two sets, actually."

"Two sets!" Minnie exclaims. She holds her hand to her forehead as if swooning. "It doesn't seem possible."

"One baby would be difficult enough for a girl in her position," Mrs. Davidson says.

"They remind me of the puppies Father found in the church last spring," Minnie says as Sophia whines in her sleep. "Look how the boy sleeps with his hands out like that. Isn't he sweet, Mother?"

"Where's Maggie?" Mrs. Davidson asks Matron.

"Which one is Maggie?" asks Mrs. Kesselman. "I can't keep all the girls straight."

"The girl with the unfortunate face," Mrs. Davidson says. "That scar that runs from here to here." She gestures from the top of her head to her neck, even though Maggie's scar is mostly confined to her cheek.

"Maggie isn't feeling well," Matron says.

"I hope *she* isn't planning on delivering twins," Mrs. Davidson says.

"Mother never eats sweets," Minnie says when Mrs. Kesselman offers the tray of cookies to her mother. She takes one for herself. "What beautiful hair the boy has. His sister will covet those curls someday."

"New girl," Mrs. Kesselman says loudly to Cora, "how are you adjusting?"

"The girls have taught me to sew," Cora says. "And I'm learning how to knit, although it's terribly difficult."

"She's a quick learner," Matron adds.

"Taught her?" Mrs. Davidson asks. "She never learned?"

"Cora had an . . ." Matron pauses as if carefully selecting from a list of words in her head. ". . . unusual upbringing. As we discussed before her arrival."

"Do the babies cry a lot?" Minnie asks Kate.

"They're both sweet-tempered," Kate says at the same time Cora says, "Oh yes, especially the girl. I'm surprised she's not shrieking now." Matron gives her a look, and Cora covers her mouth with her hand.

"I'm rather terrified of babies," Minnie says.

"Terrified? Surely not," Mrs. Norris says.

"Not of the babies themselves," says Minnie, "but childbirth. My friend Jane had a baby recently and she almost died."

I look over at Theresa and see her stiffen. I suspect she is reacting to the word *almost,* that she is wondering, like I often do, why some women live through their ordeal and others do not.

"The last time I visited Jane, the baby cried the entire visit," Minnie says, "screamed and screamed until she was red in the face. My friend can't walk more than a few steps because she's in so much pain, and I thought, *Why the rush to get married?*"

Mrs. Davidson shakes her head. "Minnie enjoys being provocative these days. It always works on her father, but I've found it best to ignore these outbursts. Women who speak as boldly and frankly as men generally find themselves alone and unmarried, and not by choice. Poor Mrs. George won't even talk to me now, after the way Minnie treated her son."

"I spared you then—you always say Mrs. George is a tiresome woman."

"You mean to never marry?" Mrs. Norris asks Minnie.

"She lost her notebook and took it as a sign she shouldn't marry," Mrs. Davidson says.

How perfect that my theft of her notebook has been interpreted as a providential warning. I bite down, hard, on my lower lip to keep from laughing.

"This is why they caution girls against reading novels," Mrs. Davidson says. "It gives them strange, fretful ideas."

"I don't read novels, Mother. I read poetry."

"Clearly it breeds the same overexcitement and peevishness."

"I will marry someday," Minnie says. "I have no intention of being a surplus woman. I simply haven't met anyone interesting enough to die for."

"What on earth is a surplus woman?"

"An old maid, Mrs. Kesselman."

"You see why my nerves are so frayed, listening to this kind of talk all day," Mrs. Davidson says.

"I've always thought it normal to fear death," Mrs. Kesselman says. "Not a day passes that I don't think of my sister Betsy, and she died nearly forty years ago in childbirth. I still have the letters we exchanged when she was expecting. She was so worried something terrible would happen to her. And then her worst fears came true. Terrible!" she shouts in Cora's face.

Her loud voice wakes Sophia. Kate picks her up and gently rocks her in her arms.

"What would she do if the boy were to start crying?" Mrs. Davidson has a way of asking questions to everyone and no one. It's a surprising trait in a woman.

"William rarely cries," Matron says. "And the girls are always eager to help each other. I'm sure you've noticed a great improvement in their manners and general bearing."

"They won't be under your watchful eye forever." Mrs. Davidson fingers the beetle by her throat and studies William with a critical eye. "Boy babies are easier to care for. They sleep more and don't have any of the digestive issues that plague girls. Better dispositions as well."

"Ruth and her husband were hoping for a son, this last time," Mrs. Norris says. "The doctor fears she isn't strong enough to carry a child to term."

Mrs. Davidson makes a noise of sympathy. "It's dreadful to think of women like Ruth who pray every day for a child, while other girls have two at a time."

Before hearing about this other Ruth, I didn't know a woman might be unable to have children. It was like learning there were birds born without wings or cats without claws. All the things I tried to rid myself of this one: chugging tea laced with pennyroyal, tightening my corset until I couldn't breathe, exercising until my head spun. Once I even lay down on my bed, knees spread apart, a knitting needle clutched in my hand. In the end, I was too much of a coward.

Mrs. Kesselman leans over to Matron. Up close she smells slightly musty, like a shawl that needs a good airing. Rather than being unpleasant, it's a comforting, motherly smell. "How is she?" Her eyes dart over to Theresa, who sits alone by the Christmas tree.

"She's still grieving," Matron says. "I see an improvement, though."

"I'm glad you warned us about her hair. Atrocious." Mrs. Davidson pats her own hair, surprisingly dark for a woman her age. I've heard of women dyeing their hair with a steeped mixture of raspberries and wine, although it's difficult to imagine Mrs. Davidson slathering such a mixture on her scalp. "You have been too indulgent with the girl. It's not as if someone cut out her tongue and she is unable to speak. She's making a choice to be obstinate. You must force her to join in conversations."

"She does all her chores and is a great help with the sewing," Matron says. "My mother used to say there is no wrong way to grieve."

Mrs. Davidson's expression makes clear she strongly disagrees with this sentiment.

"It's shocking to lose a sister," Mrs. Kesselman says. "After Betsy died, I blamed her husband. He moved to Ohio a few weeks after the funeral, and by the end of the year he had married a girl there. A girl half his age," she adds, and Mrs. Davidson tuts in disapproval. "They had six children. That girl raised my nephew as if he were her own, I'll say that."

"You know, Ruth is from Ohio," Matron says.

"Which one is Ruth?" When Matron gestures to me, Mrs. Kesselman shouts in my direction: "Is your family still there?"

"Yes, I have an aunt near Cleveland."

"She must be sorry to see you in this state."

You are not welcome in my house in that condition was the beginning of her last letter to me. "Yes, quite sorry."

"We've had quite a few ingrates pass through here." Mrs. Davidson looks over at Theresa. "A fair number of impostors and liars."

"In contrast, these current girls embrace all the opportunities they have been provided."

"You see the good in everyone, Mrs. Whitehead." Mrs. Davidson's voice makes clear this is not an admirable quality.

"Minnie dear, pass me another cookie, please," Mrs. Kesselman says. "No harm in having a third, I always say."

"I hope you are referring to cookies and not children," Mrs. Davidson says. She looks down at William, whose small chest rises and falls as he sleeps soundly. "Surely you weren't expecting her to bring two babies to your house when she comes to work. I don't see how she will get anything done."

Mrs. Kesselman swallows the bite of cookie in her mouth. "I hadn't considered twins when I offered her the job. The last girl—oh, what was her name? Agatha? Clara? She brought her baby with her."

"The last girl to work for you was Harriet," Matron says. "You were pleased with her work, as I recall. She recently wrote a letter saying she married and is living in Lexington. Isn't that encouraging news?"

"Harriet, yes. I'm surprised to hear she found a husband. She had that eye that wandered about, I was never sure what she was looking at. She had an appalling habit of sucking on the collar of her dress. What an odd girl she was. It just shows you can't account for what men find attractive. She was a hard worker, though. She brought the boy with her, and whenever he cried, she would strap an old sheet to her back and carry the boy around that way. I never saw such a thing before, although it did free up her hands to clean and cook."

"The girl won't be able to strap two babies onto her back," Mrs. Davidson says. "She's not a pack mule. I fear you'll be paying her to lounge about your house with two squalling babies."

"I was thinking that Kate would leave the babies here when she is working at your house, Mrs. Kesselman," Matron says. "We were surprised by the twins as much as you. But they are good-tempered, and the other girls can easily care for them while she is at work."

"Some babies cry endlessly when separated from their mothers."

"Don't be so gloomy, Mother," Minnie says.

"It occurs to me," Mrs. Davidson says slowly, "that we find ourselves in a fortuitous position. The girl has two babies, and Ruth"—she turns to Mrs. Norris—"has been wanting a child. There is an easy remedy sitting right under our noses."

Minnie laughs. "Oh, Mother, be serious! You aren't suggesting that Ruthie take one of these babies?"

"That's exactly what I'm suggesting."

The room grows silent, as if sound could be extinguished as easily as a candle.

"She has two while another in this city has none. A girl in her position shouldn't be selfish."

"The babies are not puppies in a church, Mother. You can't divide them up as you please."

"As president of the Board, I am forced to make all sorts of delicate decisions, and it's clear to me the girl can't care for two."

By the fireplace Kate has gone still and white, Sophia clutched in her arms.

"There are lots of places in this city where Ruth and her husband can adopt a child," Matron says. "The Home of the Innocents, for example, is full of babies who need a loving home."

"One doesn't know anything about those children, what diseases they might carry," Mrs. Davidson says. "Most of them cripples, I'm afraid."

"I can take care of them. Both of them." Kate's voice trembles in time with her body. "They're no trouble to me. As I said earlier, my mother—"

"She's a friendless woman, yes. Luckily the babies don't appear to be harmed by her poor choices"—Mrs. Davidson lightly touches William on the foot and turns to Mrs. Norris—"especially the boy. Wouldn't Ruth be a wonderful mother to him?"

"I told Ruth just yesterday that if she places her trust in the Lord, she will find comfort and strength." Mrs. Norris shifts in her seat and avoids looking over at Kate, who is openly crying now. "Ruth would provide a good Christian home for a baby."

"I have a fiancé back home." Kate turns to Matron with drowning eyes.

Mrs. Davidson flaps her hand, as if Kate were a fly buzzing about the room. "He would have married her already. In fact, it seems very likely she will fall into the same life of sin she led before, especially if she leaves the Home saddled with not one but two children. How long before she ends up back in a house of ill fame?"

"Kate did not come to us from a house of ill fame," Matron says. "Now, why don't we go back in the other room and sing carols? Have a few more cookies?"

"The real problem," Mrs. Davidson says in a voice much louder than her normal one, "is that we never established a firm policy about the babies. It's been a bit too haphazard, every girl choosing for herself whether to take her child or give it up for adoption. And now that we find ourselves with twins, we are truly in uncharted territory."

I wait for Matron to say that twins are not uncharted territory for Kate, yet she is silent.

Kate makes a loud keening cry, more animal than human.

"Ruth could buy the boy and all this worry about how the girl will care for two babies, or how she'll work, will be settled." Mrs. Davidson smiles and pats Mrs. Norris's hand. "How relieved Ruth will be to finally have a child of her own. You told her to place her trust in the Lord, and look what he has provided."

"We are not in the practice of selling babies out of this Home," Matron says. I take in the sudden firmness of her jaw and realize I have never seen Matron truly angry before.

"Ruth and her husband can make a donation to the Home, then," Mrs. Davidson says.

"I will not allow such a transaction, Eliza."

Mrs. Davidson stiffens at the use of her Christian name. "A generous donation would alleviate costs, Mrs. Whitehead. And it bears repeating that you work for the Board. Reverend Davidson is one of your most loyal and faithful subscribers. Without our financial support, this Home would not survive another month."

"Ruth can take my baby." I don't know why it has taken me so long to speak. "I don't want this child." I direct my words to Matron. "And Kate wants both of hers. It would be a help to me if someone took this baby and gave it a nice home."

"A help to you?" Mrs. Davidson asks. "All we do is help you girls! How bold you are to decide that Mrs. Norris's daughter should take your child instead of one of the twins. I'm not a mathematician, but even I can deduce that the girl can't care for two. Adoption is an easy solution to a complicated problem."

"Her name is Kate, not 'the girl.' And she wants both her children, while I don't want this one. I plan to give up mine for adoption. Ruth can take mine." There is a pleasing symmetry to this, the child being handed from one Ruth to another.

"Are you planning on delivering two babies as well?" Mrs. Davidson asks. She turns to Cora with a fearsome smile. "And what about you, dear? Will you be having twins as well? Do you also want us to take a child off your hands so you can return to a sinful life?"

"I'm not here to have a baby."

"Oh, my mistake. I thought all the girls here were whores of Babylon."

I flinch as if Mrs. Davidson slapped my cheek with those words.

"That's enough," Matron says. "I will not allow you to speak this way to the girls, even if you are president of the Board."

The anger I feel inside is reflected on Matron's face. The mask Matron usually wears in front of the Board members has slipped off her face. She looks younger than she has in months, and for a moment I imagine I am seeing her true self.

Mrs. Davidson's cheeks are the same mottled red as the beetle clinging to her throat. "I might as well light my money on fire and toss it out the carriage, for all the good it's doing here. Our efforts have been in vain, since girls of this class are unable to abandon their vulgar upbringing." She looks at Matron. "Especially if they are under the guidance of a fallen woman."

Theresa moves soundlessly across the room and scoops up William from his cradle. She returns to the Christmas tree and positions her body in front of it. Her short hair, aglow from the candles, is a fiery halo.

"Leave," she says to Mrs. Davidson. She switches William from her right to left arm. "Now."

Mrs. Davidson is momentarily speechless.

"You will not shop for babies as if this were a department store and you are in need of a new hat," Theresa says. "Go home."

Mrs. Davidson's neck is now a painful pink blotch. "The lack of restraining influences on display tonight. One girl ordering me to leave, one claiming she's not pregnant, one eschewing her maternal duties, and one refusing help. All that's missing is the scarred girl, and I shudder to think what insanity she might spout. There will be severe changes once the reverend knows the true state of things over here." Mrs. Davidson snatches up the prayer book and check.

"If you want to lecture about restraining influences, you should speak with Mr. Norris first." Theresa's eyes are dark as night as she looks directly at Mrs. Norris. "Ask him about the house on Fourth Street he likes to frequent. He always requested Catherine and me together, 'the two blondies,' he called us—never did bother to learn our names, although it was obvious my sister was his favorite. He'll be sorry to hear she's dead."

Judging by her face, this is not the first time Mrs. Norris has heard such rumors about her husband.

Mrs. Davidson stands from the couch and gives Minnie a loud look, and her daughter wordlessly rises to her feet. "When I return tomorrow, I expect the girl to be expelled or I will close this Home myself. And if that one wishes to remain here"— she turns to Kate—"she will give up the boy."

Theresa gently cups William's head. "I won't allow him to be separated from his sister." She holds him as tenderly, as fervently, as she held Catherine's dead son that day.

Theresa uses her right hand to pull something from her dress pocket, while cradling William with her left. Kate is the first to spot the knife in Theresa's hand. "Theresa, no!" she shouts, but Theresa's hand is quicker, and she makes the first gash, long and red, across her own stomach. Her hand is steady and sure. I have never seen a deer gutted, but it must look like this, an instant summoning of red where before there was none, the inside of the body suddenly on the outside. I try to shout and discover something is wrong with my throat. Same with my feet, which refuse to leave the ground.

"They can't take this one now." Theresa makes one final slice, even deeper than the first, before collapsing, William still clutched tightly in her arms.

> "Never exhibit anger, impatience,
> or excitement, when an accident happens."

Matron rips off the bottom of her own dress and presses it to Theresa's abdomen, where it promptly blooms red. I kneel helplessly beside Matron. "Ruth, I need rags. Go quickly."

I run upstairs as fast as I can. I look down to find I am running with my hands under my stomach. I fling open the linen closet, blindly grabbing at the bandages. When I enter the sitting room again, I freeze at the sight of all the blood. It's in the branches of the Christmas tree, on Minnie's painting, on the fireplace screen. It's on William's face. Kate has stripped off his clothes and wrapped him in a blanket. His cries appear to be of someone frightened, not hurt. Cora and Minnie sit side by side on the couch, both with stunned, blank faces. Cora reaches out and grabs Minnie's hand. Minnie looks down at their entwined hands in surprise but doesn't pull hers away.

The puddle beneath Theresa has grown larger. On the floor beside her is not a knife but Matron's letter opener, its handle no longer green.

I hand Matron one of the bandages, and she presses down with both hands. I briefly wonder if she's using the bandage Reverend Davidson waved about during his Egyptian lecture.

"We just need to get you stitched up, Theresa, and you'll be good as new." Matron motions for a clean rag and shows me how to apply pressure.

I press down on Theresa's stomach with both hands and

hope I am not hurting her. She moans and blood slides from her mouth into the tangle of her hair.

"You'll be fine, Theresa, you wait and see," Matron says. She presses a clean bandage against Theresa's stomach and ties it tightly. "Mrs. Kesselman, may we take your carriage?"

Mrs. Kesselman looks up at her name. Beside her, Mrs. Norris shakes and cries. "Yes, that's fine," Mrs. Kesselman says. "Mine is the largest." Her voice is no louder than a whisper.

Matron looks at me. "On three," she says.

It's hard to get a firm grip on Theresa, whose arms are slick with blood. Somehow we manage to lift her up and carry her outside. The cold air makes my eyes water, but Theresa doesn't react. She's gone slack in our arms, her head lolling off to the side in a way that I know is not good.

"Wait," Mrs. Davidson calls. She rushes past with blankets in her arms. We wait in the cold, arms shaking with effort, as she carefully arranges the blankets over the seats of Mrs. Kesselman's carriage. She helps us maneuver Theresa inside, and then Matron climbs in, cradling Theresa's head in her lap. "You foolish girl," she says, not bothering to wipe the tears streaming down her face. Mrs. Kesselman climbs in and they disappear into the night.

I look down to discover I too am covered in blood, my arms and dress slick with it. Blood smells the same, no matter the reason it is leaving the body. I don't know why this is a surprise to me.

⊗⊗

When I finally told her about the baby, Miss Voght arranged a meeting with Mr. Bullough, the president of Oberlin.

"There's no point," I said. "He won't let me stay in my condition."

"Mr. Bullough is progressive, surprisingly so," she said. "He recently formed a committee to look into opening more science classes to women." She patted my arm encouragingly. "Just because something has never been done before doesn't mean it's impossible, Ruth."

On the morning of our meeting, I scrubbed my face until it was pink and brushed my hair until my scalp tingled. I ransacked my closet for a dress that fit my new breasts.

Mr. Bullough ushered Miss Voght and me into his office. It was clear that Mr. Bullough had not dressed with the same care for our meeting: his wrinkled shirt had a yellowish stain on the collar, revealing a breakfast of eggs. The surface of his desk was immaculate, and something about its extreme tidiness—not a stray paper or pen, no sign of dust—made my heart sink as I sat across from him. This was a man who clearly believed, at least when it came to his college if not his appearance, in the ordering power of rules.

I had never spoken to Mr. Bullough directly. I knew he was well liked by both teachers and students, admired for his humble nature. There were rumors he even milked his own cow, although I never gave that story much credence. He had fought in the war and there was something wrong with his hand as a result. His good hand now rested on top of the desk, while the other stayed in his lap.

"You don't believe you deserve expulsion, Ruth."

"It's not her fault, Richard," Miss Voght said.

He held up a hand in her direction. "I'd like to hear from Ruth, please. You are with child," he said to me.

"Yes. Not by choice."

He pressed together his thumb and index finger. The fingers on his good hand were unnaturally long and thin. Surely his wife had to make special gloves to fit those fingers. The hand in his lap was shriveled and scarred, more claw than hand. Did his wife make a special glove for that hand as well? "You're saying he forced you."

"Yes."

"That's a very serious accusation."

"I find myself in a rather serious situation." At a look from Miss Voght, I added, "Sir."

Miss Voght's earrings, small blue stones, glittered in the light as she leaned forward in her chair. "Ruth is a smart girl and she's a good student. She's doing better in her studies than most of the boys in her year."

"I know," he said. "I looked over your grades this morning, and they are impressive."

In spite of myself, I fought to hide a smile. I took out the boy's handkerchief and carefully laid it on the desk. "I told him no. I said it very clearly, there was no misunderstanding me. Afterward, he threw his handkerchief at me. Those spots are my blood." I said this calmly, as if reading from a script.

He looked at the initials sewn onto the cloth, the work of a mother or sister, someone proud of this boy heading off to college. "He'll say he gave it you," Mr. Bullough said, "or that he has no idea how you ended up with it. Unfortunately a handkerchief proves nothing." Staring at it now, I saw how idiotic it was as a piece of evidence.

"Ruth has not had any discipline problems, but I suspect that's not true of the boy," Miss Voght said.

"I can't ask him to prove that she resisted."

"Why not?" she challenged.

"Would you really drag Ruth through such a degrading process? Pit her word against his, allow her character to be examined and smeared, while his remains intact? I would be an unfeeling man if I allowed such a thing." He looked first at Miss Voght and then at me. "I wouldn't be able to look my wife or daughter in the eye afterward," he said quietly.

"As long as you don't expel her, she can return after the baby is born."

I saw in his eyes that he believed me. But he also believed, and this was clearly stronger and more set, that what had happened to me would never happen to his daughter, his sister, his wife. He couldn't imagine a woman he loved crying, *No, no, don't,* in a voice not her own. And since he couldn't, or wouldn't, believe in a world where what happened to me could happen to someone he knew, I became a different sort of girl. An unfortunate girl who found herself in an unfortunate situation. I imagined his wife saying, as she listened with a sympathetic ear while he recounted our meeting, *It sounds to me like you were very fair-minded with the girl.* I would never be able to convince him I was blameless. In his mind, I was as stained as that goddamn handkerchief on his desk.

"We must take the world as it is," Mr. Bullough said, "not as we wish it to be."

With his good hand flat on the desk, he pushed himself to standing. I stared at his claw hand instead of his face. How many girls had sat where I sat? How many times had he said, "We must take the world as it is," and had he said it enough times that he now believed it?

"I wish you luck, Ruth," he said. "There's a home in Louisville that I can inquire about, if you have nowhere else to go."

"Never lend an article you have borrowed,
unless you have permission to do so."

Christmas Eve night, I dream I am walking with Sally through
the museum at Oberlin. It's night and we're not supposed to be
there, and at first this rule-breaking is amusing. We tiptoe in
an exaggerated fashion, and when I giggle, the sound is overly
loud in the dark quiet. Sally holds a finger to her smiling lips,
and I clap a hand over my mouth to stifle my laughter. Sally
walks over to the microscopes and carefully places something
under the eyepiece. She motions me over. *You see it now, don't
you?* Sally whispers in my ear. But there is only darkness when
I put my eye to the microscope, and when I turn to tell her this,
I'm alone in the museum and there is nothing funny about the
darkness now. I hear Sally crying, but I can't find her. I enter the
hallway and start opening doors. The sound of her crying grows
louder as I search room after room, all of them unfamiliar and
vast. I'm going in circles, but I can't stop flinging open doors
or calling Sally's name. At one point I drop to my knees and
crawl through the rooms. How will I reach her in time? I crawl
over something wet, and I look down to see I am on top of one
of my mother's paintings. *In time before what?* my mother asks
before deftly pulling her painting out from under me.

When I wake on Christmas Day, it's from the sound of a
crying baby, not my old roommate, Sally. The door to Kate's
room is open, her bed empty. Sophia is alone in the cradle. I

call for Kate, and when she doesn't appear, I change Sophia into dry clothes and bring her with me. We pass Maggie's room, empty as well, the quilt from her bed crumpled on the floor. Maggie takes pride in always keeping a clean room, and I swallow hard as I head downstairs.

A woman I don't recognize is on her hands and knees in the sitting room, scrubbing furiously at the rust-colored stains on the floor. She dips a wire brush into a bucket of strong-smelling water that makes my eyes and throat burn and moves the brush in small, tight circles.

"Where's Matron?"

The girl doesn't look up from her work. "Kitchen."

I find Mrs. Davidson in the kitchen, Matron's apron tied snugly around her small waist. She walks past with a sack of sugar and places it next to a growing pile of food: leftover Christmas cookies, bacon, honey, pears, jellies. "Part of the problem," she says, as if we were in the middle of a conversation, "is the diet here. All these fatty foods."

Instinctively I pull Sophia closer to me. "Where's Matron?"

Mrs. Davidson opens and closes cabinets, peering inside. "There will be some changes around here. Dietary changes. Changes in chores. Which hopefully"—she stands on her toes to pull down a tin of black tea—"will lead to significant changes in temperament and decorum."

"Is she at the hospital with Theresa?" I ask this even though I think Theresa is likely at the morgue.

Mrs. Davidson returns to the cabinets without looking at me. "I know you were fond of Mrs. Whitehead, but last night showed me what happens when there is a laxity of rules."

I shift Sophia to the other arm. She snuffles against my shoulder as if searching for food. She makes a whining noise that I know will escalate into full-fledged screaming if she isn't fed soon. "I can't find Kate, and her daughter is hungry."

"The girl is at the asylum. She refused to see the wisdom of giving her son a better life. Those who have made their beds must lie in them."

What I know of asylums comes from novels. They are not a place for someone like Kate. "You can't send a person to the asylum simply for disagreeing with you."

She turns to me and wipes her hands on Matron's apron. "There is a devil-may-care tone in your voice that I don't appreciate."

I step away from her. "And Maggie?"

"The scarred girl is at the hospital. She went into labor early this morning, and after what happened last night, I thought it best she deliver there."

Mrs. Davidson bends down to look through the cabinets by the stove. I imagine shoving her inside, like she is the witch from "Hansel and Gretel." I imagine snatching a knife and slashing at her the way Theresa did her own body. I imagine a different girl cutting out an article from the paper before pasting it in the black book: *Two women sent to insane asylum, one to hospital, one to the city morgue.*

Sophia begins crying, loud hiccuping sobs. Mrs. Davidson hands me a tin of powdered milk and a bottle. "I have a headache. Please take her out of here."

⟡

After breakfast, Mrs. Davidson's girl searches our rooms. In Theresa's, she finds an empty brown bottle and shears from the kitchen. When the girl brings down Minnie's book and lays it on the table beside the other contraband, Mrs. Davidson closes her eyes, pressing her fingers to her temple. "Where did you find that?"

"The room at the end of the hall, ma'am."

"My room." I hope she hears the devil-may-care tone in my voice.

"Would you like to explain how my daughter's notebook ended up in your room?"

"I took it."

"This means expulsion."

The moment is eerily familiar. "Third-year girl expelled for curfew violation," reported the *Oberlin Review*. I suppose I should be thankful I'm not being sent to the asylum. To be honest, I'm too tired to feel much of anything.

⚭⚭

Mrs. Davidson's girl packs my bag. She doesn't look at me as she hands it to me, and I don't look inside. When I hug Cora goodbye, I slip Dr. Munro's letter into her dress pocket. "Read this when you're alone," I whisper in her ear.

Mrs. Davidson walks me to the door. "I take no pleasure in your expulsion, Ruth. Especially not on Christmas Day." The door clicks shut behind her.

The coin doesn't land on tails every time, Ruth, Miss Voght had said after our meeting with Mr. Bullough. I find comfort in the words today, even though I didn't all those months ago. It's statistically impossible for a coin to land on tails every time.

It's cold outside, but my body is warm, mostly from the baby. No one told me that about being pregnant, the continuous warmth. How can I be a friendless woman when inside me is a constant companion?

I wonder if I will discover I am a cat who always lands on her feet or a bird who, once banished from the nest, falls to her death.

We must take the world as it is, Mr. Bullough said.

I hope the next girl who sits across from his desk brings more than a soiled handkerchief. I hope the next girl fights to stay, that she refuses to take the world as it is, because the world is ever-changing. "The world is ever-changing," I say quietly, and then I shout it up into the cold morning sky. My feet carry me toward the park.

Freedom smells the same, no matter the circumstances by which it is granted. This is not a surprise to me at all.

THE LOUISVILLE COURIER-JOURNAL

AN INTERVIEW WITH VENERABLE WORKER LUCY STONE—WHAT WOMEN WANT

Though sixty winters have passed over the head of Mrs. Stone, she is still a hale and hearty woman, and expects to live to see the object of her labors, partially at least, accomplished.

> Q—Is the cause of woman suffrage gaining the interest of women?

> Mrs. S.—Most assuredly, but they are slow to come out and acknowledge it in public.

> Q—Do you expect it to be sustained in Wyoming, when she forms a State Constitution?

> Mrs. S.—Certainly.

> Q—What about in other Territories or States?

> Mrs. S.—We don't expect anything, but we hope everything.

> Q—Do you think that wives would be free voters?

> Mrs. S.—Men who are tyrants now would be tyrants over the voting of their wives. And the sooner women get to respecting their own rights, the sooner their husbands respect them.

Q—If the wife is merely to duplicate the man's vote, would that be any gain?

Mrs. S.—She will not duplicate it always. It would be a gain to have two votes for a good measure.

Q—There is a general conviction that suffrage has been debased by too great extension into the ignorant and improvident classes; do you not think that woman suffrage, in its practical working, in which the worst would be sure to vote, and the better sort might neglect, would cause still further debasement?

Mrs. S.—I am reminded of the man coming home late at night drunk. He says, "If my wife is up, I'll lick her. What right has she to sit up so late at night? And if she's abed, I'll lick her. What right does she have to go to bed before I get home?" The opponents of women's suffrage are like this drunkard. They are equally dissatisfied whether the best or worst class of women vote.*

---

* November 1879.

PART II

Belle

*We fear that Belle has returned to
her former life of shame.*

"There will be times, alas, when a woman's health makes her cross and petulant."

———————————

"You want to tell me already?" Fay asked. This was early March. I was lying on my back, breathing deeply and attempting to focus on the dimpled pattern in the ceiling to calm my stomach.

She was referring to the incident with Mr. Dreck. He refused to pay after I slapped his face when he went to touch my breasts.

"In my experience, there's only one reason a woman won't let a man touch her nipples." Fay stood next to the bed, hands on her hips.

"I don't know how this happened."

Fay made a dismissive noise.

"You should get that water stain looked at before the roof caves in." I rolled over to face the wall and swallowed, hard, to keep my supper down.

"You'll have to leave when you start to show," she said, "which ought to be any day now, I reckon."

"I'm not going to that religious home you banished Ruby and Phoebe to last year."

"If you have a better idea, please share it."

"Abortion."

"You want to die like Evelyn?"

"I'll take those Spanish pills Charlotte has."

"Sugar-coated poison."

"I don't know a goddamn thing about being a mother," I said to the wall.

"It is what it is, Belle." As the owner of her own brothel, Fay was nothing if not practical.

"Behold, I stand at the door and knock."

———————

A week later I found myself in the parlor of the religious Home, wearing my most modest dress, seated across from two women, one old and one young. The house was quiet for a house full of women and children. A young girl with a shockingly huge belly entered the room, a tray with coffee, sugar, and cream gripped tightly in her hands.

The girl offered a cup to the older woman first. "Sugar?" she asked. I heard in that one word that she was not from the city.

The old woman shook her head. "None for me, Hattie, or for Miss MacCorkle today," she said when the pregnant girl turned to her younger companion.

"I'll take sugar," I said. Mrs. Clarke frowned, but she didn't object when the girl added a heaping teaspoon to my cup.

Mrs. Clarke carried herself like she had been beautiful once and expected to be treated as if she were still a pretty young thing, even though her hair was gray and her eyes sunken in by old age. She looked me over as she sipped her coffee. The young one, Miss MacCorkle, had colorless thinning hair and close-set eyes offset by dark, unruly eyebrows. The hairs grew angrily together before fanning out like wings on a bird. Fay would never have allowed such eyebrows at her place. Miss MacCorkle took the world's smallest sip from her un-sugared coffee and grimaced slightly.

"Now, Belle," Mrs. Clarke began, "this is not an inn on the highway of vice. You must be committed to leading a better life."

Agree with everything they say, Fay told me before I left. Your choices are their charity or the street.

"I am very committed."

"The drink curse and the social evil are twin monsters, and we cannot separate them," Mrs. Clarke said. "Do you promise to abstain from all intoxicants, Belle?"

She sounded like the woman we called Mrs. Rum Curse who stood across the street from Fay's all last summer, waving a Bible and shrieking to all who entered and left, Abstain and repent! Fight the rum curse!

"Yes, ma'am." I gave my newly rounded stomach what I hoped was a motherly pat.

"You must promise to stay in the Home for a full eighteen months. We have learned from experience that we cannot depend upon the stability of a reformation that cannot endure that long a test."

Eighteen months. Fay had failed to mention that important fact. No way was I staying here a year and a half. Still, I nodded, as if the idea were simply too delightful to merit mere words.

"Yes or no?" Mrs. Clarke asked. "A head nod is insufficient."

"Yes," I said loudly.

"Religion will not be thrust upon you. But we have found that all women, from their first day in the Home, intuitively turn to the worship of God."

"Intuitively," Miss MacCorkle echoed, before braving another sip of her bitter coffee.

"Have you attended church services before?"

"When my mother was alive, we attended Mass at Christmastime."

Miss MacCorkle's eyes grew wide while Mrs. Clarke's narrowed. My heart sank when she set down her coffee and sat up straight. "God forgives, but he is not always ready to forgive the sins of idolatry. Should you bring any sort of Papist sensationalism into this Home, you will be removed."* I didn't know idolatry from Adam, but I could tell from the new tightness of her mouth that it was not a good thing.

"I won't bring anything like that with me."

"Do you promise to read from the Bible nightly?" Mrs. Clarke asked.

I was starting to think Mrs. Clarke might be Mrs. Rum Curse after all. "Sure," I said.

"Finally, and this is by far the most important," Mrs. Clarke said, "you must agree to keep your child. We used to allow the girls to put their children up for adoption, but that practice has been abandoned. Motherhood will hold you to a better life and act as a safeguard. Prevent you from returning to sin."

I think you'd make a great mother, Rose once told me.

Motherhood didn't seem like the worst thing in the world. It generally involved a husband, though, and I didn't want any part of that.

I thought of Fay's advice again, and I finally said, "Yes, I agree to keep my child."

The young one had been staring blankly into her coffee, but when I said yes, her head snapped up and she wiggled happily in her chair. I was starting to wonder if there wasn't something a little off about her.

"While all the world might see you as incorrigible, we believe in your potential salvation, Belle. Now that you have

---

*   Adapted from "The Betts Lecture," *The Louisville Courier-Journal,*
April 15, 1889.

heard about the drudgery and hard work, do you still desire admission?"*

"I'm no stranger to hard work, ma'am."

Mrs. Clarke solemnly handed me a Bible. "Welcome to the Home, Belle. Miss MacCorkle will show you to your room."

---

* Adapted from "Friends of the Fallen: A Charity the Fruit of Whose Good Work Will Ripen in Eternity," *The Louisville Courier-Journal,* February 26, 1887.

"For every ~~man~~ woman shall
bear ~~his~~ her own burden."

That first week, I learned a person could sleep anywhere, if offered a warm bed. I'd learned years ago that the body needs what it needs but will take what is offered.

The girl in the room next to mine, Mary Ann, was always grumbling about the chores in the Home, but I'd never had this much free time in my life. Memorize a few Bible verses, sew curtains, and work in a garden—there were worse things a woman could be asked to do in this life, trust me. I dove headfirst into the chores. First to rise, last to bed. I worked in the garden all morning, the laundry room all afternoon, and I sewed curtains at night as if the devil himself had requested a completed set by the end of the week.

In the garden I would kneel in the dirt, my belly daily growing as round as the bulbs I planted. Sometimes I would slip off my gloves and plunge my hands far beneath the sun-warmed top layer, to grasp something cold and solid. The lady managers believed that if we worked our bodies to exhaustion, our minds would be open to salvation. I wasn't looking for salvation, but an exhausted body meant an exhausted mind, which sounded pretty damn good to me.

Mrs. Clarke was fearful I would return to my evil ways after the baby was born.

"Fay doesn't let mothers work at her place," I told Mrs. Clarke when she cornered me outside one morning.

"You must pray for forgiveness and the fortitude to resist the pull of your former life."

"The only pull of my former life was money," I said.

"Dishonest money dwindles away, but whoever gathers money little by little makes it grow."

Dishonest money put food in your belly and clothes on your back just as well as honest money, in my experience.

Mrs. Clarke looked at me expectantly.

"Wise words, ma'am," I said as I lovingly patted dirt around the black-eyed Susans.

☙❧

At the end of my first week, there was a loud knock on my door at bedtime, and before I could get up, Mary Ann walked in.

"I need to have a word with you, new girl. May I?" She nodded at the rocking chair by the window and lowered herself into it, the wood protested loudly at her weight. She was a short woman with strictly parted dark hair. I hadn't talked to her since my first day, when she told me she was a widow. I had a knack for spotting former fame girls, since I used to help Fay with the screening at her place. Girls like Mary Ann, whose figures were on the thick side or whose manners were a little too uppity, we sent to Hannah Daily's over on Lafayette. Fay said I was the best at sniffing out the girls who thought they were too good for the job. I knew right away Mary Ann was no widow, that she was at the Home for the same reason as me.

"You're making us look bad." She was so short her feet didn't touch the ground while in the rocking chair. "You're working too hard."

When I laughed, she shot me an angry look.

"I'm serious," she said. "Don't set a pace that the rest of us can't keep up with."

"I'm just trying to keep my nose clean and stay out of trouble."

She heaved herself out of the rocking chair and waddled over to the painting hanging next to my bed. "Where did you get that?"

Earlier that day, I found a painting stashed behind the drying racks in the basement. The frame was old and rusted, brownish red in places. It was of two blurry figures on a path. I decided the figures were girls. These girls were not out for a leisurely stroll; their walking was purposeful and deliberate. They were happy. Above their heads were yellow smudges. Hats or halos? Halos, I decided. Ahead of them loomed a gray house. I studied that painting for a long, long time before carrying it upstairs to my room.

"Found it. What's it to you?"

"We're not permitted to hang art on the walls."

"Then I'll take it down when I'm told to."

"Consider yourself told." She lifted the painting off the wall and held it defiantly in front of her.

"Put that back where you fucking found it or you'll regret walking in here."

Something in my face must have told her she was on the wrong side of the fence. She flung the painting onto my bed. "You don't want to get on my bad side, Belle," she said, slamming the door on her way out.

"Bitch." I'd known plenty of women like Mary Ann, and in my experience, they only ever managed to scare themselves with their big feelings.

After Mary Ann left, I lay on my back and thumbed through the book on Kentucky birds Rose left behind last December. I had learned a lot about birds in her absence. I'd never in my life gone to bed as early as I did here, and most nights, while I tried to fall asleep, I would drape one of Rose's dresses across my stomach and talk to that dress as if it were Rose herself. I told her that my gums bled when I brushed my teeth, that sweat collected under my breasts and behind my knees, that one day

I woke to discover my swollen feet no longer fit into my boots. I told her that Mary Ann was a liar but that the other girls weren't so bad. Rose's dress was a comforting presence there on my stomach, which occasionally rolled like the waves of the ocean we never did visit.

You can conjure a person's smell from her clothing, but if you're not careful, you can overhandle her memory, turning her into a person who never existed. Still, I clung to what I remembered.

"Maybe the baby will have dark hair like you," I said to Rose. "Your hazel eyes."

The real Rose would have said, *Silly Bells. It doesn't work that way.*

But what if that was exactly how it worked?

"I don't know if I can do this," I said to Rose's dress that first week. *This* referred to staying in the Home and living without her and becoming a mother. What did I know about motherhood?

Rose's dress said, with Rose's characteristic shrug, *What other choice do you have, Bells?*

"You sound like Fay," I said with a sigh.

"God is our refuge and strength,
a very present help in trouble."

The Home and Fay's place over on Fourth Street were only a few blocks apart. Fay used to tell us girls what to do with our hair and our bodies, and now it was Mrs. Clarke. Even the exams from Dr. Shippen were the same. Mrs. Clarke would not be happy to know that despite the religion lessons and lack of colored girls, at the end of the day, her home wasn't so different from Fay's.

I passed a month in the Home and then two. For years I had been forced to unnaturally groom my body. No hair down below, abundant hair on top. A small waist. But not too small! A good-sized behind. But not too big! The trick was to appeal to the majority of men—an impossible task. And now I watched my waist grow less small and my bottom grow bigger, and there was a surprising freedom in this complete surrender of my body.

Once the chill of spring passed, I made a point to sit in the chair by the window during sewing time so I could feel the sun on my face as I worked. I wasn't happy exactly. But there were times, as the days blurred together, that I was content. Happiness and contentment are not the same, although if someone were to peer in through the Home's window and see me balancing my sewing on my ever-growing stomach, the sun warming my face, they might mistake the one for the other.

On the day Hattie went into labor, I was seated by the window, so I could keep an eye out for Mr. Goss's carriage. Every Friday afternoon he brought over a bag of caramels to the Home. He claimed they were the ones he didn't sell in his sweet shop that week, but the candies were too buttery and fresh tasting to be a week old. When we saw him on our Sunday walk to church, he would wave: Did you enjoy the caramels, girls? I used to hate caramels, but pregnancy makes you crave weird things. One of the other inmates, Annie, told me that when she was pregnant, she would eat dirt. Big handfuls straight from the backyard garden. So there are worse things a woman could crave.

I was looking forward to the caramels after spending the morning in Hattie's room. She had been in labor since late the night before. Even though Dr. Shippen didn't say anything, I could tell he was worried about how long it was taking from the way he paced about, rolling and unrolling his shirtsleeves. At Fay's, he would come to the house every six months to inspect us, make sure we weren't carrying the French disease. Time for our French exam, I used to say when Dr. Shippen arrived.

Technically it was Miss MacCorkle's job to assist Dr. Shippen on birth days in the Home, but ever since the disaster that was Caroline's birth, when Miss MacCorkle vomited all over Caroline's bed and poor Caroline herself, after the baby's head emerged, she had been banned from the birth room. I certainly didn't enjoy being in the room with a woman as she pushed out another human being. If I could learn to vomit on command to get out of helping on birth days, I would.

"Mr. Goss is here with the caramels, thank God," I said as his carriage pulled up next door. As soon as I said *thank God*, Mr. Goss's horse suddenly reared up, and Mr. Goss, one foot in and one foot out of the carriage, was tossed unceremoniously to the ground. He lay motionless, his legs splayed out in a way that was clearly not right. The paper bag landed upright by his head, and I watched in horror as the horse's hooves landed in quick succession, first on the bag and then on Mr. Goss himself.

"Oh hell," I said. From upstairs Hattie screamed, "*I can't, I can't.*"

"Don't tell me he forgot the caramels," Mary Ann said. "I've been thinking about them all week."

"Go tell Dr. Shippen he's needed next door," I said. "And be quick about it."

⚮

When we retired to the front room after dinner for needlework, Hattie was still at it. This time I avoided the chair overlooking the street. Mr. Goss's body had been taken away hours ago, but there were still blood and caramels in the street.

"'Aged Man Thrown from His Carriage, Sustaining Fatal Injuries,'"* Annie read aloud from the evening paper. She carefully snipped out the article with her sewing scissors. "Poor Mr. Goss." Annie's favorite column in the newspaper was the Devil's Diary, an annual compilation of all the murders from the year: 57 persons killed by thieves, 253 men killed in common quarrels, 4 killings on account of dogs, 64 on account of wives, et cetera.

"He had a nice long life," Caroline said. She looked over at her son, Phillip, lying placidly on a blanket beside her chair. "We can take comfort in that. I'd like to pray for him before we begin sewing."

Caroline and I were both new to religion, but her prayers had an embarrassing earnestness to them. I kept my eyes open and stifled a yawn as she began.

---

* Adapted from *The Louisville Courier-Journal*, August 6, 1899.

Bless the Lord, O my soul,
For I am a grave sinner,
Yet he forgives all my sins,
He heals all my diseases,
And redeems my life from the pit.

"What could be worse than being trampled to death by your own horse?" Mary Ann asked after.

"It wouldn't be better if the trampling was done by someone else's horse, if the final outcome was still death," Annie said. At forty-eight, Annie was the oldest woman in the Home, and unlike the rest of us, she was not pregnant. Her daughter, Tabitha, age eight, lived in Indiana and sent Annie a letter once a month addressed to *Aunt Annie*. Other girls stayed their full eighteen months in the Home and then left, generally with a husband or a job. But not Annie. She was a good cook and liked to take care of the babies in the Home when their mothers went off to work, and somewhere along the way she became a permanent fixture in the Home. I'd rather take my chances on the street than live here forever under Mrs. Clarke's watchful eye.

"Would you rather be trampled by horses or die in childbirth?" I asked.

"Oh, Belle, really," Mary Ann said. "Don't be so gruesome."

"Horses," said Annie. "A quicker death."

"Speaking of death, I received a letter from my cousin Constance today," said Mary Ann. "It's been one year since that man in London killed all those women, and they still haven't caught him. Constance fears they never will."

"And you call me gruesome," I said. It was a real struggle to be patient with Mary Ann. The last time Mary Ann told her ridiculous lie about being a widow, I lost my temper with her and she cried until she gave herself the hiccups. All I said was: I don't care where you came from, but you're no widow.

Miss MacCorkle grew worried Mary Ann's baby would come early because of all the hiccuping and carrying on, and after Mary Ann calmed down, Miss MacCorkle and Mrs. Clarke were angry with me. The most infuriating part was they weren't angry with Mary Ann for lying about being a widow. I apologized when it became clear that was my only option if I wanted to remain in the Home. But you can bet I never forgot what that girl really was.

"Of course, Constance isn't worried, because this man in London only killed a very particular kind of woman. What some might call a *doubtful* woman." Mary Ann squinted over at me. She desperately needed glasses and was too vain to wear them. "Isn't that terrifying, Belle?"

"Terrifying," I agreed. "It's doubly worse for those thick-skulled broads who didn't even realize they were a target for this man. Women who lied about being a doubtful woman."

"Men murder women all the time," Annie said. "They murder each other and their own sons as well. You don't have to live in London to know that."

The last newspaper article about the Home included a paragraph about Annie: "An interesting character occupies the room furnished by the Trinity Methodist women. Her former life of dissipation has bleached her black hair and given her a prematurely old expression. She is called 'Annie' and has been in the Home for over eight years, never having been beyond its doors during that time."[*] Annie attended Sunday services with the rest of us, and her hair looked just fine for a forty-eight-year-old woman, but I supposed that kind of honest reporting didn't sell as well.

"The things this man did to those girls," Mary Ann said about the London murderer. "How he cut them up, the parts he took and the parts he left behind." She smoothed the cur-

---

[*]   Adapted from *The Louisville Courier-Journal,* May 29, 1894.

tains in her lap. "I'm still haunted by what Constance wrote in her letter, so I'll spare you the details. Don't bother asking. Bodies left in the street like garbage. Insides on the outside of the body."

"He'll be caught," I said. "One day he'll try to mess with the wrong woman, and then it will be his body we'll read about in the papers."

"That can't happen soon enough," Mary Ann said. "I share a name with one of the murdered women."

"Did he take their eyes?" Annie asked. Instead of sewing curtains, she was mending the quilt from her bed. Last month, the women of the Trinity Methodist Church donated new quilts to the Home, and Miss MacCorkle tried to convince Annie to trade in her quilt, with its strange, clashing colors and uneven squares, for one of the nice new ones, but Annie refused. She said she felt a real kinship with the woman who made her quilt, because when she was a young girl, her first quilt came out rather lopsided, and her mother had threatened to hold her hands over the stove if she ever did such a poor job of sewing again. I'd prefer to mend this one instead of trading it in for a new one, Annie said to Miss MacCorkle, who nodded quickly with wide eyes, her typical response to hearing one of Annie's stories about her childhood.

"Along with other parts that should not be mentioned in polite company," Mary Ann said. "I'm sorry to report that you also share a name with one of the women, Annie."

Annie nodded, as if she'd been expecting such a report. "I bet he took their wombs. Men like that always do."

Mary Ann made a slicing movement across her abdomen. "Last thing I'll confirm."

"My womb fell out years ago," Annie said.

"How do you know that?" Mary Ann asked.

"There's no mistaking it for something else," Annie said.

I thought of the farmer from Carroll County, the one who

choked me in my own bed. Months later, I sometimes still woke in the night gasping for air. It took a week for the bruises to fade and two weeks for my voice to return. Mary Ann and Caroline would be easy prey for that London man. Rose too. But not me. If I ever saw that bastard from Carroll County again, he wouldn't be long for this world. I knew what it was to point a gun at a man, to pull the trigger, to feel nothing but relief as he bled out. After being forced to read the Bible every day, I'd learned a few things, namely that people always got what was coming for them. And you can't say they weren't warned either. Deuteronomy 32:35: "In due time their foot will slip; their day of disaster is near and their doom rushes upon them." Some nights I fell asleep imagining what the farmer had waiting for him. "It is mine to avenge."

"Oh, God, come to my assistance!" Hattie screamed from upstairs.

THE LOUISVILLE COURIER-JOURNAL

WOMEN'S CHRISTIAN WORK:

THE TREASURER'S ANNUAL REPORT ON THE HOME FOR FRIENDLESS WOMEN

General expenses	760 00
Matron's salary	220 00
Rent	339 00
Coal	50 00
Gas	8 40
Plumbing	5 00
Curtain stretchers	2 60
Cash on hand	$116.76

The health of the Home is thought to be good considering the broken-down condition in which so many of the girls enter our Home. The managers are at present occupied with the effort to raise money for the completion of a new building, which is to cost $24,000 when completed. The report of the treasurer was read by Mrs. Edward Shippen.

THE LOUISVILLE COURIER-JOURNAL

HOUSES OF ILL FAME:
A LETTER TO THE EDITOR

I am writing, as the wife of a physician, to express
my support for the amendment to the city charter
which would grant licenses to houses of ill fame.
While some have expressed doubt that this would
curb the social evil in our midst, I believe a law could
be framed to very much restrict it. All attempts at the
extinction of prostitution—of which there have been
many—present one unbroken record of failure. There
are a class of impractical clergymen and a number of
enthusiastic and well-meaning women who believe
such an amendment, rather than suppressing the vice,
would be seen as a protection and endorsement of this
social evil. Two and a half million syphilis cases in the
United States is of itself an argument cogent enough
to overcome all opposition to the enactment of a law
with an eye to public welfare. We can suppress the
vice or we can continue as we have, and lament the
increase of seductions, illegitimacy, criminal abortion,
and infanticide. Much more can be said on this subject,
but I will close with the idea that the legislature could
not pass a more beneficial law than one having, for its
object, the regulation of houses of prostitution.

Sincerely,
Mrs. Edward Shippen*

---

* Adapted from a letter to the editor in *The Louisville Courier-Journal*,
"Houses of Ill Fame," February 8, 1888.

"~~He~~ She healeth the broken in heart,
and bindeth up their wounds."

I passed Dr. Shippen in the morning as he was leaving Hattie's room.

"The baby's name is Joseph," Dr. Shippen said. "She's resting now if you want to visit her." His shirt was dark with sweat, his blue eyes threaded with red. He looked like he was struggling to keep them open. Annie said he offered his services to the Home for free because his first wife died in childbirth. His second wife, Regina, was on the Board. She was thirty and childless, and unlike the other lady managers, she always remembered our names.

During my first exam at Fay's, Dr. Shippen had asked how I was doing.

Fine, I lied.

Are you getting enough rest? he asked.

I was the new girl and I had a different client every night, sometimes two a night. I'm fine, I repeated.

I don't know what Dr. Shippen told Fay, but the following week, I didn't have to see any customers. Instead, I did the laundry and shopping for the house, and I spent my nights alone in my room, sewing a new dress. It was one of the best weeks of my whole life, and I've never forgotten what Dr. Shippen did for me.

"You were worried about her," I said. "Hattie."

"Labor is hard on girls her age."

I had never thought to ask Hattie's age, I realized.

"Sixteen," he said in answer to my silent question.

Ten years my junior, I thought with a shiver. "It's my birthday today." At Fay's, you got the day off when it was your birthday. When it had been Mary Ann's birthday last month, Miss MacCorkle made us hold hands before supper so we could say a prayer of thanks for Mary Ann. A piece of cake would have been nicer, Mary Ann grumbled that night during sewing time.

"Happy birthday, Belle," Dr. Shippen said now. "I wish I had known. Regina would have sent me with a cake for you."

"My mother used to make me a coconut cake. She would let me eat a slice with my breakfast." I'd never told anyone about the birthday coconut cake, not even Rose.

Dr. Shippen smiled in delight. "My first wife used to make a coconut cake for my birthday. She would spell out my age with raisins."

"My mother used raspberries." I thought of the last cake my mom ever made, the raspberries perched on top like cardinals in the snow. Every year she'd ask me a little anxiously, as I took that first bite, Does it taste all right? And every year I told her, It's perfect, just perfect. On my twelfth birthday, I didn't know, as I ate it, that it would be the last cake. I assumed my mother would be there year after year, because who can imagine a world without their mother?

"I hope you have a wonderful birthday, Belle." Dr. Shippen patted my arm, a fatherly gesture, before walking downstairs.

I stood at the upstairs window a moment, my hands resting lightly on my stomach, and watched him walk home, his shirt darkening in the falling rain. I imagined his pretty wife waiting up for him, ready to draw him a bath and fix his breakfast after such a long night. Maybe sometimes he came in from a particularly bad delivery and went straight to his bed, and

Regina would lie beside him. Maybe on those days, as she said a silent prayer of thanks she was childless, she would wrap her arms around him and whisper in his ear, You did everything you could. I hoped he believed her. If you had to marry a man, there were certainly worse ones than Dr. Shippen.

"A woman's home should be
a reflection of her inner life."

———————————

In the laundry room: WASH YOU, MAKE YOU CLEAN; PUT AWAY
THE EVIL OF YOUR DOINGS FROM BEFORE MINE EYES; CEASE TO
DO EVIL.

In the kitchen: LET ALL THINGS BE DONE DECENTLY AND
IN ORDER.

In the nursery: FOR GOD HATH NOT CALLED US UNTO
UNCLEANNESS, BUT UNTO HOLINESS.

In the sitting room: BUT IF THE WICKED WILL TURN FROM
ALL HIS SINS THAT HE HATH COMMITTED, AND KEEP ALL MY
STATUTES, AND DO THAT WHICH IS LAWFUL AND RIGHT, HE
SHALL SURELY LIVE, HE SHALL NOT DIE.

On an embroidered pillow in the sitting room, featuring a
mother cradling her baby: HE MAKETH THE BARREN WOMAN
TO KEEP HOUSE, *AND TO BE* A JOYFUL MOTHER OF CHILDREN.

The woman didn't look unhappy, exactly. But my idea of joy
was clearly different from hers.

"Wives, submit yourselves unto your own husbands, as it is fit in the Lord."

———————

The other girls and I wanted to attend Mr. Goss's funeral, but Miss MacCorkle said her nerves were too frayed to attend herself and we absolutely could not attend without a chaperone. She said a flock of friendless women descending on the funeral would frighten his poor family, and hadn't they suffered enough?

"But we want to pay our respects to Mrs. Goss. We wouldn't frighten her," I said. "She knows us. Likes us, in fact."

"It would be unseemly for you girls to run about town in your present conditions."

"I'm asking to attend a funeral next door for a nice old man who brought us candies every Friday. That's not 'running about town.' And I don't need a chaperone to go where I want."

"I said no," Miss MacCorkle said in her firmest voice, which was not all that firm, and when I kicked the wall in anger, Miss MacCorkle sent me to my room like I was a naughty child. "And oh yes you do need a chaperone to leave this house," she called after me.

I stood at my bedroom window and watched Mr. Goss's friends file in to pay their respects. A flock of friendless women indeed. Did Miss MacCorkle picture us as a flock of yellow-rumped warblers? Ruby-crowned kinglets? Honking geese, more likely. Maybe even a white crow, the unluckiest bird out there. On Miss MacCorkle's wedding day, I hoped a white crow flew into the church and flapped about, frightening the guests and bestowing bad luck on the bride and groom.

Before heading down for supper, I saw a gaggle of geese alight in the Gosses' front yard. "Rest in peace, Mr. Goss," I said as the birds staggered about in clumsy circles.

⊗⊗

I'd prepared the meal myself—fried chicken, green beans, and mashed potatoes—and I looked defiantly at Miss MacCorkle as I gave myself an extra heaping of potatoes.

She frowned at my plate, but rather than scold me, she turned to Caroline. "Caroline, I believe you have some news to share."

Caroline pressed her hands to her freckled face. "I received a marriage proposal today."

"From a man who frequented Mollie's?" Annie asked.

Caroline came to the Home from Mollie Burns's over on Grayson Street. Last year, after an argument with a male companion, Mollie swallowed a two-ounce vial of laudanum and declared, Death awaits me. Caroline said this was not unusual behavior for Mollie. An hour later, though, the unmistakable purplish color of poison stained Mollie's face and she grew insensible, which is how Caroline and the other girls came to be pallbearers at her funeral, which is where she met Reverend Perkins, who shared with them the story of the fallen Magdalen. Though outcast from society and exiled from the better class of people, Magdalen was redeemed by Christ's love. After the service, Caroline, who was already with child at the time of Mollie's death, asked Reverend Perkins if she too might be redeemed, and that day she packed her bags and left Mollie's place for good and chose to dedicate herself to Christ and life everlasting. We all knew this story by heart, since Reverend Perkins shared it every time he came by the house. He even called Caroline "my Magdalen," which I found bizarre, to say the least. Caroline, being Caroline, found it sweet.

"Oh no," Caroline said. "Fred lives in Jacksonville."

"Jacksonville? In Florida?" Mary Ann asked. "How does a man in another state ask for your hand in marriage?"

"We haven't officially met," Caroline said. "Reverend Perkins knows Fred's family and says Fred is a good Christian. We've been exchanging letters for a few weeks now. His wife died last winter. Childbirth." She lightly touched her stomach. "He has a daughter Phillip's age, and a woman from town has been staying with him, but this woman's daughter is about to give birth in Kansas. He needs a wife and his baby needs a mother. Her name is Isabella. The baby, that is. Isn't that a lovely name?"

Caroline and her son, Phillip, were a strange combination. She was tall with a round freckled face and pale green eyes, while Phillip was squat with dark eyes and black hair. Even when she was days away from giving birth, her stomach remained small and high, as if she were smuggling a sack of flour under her dress.

"Shouldn't Caroline be seeking work here in Louisville instead of husband hunting down in Florida?" Mary Ann asked with a frown. "Caroline won't have stayed the full eighteen months if she marries this man this year. Mrs. Clarke was very clear about the rules of the Home."

Technically Miss MacCorkle was the mistress of the Home, although everyone knew Mrs. Clarke, her future mother-in-law, was the one in charge. Mrs. Clarke clearly derived great pleasure from undermining her future daughter-in-law's decisions, disagreeing with her on everything from nursery wallpaper patterns to how to decorate the sitting room. As for Miss MacCorkle's gardening attire—the less said about those bloomers, the better. Miss MacCorkle was unnaturally gracious when accepting Mrs. Clarke's advice; someone like Rose might say this made her wise beyond her years, but it was clear to me, after only a few months here, that Miss MacCorkle was profoundly stupid.

"Mrs. Clarke says it will be a real success story for the Home," Miss MacCorkle said. "A husband is always better than a job."

"Not true," I said, and Miss MacCorkle looked over at me and shook her head.

"The rules." Mary Ann followed this with a loud hiccup. "She's not even an older girl yet."

The girls nearing the end of their time in the Home, the ones who had given birth already and who had jobs in town, were known as the "older girls." They were allowed to spend their evenings making baby clothes instead of mending curtains. The three currently living upstairs—Rachel, Helen, and Christie—generally avoided us, as if our condition were contagious and we might reinfect them. Annie's room was also on the top floor, but no one considered her an older girl.

"I sent Fred a sketch of Phillip, and he said he was a handsome boy," Caroline said. "He said it was a great comfort to know I was a healthy woman who had not been weakened by childbirth."

Mary Ann stabbed one of the green beans on her plate with such force the table shook. "What a glowing recommendation—you didn't die giving birth. I hope the older girls aren't offended by this blatant show of favoritism."

"Rachel will be moving back home to Paducah to care for her mother, and Helen will return to Frankfort, where she will work as a laundress at the new Buhr Hotel."

"And Christie?" Mary Ann asked. "Her time at the Home is drawing to an end, and wouldn't it be better for her to have a nice Christian husband?"

Caroline looked anxiously from Miss MacCorkle to Mary Ann.

"Christie has been working with Mrs. Clarke to find a suitable place of employment."

"Christie wants to be a dentist," Annie said, "in New York."

"A lady dentist!" Miss MacCorkle exclaimed. "I can't picture such a thing."

Mary Ann squinted across the table at Caroline. "Did you tell this man in Florida about your freckles?"

"No."

"Well." Mary Ann took a sip of water, dabbed at her lips, and violently hiccuped into her napkin. "Some men find freckled women very displeasing."

Caroline had tried all the remedies to remove her freckles: sugar and honey, powdered borax, friar's balsam and rosewater. The sugar and honey mask didn't take off the freckles, although, unlike the powdered borax, she said it made her skin smell nice.

"Most men find malicious gossipmongers more displeasing than a few freckles on an otherwise pretty face," I said. "But the real question is, do you want to marry this man? Or are you only doing it to make Reverend Perkins and Mrs. Clarke happy?"

"Caroline wants to marry this man," Miss MacCorkle said. "Don't go planting any of your pernicious ideas in her head, Belle."

I ignored her and turned to Caroline. "Caroline? Do you want to marry this man?"

"He said he thought I sounded like a good mother," Caroline said, "and a good woman. I've never had a man tell me that before."

"Of course he's going to say nice things," I said. "He wants something from you."

"I believe him, though," Caroline said. "And I've always wanted to visit Florida."

Mary Ann viciously stabbed another green bean. Her hiccups were gaining speed. "Yellow fever is sweeping across Florida. The things I could tell you about yellow fever would raise the hairs on your head, Caroline."

"We should avoid sharing medical stories at the dinner table," Miss MacCorkle said. "Mary Ann, you're getting agitated."

"Maybe yellow fever isn't a problem where he lives," Caroline said.

"It's a problem everywhere in Florida," Mary Ann said. "Far be it from me to dissuade you." *Hiccup.* "Just because I personally wouldn't marry a man who wants to lure a poor, hapless woman to Florida to bear him children doesn't mean that you should base your decision off anything I relay."

"Caroline might not get another proposal," Miss MacCorkle said. "It would be foolish—foolish and foolhardy," she said earnestly to Caroline, "to throw away such an opportunity. Think how disappointed Reverend Perkins would be if you led on this poor man without any notion of marrying him. You told me yourself how despondent Fred has been since his wife died. Men are so helpless with children. I can't bear to think of little—what's her name again?"

"Isabella," Caroline said.

"What kind of woman might little Isabella become without your strong maternal influence?"

"I'm glad you didn't recommend me to this Florida man, Miss MacCorkle," Mary Ann said. "My cousin Ida has a friend who lives in Florida, and she told Ida that yellow fever is all anybody down there can talk about. Every night they burn tar fires outside the city limits to disrupt the miasma, and the smell of these fires is enough to make a person sick. Doctors are telling people that fear is more contagious than the fever and that worrying about death will only hasten it. If that's true, then Ida's poor friend will be the next to go. Ida said she frets about yellow fever in every letter. You don't want to hear how it ravages the body, Caroline." Mary Ann shook her head and a double hiccup slipped out. "First, chills. When I say chills, I mean a shaking so fierce your bones break. Then vomit, black and thick as tar."

Both Caroline and Miss MacCorkle pushed away their dinner plates.

"We'd never be able to visit you and Phillip. Yellow fever is not something I will risk, even for a dear friend like you. I hope no girls from Florida seek shelter here. Imagine yellow fever sweeping through the house!" *Hiccup.*

"If we're lucky," I said, smiling across the table at Miss Mac-Corkle, "yellow fever would kill only the nasty ones."

THE LOUISVILLE COURIER-JOURNAL

A PROTEST AGAINST PROSTITUTION:
A LETTER TO THE EDITOR

Will you allow us to add our hearty disapproval to the letter you ran last week, on the subject of granting licenses to houses of ill fame? It is safe to say that every utterance in the aforementioned article will meet with the unqualified disapproval of religious and moral people everywhere. It seems shocking, in this enlightened age, to every lover of morality and pure life, that the city council of Louisville should even propose such a measure. The idea that the evil will exist and that we must, therefore, legalize it is simply monstrous. Why not legalize and grant men the right to commit murder? As men will gamble in defiance even of law, why not grant them, under cover and protection of law, the right to gamble? Why bother passing laws to regulate disgraceful and degrading business at all? The proposition by the city council should be met by our own lawmakers with a stinging rebuke. They can afford to do nothing less. The Bible is full of denunciations of this evil and body-destroying sin that leads hapless men and lewd women to these places of destruction. Many strong men have been slain in these houses of cruelty and vice. Such establishments are, to speak plainly, the fastest way to hell.

Faithfully signed,
Women of the Trinity Methodist Church*

---

* Adapted from a letter to the editor in *The Louisville Courier-Journal*, "A Protest Against Prostitution," February 17, 1888.

"For the wrongdoer will be paid back
for the wrong ~~he~~ she has done."

———————

Miss MacCorkle studied the thermometer in her hands.
"Sixty-five on the nose!" she crowed. "Mrs. Clarke said Leo is
very sensitive to changes in temperature and that I should get
in the habit of ensuring the bedroom remains a constant temperature. The last few mornings it's been closer to sixty-nine,
which, according to Mrs. Clarke, is not an ideal temperature
for young men."

As if that dried-up cunt knew what men wanted, I thought.
My punishment for talking back and kicking the wall on the
day of Mr. Goss's funeral was to rise early and help Miss Mac-
Corkle get ready for the day, like I was her personal maid.

Everything in Miss MacCorkle's bedroom was pink: the
curtains framing the dressing table, the wool rug at the foot of
the bed, even her quilt, which was a medley of dark and light
pink squares. Her dressing table was covered with pink bottles
holding hairpins, creams, and scent.

Miss MacCorkle handed me a thick-handled silver hairbrush and sat down at her dressing table. It's from France.
Horsehair. At the shop they said it's what the best hairdressers
in Paris use, she told me the first time she placed it in my palm.
As I'd started brushing her hair, she asked, Why is horsehair
the best?

Prevents breakage, I replied.

Everything I learned about hair, I learned at Fay's. On Sundays we slathered egg whites onto our scalps to keep our hair shiny and strong. A girl once rinsed out the egg with hot water. Lord, what a mess that fool cooked up in her own hair.

Miss MacCorkle's hair used to be in dreadful condition—dandruff, greasy scalp, dry ends. All that was under control now, thanks to me, but the bald spot right smack in the middle of her head had recently grown from nickel- to half-dollar-sized, and soon, no amount of combing and twisting would mask it. Last week I had her try false hair, but she claimed it made her feel overheated and faint. And what if it's the hair of someone in prison? she had fretted. Or the hair of a you-know-what? I've read about such things, you know.

A prostitute would never donate her hair, I had said.

The brush handle was cool in my hands. It had a pleasing heft to it; she had clearly spared no expense.

"We have exactly one month until the wedding to get rid of that spot," Miss MacCorkle said anxiously to her reflection. Miss MacCorkle's future husband, Leo, was ten years her senior, completely bald, and several inches shorter than her—and still she worried he would find her unappealing.

I massaged her scalp, applying light pressure around the thinning hair to stimulate blood flow. "At least Leo is shorter than you are. No chance of him looking down at the top of your head during the ceremony."

"Oh, Belle, don't tease. The problem is all that time I spent attempting to curl my hair when I was younger. Sometimes my hair would smoke. What an appalling smell, burning hair. When Mary Ann was talking about the fires in Florida, that was the exact smell I thought of." She relaxed in her chair, closing her eyes as I brushed and brushed. "I used to have the most beautiful hair as a child. That's what Mother always told me."

For Miss MacCorkle's tenth birthday, the last birthday her mother was alive, her mother gave her a doll with a real silk dress. Miss MacCorkle said that doll's dress—pale blue, shimmery—was nicer than any dress she owned. She wasn't allowed to play with this doll, in case she ruined that silk dress. And you never once played with that doll? I asked in astonishment. You never even took her out of the cabinet when no one was looking?

Never, she said proudly.

I made a promise to my baby, there in Miss MacCorkle's pink explosion of a room, that I would never give her a present she couldn't enjoy.

Miss MacCorkle picked up a hairpin from the dressing table and ran her fingers across its amber-colored surface. "Mrs. Clarke gave me this yesterday. It's tortoiseshell. She said the belly of the tortoise yields the highest-quality jewelry. You'll never guess how much it cost. Four whole dollars. She thought I might want to wear it at the wedding." She rubbed the gold top of the hairpin between her fingers. "I've never worn a tortoiseshell hairpin."

All the things I would do with four dollars. And to spend it on a hairpin made from a turtle's shell? Mrs. Clarke was clearly as fool-headed as her bald son.

"I wonder, though—is it the right accessory for such a special day? How can a girl be sure, on her wedding day, that she is ready to have such a pin inserted in her hair?" Miss MacCorkle said this in a rush, as if the words had been hiding beneath her tongue all morning.

"No woman likes having a pin inserted in her hair." I met her eyes in the mirror to show I understood what she was really asking. "Not the first time, anyhow."

"I'm very tender-headed. More so than most."

"Then you shouldn't be shy telling a man how you like to have your hair styled. If you would want him to brush your hair before he jabs in a hairpin, then speak up. If there's one thing I learned about men, it's that they aren't mind readers."

Try to be on your stomach the first time, a girl at Fay's told me. That way if you cry, he won't see and try to get out of paying.

"If a man doesn't like how his wife styles her hair, he might be tempted to visit an establishment where the women allow any old hairpin to be inserted into their hair, as long as the man is willing to pay."

I'd always wondered what Miss MacCorkle knew about her fiancé's past. When I knew him, Leo played the piano at Fay's every Thursday and Friday night, and he'd probably still be there if he hadn't gotten it in his bald head that he was in love with my friend Genevieve. He even proposed marriage to her. Once Fay learned that, she fired him on the spot. She said any man reckless enough to propose marriage to a prostitute was nothing but trouble, and her daddy used to say trouble rode a fast horse. And I won't be inviting trouble into my house so it can stampede around and destroy shit, Fay said.

If you were drunk and in a dark room, you might be able to convince yourself that Miss MacCorkle, with her pale, thinning hair and nervous blue eyes, resembled Genevieve. I thought of the song Leo performed for Genevieve's birthday:

Leo gave me apples,
Leo gave me pears.
Leo gave me fifty cents
To kiss him on the stairs.

I gave him back his apples,
I gave him back his pears.
I gave him back his fifty cents
And kicked him down the stairs.

"Have you ever been in love, Belle?" Miss MacCorkle asked now.

"No," I lied.

"I hope you're not jealous of Caroline. We might be able to find you a husband too. Although you will have to do something about that sharp tongue of yours."

"I'd prefer a job over a husband any day."

"You say the strangest things sometimes." She picked up her hairbrush and started plucking at the pale hairs caught in the bristles. "Leo told me all about that nasty girl, you know. How she led him on and teased him mercilessly. What a vulgar name, Genevieve."

"Careful who you call vulgar." The night before her wedding, Genevieve gave me her old dresses, since her husband had ordered her a new wardrobe from New York. Genevieve and I weren't the same size, but I took them apart and saved the lace and velvet and embroidered bits. The last time I saw Rose, she was wearing a skirt and blouse I made from one of those dresses. "Besides, she's married now and no threat to you."

Miss MacCorkle leaned forward and violently swept the hairpins off her dressing table. "Pick those up, Belle." Her eyes were dangerously wet when they met mine in the mirror.

"You're a real imbecile sometimes."

"You can't talk that way to me. Pick them up!" she shouted at my retreating back. "Belle, get back here!"

I saw the tortoiseshell pin by the door, and I kicked it into the hallway. When I walked by it, I bent down and slid it into my pocket. My curly hair was too thick for such a delicate pin, but it would look just fine on someone else. Four dollars for a pin!

A fool and his money are soon parted, Fay often said.

"Wash me, and I shall be whiter than snow."

The shelf above the washer held boxes of James Pyle's Pearline soap. Forty-seven boxes, to be exact. A former inmate had married a relative of Mr. Pyle, and now Mrs. Cora Pyle sent the Home a crate of laundry soap every year. *It is my sincere desire that future girls will see these boxes of soap and be reminded that they too can be washed clean.*

The soap promised to remove stains with no rubbing whatsoever. I never tried this no-rubbing method, but judging by the numerous stains on the shared baby clothes, quite a few girls before me had. The piles of laundry in the Home never diminished; wash one load, and three more appeared, a predictable incoming tide of dirty linens and diapers, a sea of threadbare dresses. There were some chores I balked at. Never laundry, though. It was the only place in the Home where I could be alone and in peace.

To remove bloodstains: submerge the clothing or bedsheets in boiling water with an ounce of cream of tartar and an ounce of oxalic acid. Wait two minutes and then rinse with cool water. If the stain is stubborn, make a paste of soap and starch, spread it thinly on the blood, and scrape off when dry. The day after Mr. Goss died, Annie spent the morning attacking the spots in the street with a scrub brush and a bucket of watered-down Pearline soap.

ᏩᏦ

A memory: age ten, helping Mother with laundry. I was a surprise baby, conceived after the war. Your father wasn't always
like this, my mother would say, which didn't mean anything to
me. According to Mother, he looked the same when he came
back from the war. But something important was missing, and
his way of reclaiming the missing part was to beat her senseless.

"There are women who think the world owes them something," my mother said that day as she scraped shavings of soft
black soap into our washtub. The water steamed and shimmered
blue, then gray. My mother and I shared the same thick hair,
the same strong arms, although under her dress, her arms were
covered in bruises fading to the color of the black-eyed Susans
growing in the windowsill. "And others who don't think they
deserve the scraps they are given. Which one are you going to
be, Belle?"

My mother said another baby would surely kill her, and
the day after my twelfth birthday, she died. Not from a baby,
though. That day, my mother sent me outside after breakfast.
My father was in one of his moods. I climbed high up into the
tree next to the kitchen window, and I waited for her beating
to end. The last time I tried to get in the middle, I wound up
with a broken arm, and afterward, my mother said the best way
to help her was to wait quietly in the tree, and she would give
a signal when it was safe to come inside. On that particular
day he reached for a knife instead of using his fists, and when I
saw her lying so still on the kitchen floor, I knew there was no
signal coming for me.

He was kneeling beside her, covered in her blood, when I
walked inside. She didn't look like anyone I knew anymore. I
took his gun off the wall and pointed it at him like he was a
turkey in the wild. I'd often imagined this moment, while I sat

helplessly up in the tree. In my imagination I was shaking and crying when I held the gun, but that day I was deadly calm.

"Belle," he said quickly, "don't—" and then he was on his back and there was a sea of blood in that small kitchen.

That night I buried my mother as best I could. Him I left on the floor.

The next day I pulled the washtub out into the yard and took a freezing cold bath. I donned one of Mother's dresses I found pinned to the wash line and made my way into town, where I answered a help wanted ad at a laundry. I told the owner I was sixteen. He didn't believe me, but he didn't ask too many questions either. I slept in a room above the laundry, and nearly all my wages went to pay for that pitiful room. I didn't know how to sleep, that first night, in the too-quiet room. I opened the windows so I might feel surrounded by others, and my lullaby on those nights was the sounds of a busy city street. When I thought about those years, it was like hearing a story about a stranger who shared my name. That Belle was very brave. How fast she had to grow up. She quickly learned that lonely and being alone are not the same thing at all. Everything she learned, she learned fast, and the price of that learning was a thick scar, deep inside. Most people couldn't see what was right in front of them when looking at her, though. A mixed blessing.

When I was seventeen, a woman brought in a silk handkerchief dress to the laundry. She wanted to know if I could remove the grease stain on the right sleeve. It was the nicest dress I had ever seen, much less touched. The dress was the color of the black-eyed Susans my mother had loved so dearly, the color of the bruises on her arms. "Yes," I told the woman with the silk dress. "I can remove that stain for you, ma'am." When Fay Sewell returned the following day, she examined the sleeve from every angle before giving me four dollars and a job offer.

That day I traded my cramped room above the laundry for a room in a mansion on Fourth Street, and that night I let a man enter me for the first time, and after he left, I tucked the crumpled bills inside a pair of flannel stockings. It was more than a week's wages at the laundry. Money meant choices, I told myself night after night, as I filled up one pair of stockings and then two more.

It's not always possible to view your life from afar, to see how small decisions add up to something larger. This must be why we whisper our lives in the dark, why we ask someone else to receive what we once fiercely guarded in the silence of our hearts.

What kind of woman are you going to be, Belle?
The kind who thinks she's worth something, Mother.

Dear Sir:

Can you please deliver this letter to the person who wrote the article on December 21 "May Lead a Better Life: Wealthy Farmer from Carroll County Marries a Fallen Woman"? I'm looking for the woman, Rose Walzer, who married that man, because she's in danger. Do you know their address in Carroll County? Do you know how I can find her? Send a response as soon as you can to Fay Sewell's, 624 Fourth Street.

Thank you,
Belle Queeney

"Cultivate a happy temper; banish the blues."

Hattie looked with dismay at the food on her tray: mushy oat-meal, boiled potatoes, a glass of milk. Mrs. Clarke believed new mothers should eat a bland diet to regain their strength and calm their nerves; the meal looked about as appetizing as a bowl of dirt.

Hattie's room was damp and sour smelling, a stew of sweat and old milk. I breathed through my mouth as I went to open the window. It had started raining again. Ten days since we had seen the sun. Somewhere in the house I heard a baby crying.

"How do you feel today?" I asked.

Hattie's face was creased from the pillow. When she looked at me, her eyes were bloodshot.

The crying grew louder, shriller. I peered into the cradle beside her bed.

"Where's Joseph?"

"They thought I wouldn't notice what they did to him. But I'm not stupid." Her eyes flickered over to the closed closet door.

A naked Joseph lay on the hardwood floor of the closet, the blanket underneath him wet.

"Come here, it's okay," I murmured. His body was cold and damp when I picked him up. "Hattie, why is he in the closet?"

"He hates his cradle. He cries and cries when he's in there."

"Babies can't sleep on the floor. He needs clothes and a blanket."

"He doesn't like clothes. He cries when he has them on."

"Babies usually cry for a reason," I said, wrapping him in a clean, dry blanket. He scrunched up his face and cried louder as if to prove my point. "Like when they're hungry."

Jagged wet spots bloomed on the front of her nightgown in response. She took him from me and wordlessly lifted her nightgown. Dried blood crusted her nipples. Joseph made a noise that was part sigh, part squeal as he clamped down on her nipple. She grimaced as he began sucking in earnest.

"I think there's something wrong with my milk. He spits it up after he eats."

"Are you patting him on the back afterward, the way Annie showed you?"

"Maybe it's poisoned."

"Your milk isn't poisoned."

"I don't know what to believe anymore." Tears dripped down her face and fell onto Joseph's head. He stopped nursing in surprise, and a thin stream of milk dribbled out of his mouth. "He said I dreamed the whole thing and then she said it was my fault, but I didn't do anything, Belle. All I did was answer that ad in the paper."

"What ad?"

"'Wanted: Girl of about sixteen years of age to look after children.' I was only fifteen, but he said that was fine, and I was there for only four months, and everyone thinks I'm crazy but I'm not."

She was crying and shaking so hard I was afraid she would drop Joseph, so I took him from her and briskly patted him on the back until he let out a loud belch. He didn't protest when I dressed him in a clean gown and laid him back in his cradle.

"I'm not crazy." She made no move to wipe the tears streaming down her face. "I really do know the difference between waking and dreaming."

"Sure you do," I said. "You're a smart girl."

"I won't go back there. He said after the baby was born I could return, but I won't."

"You're not going anywhere you don't want to. I'll make sure of it."

She rolled over on her side and pulled up her legs so she was curled up in a ball. "Would you rub my back?" she whispered. "Please."

I sat beside her and rubbed her back in small circles and hummed a wordless tune that my mother used to sing on wash-days. Even after I knew Hattie was fast asleep, still I hummed that tune, as if it might keep her asleep just a few minutes longer.

છ∕ભ

I found Miss MacCorkle in the study, two different clippings from the newspapers spread out in front of her. "I like the lace on this veil," she said, "but I wonder if this one with the flow-ers would better hide the bald spot. What do you think, Belle?" She pointed to the two advertisements. Neither bride looked much like Miss MacCorkle, and neither of those veils would do a damn thing to hide her missing hair.

"Flowers," I said. "Listen, there's something wrong with Hattie. I think she needs to see Dr. Shippen."

"There's something wrong with all women after they give birth," she said. "It's a dreadful, nasty business." Miss Mac-Corkle picked up the advertisement for the flowered veil and set it down with a sigh. "I swear you girls invent reasons for the handsome doctor to pay a visit." She grinned mischievously at me, and I thrust my hands behind my back to keep from smacking her face.

"I was wondering where Hattie was living before she came here."

"Somewhere in Tennessee. She was working for a doctor there. I remember he said that friendlessness is a real epidemic in Tennessee and he's so thankful for our Home and the refuge it provides these young women. The poor man has been forced to escort a number of young women here. And each time he brings a generous donation. Out of his own pocket even."

"What's this doctor's name?"

"Dr. Munro. Why?"

"We ought to send him a letter, let him know how Hattie is doing. I know you're so busy these days, what with the wedding. I'd be happy to write the letter. As penance for my tantrum last week."

"A wonderful idea." She opened her desk drawer and pulled out a stack of letters tied with a satin ribbon. "All these young girls moving to the city. Some of them just can't resist the temptations." She printed the address on a piece of pink paper and handed it to me. "Thank you, Belle. Your efforts at repentance are noted and appreciated."

Back in my room, I unfolded the piece of paper and read the name aloud: "Dr. William Munro." I'd known plenty of men like the good doctor, men whose mouths said one thing, their hands another. He was my father and the farmer from Carroll County. He was the men who came to Fay's with a Bible in one hand, their prick in the other. Men like that didn't understand when a woman said no. No, it was simpler than that—they didn't care what a woman said, as long as they got what they came for.

Dr. Munro's name didn't mean anything to me, but someday I'd make sure my name meant something to him.

THE LOUISVILLE COURIER-JOURNAL

WOMEN AND POLITICS

It is difficult to speak with calmness and courtesy on the subject of woman suffrage, because the insults offered to the vast majority of women by its advocates have worn out their patience. Women are told they oppose suffrage because they are ignorant, because they are slaves. All the arguments in favor of women's voting are puerile and silly; we would indeed be ignorant to be influenced by them. Suffrage as a natural right? No. It is a duty which society imposes upon such citizens as she sees best. The expression which arouses the greatest ire in the hearts of women generally is when the advocates of woman suffrage claim to be "fighting for our homes." It is uncharitable, perhaps, but other women can't help wondering, as they see said advocates continually wandering to and fro upon the earth, whether they have any homes worth saving, and if they have, why they do not stay in them occasionally.

—Emma Walton Clarke*

---

* Adapted from "Women and Politics," *The Louisville Courier-Journal*, May 13, 1888.

"Do not fear those who kill the body,
for they cannot kill the soul."

———————————

"My cousin Irene sent a letter today," Mary Ann said.

"I don't want to hear any more stories about murdered women," I said. "I have enough troubles of my own. And when you talk about your cousins, you stop sewing. Mrs. Clarke is coming on Friday to pick up the curtains, and without Hattie to help, we're falling behind." Earlier that evening I had tried to coax Hattie downstairs. You don't have to sew, I told her. Just come sit with us downstairs, a change of scenery would do you and Joseph a world of good. And you know Annie loves snuggling new babies.

Not tonight, she said. But for once she wasn't crying, and she had brushed her hair and found a clean dress to wear, all of which made me hopeful she was on the mend.

"We can't possibly be behind," said Mary Ann. "I've never seen a woman sew as quickly as you do, Belle."

"Compared with you, everyone is a fast sewer."

"In the time I have been here, we have repaired 853 garments, mended 2,617 pairs of lace curtains, and made 65 quilts," said Annie.

"I don't know how you know that, Annie, but I believe you," Caroline said.

Mary Ann held up the needle in her hand and made a show of sewing the striped curtains in her lap. "Constance lives in London. This letter is from *Irene*, who lives in Washington. In her letter, she told me all about a delightful new game she's been playing with her friends."

When I was inclined to feel sorry for Mary Ann, which was never, I would wonder why she hadn't been invited to live with one of these many cousins during her pregnancy. Why did her family send her here, where she was forced to sew curtains with a bunch of former whores every night?

Mary Ann pulled the letter from her dress pocket and held it underneath the lamp's flame to better read the cramped writing.

"You'll end up with wrinkles, squinting like that," I said.

She ignored me, moving the paper dangerously close to the flame.

My dearest Mary Ann,

I wanted to let you know about a new kind of game that's all the rage in Washington. Bean bag parties! Society belles are becoming very expert at this new game. At one end of the parlor is placed an inclined board with a square hole in it. Standing at the other end—and the farther away from the board the more fun there is in the game—the players pitch ten bean bags toward the hole. A regular score is kept, and if the ten bags fall in the hole, it counts 100, or 10 for each bag. Another bag, double the usual size, is also provided, and if this is also thrown into the square opening it adds 20, making 120 the highest possible score. Should any of the bags remain on the board they count 5 points apiece, but for every bag that is thrown upon or falls to the floor, 5 points are subtracted. The big bag, or Jumbo, counts double, or 10 in each case. I have become quite expert at pitching these little bags. You would be astonished at my excellent skill in accurately gauging the distances and the strength

necessary to be exerted! The sport is full of interest, and bean
bag boards are now found in every fashionable household
which expects to be considered up to the times. I wish you
*could see how handsomely embroidered my Jumbo bag is.**

Mary Ann dropped the letter into her lap with a sigh. "It sounds like enormous fun."

"What kind of beans go in the bag?" Annie asked. "Kidney? Navy? We have a surplus of black-eyed peas in the Home, but those might not be considered a bean."

Mary Ann waved her hand impatiently. "The type of bean isn't important."

"The type of bean is always important," Annie said.

When Annie was a child, her mother would give her a jar of beans in the morning and tell her to sort them by color before bedtime, and then at bedtime, she would watch as her mother dumped the beans back in the jar for the next day. Once I came across a half-black, half-red bean, and I knew it was there as a test, Annie said.

A test of what? I asked.

A test, she repeated with conviction, and I nodded like I understood, because it suddenly made sense why Annie would choose to stay in a place like this, where the chores, while endless, at least had a purpose.

"What I wouldn't give to have a bean bag party here," Mary Ann said with another sigh. "I would embroider my initials in red thread on my Jumbo bag, to prevent cheating."

"I would never cheat at bean bags," Annie said.

"Maybe Mrs. Clarke would allow us to have a bean bag party here," Caroline said.

---

* Adapted from "Woman's World and Work: A New Game for Young Ladies," *The Louisville Courier-Journal*, February 12, 1888.

"We could have one to celebrate your wedding," Annie said.

Mary Ann pressed her lips together and rapidly moved her finger up and down between her nose and mouth.

"What on earth are you doing?" I asked.

"Pretending to sew a button onto my mouth so I will not say another word about this Florida marriage proposal. It's clearly none of my business."

"It would make more sense to simply sew your mouth closed with thread and forgo the button altogether," I said. "I'd be happy to do it for you."

"I told him yes," Caroline said. "There's no need for any-one to sew their mouths shut." At Mary Ann's urging, she had applied lemon juice to her freckles, and for the last two days, the skin on her cheeks was a sea of tiny red and white bumps.

"You'll be forever in his debt," Mary Ann said. "Every time you disagree with him, or he's unhappy about your cooking, he'll say, 'This is what I get for marrying a fallen woman.'"

"If Fred called me a fallen woman every time he was angry, that would say more about the kind of man he is and very little about the woman I am. I deserve forgiveness too. Reverend Perkins says even the lowest among us deserves forgiveness."

Reverend Perkins said a lot of things. That man certainly liked to hear himself talk.

"I disagree with Reverend Perkins," Annie said. "Not about forgiveness," she said at Caroline's look of shock, "but about calling you 'his Magdalen.' Did you know Mary Magdalen is mentioned fourteen times in the Bible, and not one of those fourteen times is she called a prostitute?"

"The disciples would never have used that word," Caroline said.

"They don't call her a woman of the town or a courtesan either. She didn't come from a brothel or bawdy house, sport-ing house, bagnio, house of ill fame, dive, or assignation house. I don't think she was a fallen woman at all."

"What do they say about her, then?" Mary Ann asked.

"That Jesus drove seven demons out of her."

"There you go," Mary Ann said. "That was their way of saying doubtful."

"Is she truly mentioned fourteen times?" Caroline asked.

"And in eight of the fourteen mentions, she's named first."

"She was important then," Caroline said, "doubtful woman or not."

"We are doubtful women doubting that Mary Magdalen was a doubtful woman. Say that ten times fast," I said.

"Belle, really," Mary Ann said, but even she laughed.

"Hattie?" Annie asked uncertainly. "What happened?"

I turned and saw Hattie standing in the doorway, naked except for Joseph's baby blanket, which was tied tightly across her soft stomach. Mud coated her arms and legs, and water dripped from her hair. "They tried to poison my milk," she said grimly. "So I took care of it."

"For I have no pleasure in the death of anyone."

"There were no warning signs," Mrs. Clarke said to the doctor who came to take Hattie to the asylum that night. When he arrived, the first thing he did was give Miss MacCorkle something so she would stop screaming.

"There were loads of warning signs," I said from my spot by the fire. My hands and feet were ice-cold. I feared they would never warm up. "I told her something was wrong with Hattie, and she didn't do a goddamn thing."

"Language, Belle," Mrs. Clarke said. But her heart wasn't in it.

"That's the unfortunate thing about hysteria," the doctor said to Mrs. Clarke. "A woman is fine until she isn't."

Mary Ann, Annie, and I watched from the window as the doctor loaded Hattie into his carriage as if she were an unwieldy sack of potatoes.

Dr. William Munro, Nashville, Tennessee, I repeated silently as I rubbed my hands before the fire.

The girls and I spent a long time that night looking for Joseph. Mary Ann finally found him in a shallow mud puddle by the back fence. She called me over, and we knelt beside his small body as the rain slid down our faces and necks. Hattie had dressed him in his baptismal gown. My tears mixed with the rain as I pulled him from his muddy grave, and I thought of his mother's tears falling onto his head.

❧❧

The day of Joseph's funeral was breezy and sunny. After so many days of rain, it was a relief of sorts. Maybe those who suffered the most in life were finally granted peace on the day of their funeral, and the shining sun was for those left behind, a sign that everything was okay for their beloved. I believed this and didn't believe this. Evelyn's funeral had taken place on a similar day two years ago. Fay had to call in some favors to find someone to preside over it. The man she found did not talk about Evelyn's botched abortion, and he didn't try to convert us magdalens, like Reverend Perkins might have. Instead he spoke about the cleansing blood of the lamb. I couldn't get those words out of my head for weeks after her funeral. The day after her abortion, I found Evelyn on the floor next to her bed. Blood everywhere, a familiar sight for me, and not a cleansing thing about it.

Mrs. Clarke had chosen a headstone with a lamb for Joseph. Wherever she was, I hoped Hattie was too far gone to understand what she had done.

"She used to call him her little lamb," Annie said.

"I didn't know that."

"I don't know if she said it out loud," Annie said, "but I could tell she thought it."

I looked over at Mrs. Clarke, standing in a tight circle with the other lady managers. "At least the weather cooperated," she said.

I'd seen terrible things in this life. I'd done terrible things too. But I liked to think I knew what I didn't know, and what the Board members didn't know about us would fill a thousand cemeteries.

Embrace religion, they said, and so we did. Sew these curtains, take this job, marry this man, keep this child, and when it inevitably went wrong, they decided the problem lay with us, not with their rules.

"She was only sixteen," I said. "She should have given him up for adoption and gotten on with the rest of her life."

"Only eight years older than Tabitha," Annie said with a shiver.

☙❧

Before we left, Mary Ann led me over to a gravestone.

"That's my cousin Oscar," she said. Her face was a calm blankness. "My mother told me to tell everyone I'm a widow, but the funny thing is, I never felt like I was lying. He said we would marry. You can believe something is real, even if it doesn't happen."

"I'm sorry," I said. This time I meant it. I rested my hands on my stomach, as if I could protect this baby from all the world would throw at her.

"He shouldn't have been allowed a Christian burial. The Church is very clear about that. His family has money, though."

Rules were not for those with money. More than power, money gave you the cover of respectability. When Genevieve left Fay's, she said to me, I don't want to live like this forever. What she meant, I suddenly saw, was that she didn't want to be powerless anymore. Wasn't that what we all desired? To be seen as a person. To be treated with dignity. To make decisions about our own bodies, our own lives. Girls with money had unexpected pregnancies too, no doubt. But only poor girls were friendless.

The cemetery was a sea of gravestones. So many Marys and Elizabeths, Johns and Josephs, beneath our feet. They were remembered as devoted mothers and loving wives, adored sons and beloved husbands. Who would remember me in death? In spite of the many unlovable and unlovely things inside me, I too had once been someone's beloved.

I paused before a grave marker with the names of two

women: HAZEL LAWSON AND LILLIAN ECKARD. DEAR FRIENDS UNTIL THE END. Above their names was an etching of two clasped hands.

Belle Queeney and R. Marie Walzer. Dear friends until the end.

Why is it people can't see what's right in front of them? When I sank to the ground crying, Mary Ann gently patted my back and let me cry. "There, there," she whispered, just like I had for Hattie. "It's going to be all right."

THE LOUISVILLE COURIER-JOURNAL

MEDICAL

The only perfectly safe and effectual remedy for female irregularities, Dr. Bernardo's Spanish Female Pills are compounded from ingredients known only to Dr. Bernardo, the famous Spanish Physician. Thousands of ladies in the U.S. are using them regularly and pronounce them Safe and Sure. Those who have used them recommend them to friends. Youth, health, and beauty retained by their use. Agreeable to the taste; purely vegetable; prompt in effect. Price $2.00 per package. Sent by mail in plain wrapper, securely sealed, to any address. Remember Dr. Bernardo's Spanish Female Pills are the only reliable pill for female irregularities. Mention this paper.*

---

* Adapted from *The Louisville Courier-Journal*, August 1, 1890.

"The Bride Passed Out Cold: Part 1"

———————————

On her last day at Fay's, Rose told me she didn't think she could have children. She teared up when she revealed this, but she admitted it was lucky, considering our present circumstances. "I would make a good mother," she said.

"How do you know such a thing?" I was asking about her inability to have children, not the good mother part.

"I don't bleed every month," she said. "I never have. Something is wrong with me on the inside." And then she was quiet as I kissed the places on her face where her tears had fallen, and I told her that in my eyes, there wasn't a thing wrong with her.

The other girls were gone for the day, a shopping trip for new boots and gloves followed by sledding at Central Park. December was a notoriously slow month. Leading up to Christmas, men were more likely to spend money on gifts for their family; it meant we had the whole day to ourselves.

Don't get so distracted by each other you don't hear a customer knocking on the door, Fay said.

Rose mock saluted her, and Fay smiled. Rose could always get away with that kind of thing. Everyone loved her.

"Sometimes I worry that we won't ever think we have enough money to leave," I told her that day.

"No," she said with a shake of her head. "We'll know it when we have it."

I told her that I wanted to live somewhere so cold we had to pile blankets and thick furs on the bed to stay warm. I wanted us to have our own garden and lots of trees. She wanted us to live somewhere sunny, where we could have an orange grove and swim in the ocean, and every morning she would sing the song "Gathering Shells from the Sea Shore." She hummed a few bars. "That's the first song I ever learned by heart on the piano." She said that as a child, she asked her uncle if the Pacific Ocean looked like the Ohio River, and he told her it was a color she'd never seen before, not exactly green, not exactly blue. He said ocean water was as different from river water as a crimson finch was from a cockatoo.

"Trust me," she said, laughing at my face, "they're very different birds."

"I'll live anywhere with you, Rose Marie Walzer," I said as I laid her out on the red velvet divan, the one Fay insisted was for customers only.

"It's soft but not terribly comfortable," Rose said about the couch.

"That's what some men say about my pussy," I said, and I felt it in my chest when she laughed.

"A man better not say that in front of me," she said, and then it was my turn to stretch out on the sofa.

Afterward, she poured us both a glass of wine and sat before the piano. "Why doesn't anyone play?"

"Leo used to play on Thursday and Friday nights. Then he fell in love with one of the girls, and Fay didn't want that kind of trouble."

"Which girl?"

"Genevieve. She later married a man who bought her two hummingbirds as pets. She invited us over after her wedding, and the birds were flying all about the parlor. They built their nests in the lace curtains. Every day, the florist brings her a basket of flowers so the birds can drink the honey."

"Every day?"

"Every single day. Her husband said that as long as the birds made her happy, they could build nests all over the house."

"He sounds rich."

"Old too."

Her fingers explored the piano keys. In her quiet confidence and skillful playing, I saw the piano lessons her uncle had paid for.

Maiden, that read'st this simple rhyme,
Enjoy thy youth, it will not stay;
Enjoy the fragrance of thy prime,
For oh, it is not always May!

"Hello?" a male voice called from the foyer. "Hello? Is anyone here?"

Rose quickly closed the piano. She squeezed my hand—once, twice—before arranging herself on the sofa. I stood beside her. A big man in overalls stopped abruptly in the doorway to the front room. Straightaway I noticed his eyes, one of which watered painfully.

"The door was unlocked," he said. "I didn't know if it was all right to come in." His hands were red and chapped, as if he had been doing laundry all morning. He clasped them behind his back before sliding them into his overall pockets. "I'm not from here. I read about this place in the sporting guide."

I knew the entry he spoke of: "The house at No. 624 is kept by Fay Sewell and boasts seven ladies ready to receive gentlemen into their tender arms. The house is conducted in the best manner and is first-class in every rate." When the new sporting guide came out, Fay bought us all monkey skin muffs in celebration. Mine was at the back of the wardrobe, unworn—I didn't like the thought of monkey skin covering my own.

"Where are you from?" Rose asked the man.

He drummed his fingers against his thick legs. "Carroll County. I'm a farmer there. I live alone."

Of course you do, I thought. I could feel the beginnings of a headache from the wine I'd had at lunch. I was not in the mood for this man to interrupt our day of freedom. Men from out of town sometimes felt a little too free in their demands; you had to be firm with them.

"I like that skirt you're wearing," he said to Rose. "It looks very soft."

She stood up. "It's velveteen. Would you like to touch it?"

He sank to his knees and crawled over to her. He lifted her skirt up and settled it around his head. I knew exactly how Rose's skirt felt and smelled when settled around your head. "Oh yes," he said from under her skirt. "It's the softest thing I ever felt."

Rose looked at me and made a face. "Shall we go upstairs?"

He crawled backward to get out from under her skirt and nearly knocked her over. I instinctively reached out to catch her, and she squeezed my hand in thanks. "Marry me instead," he said. He thrust those red hands in front of his face and pleaded. "I'll go crazy if you don't."

This was not the first time I'd seen the effect Rose had on men. It never bothered me before, but it did that day. There was an unpredictability about him, simmering just below the surface, and I didn't like it.

He dabbed at his eye with a not-so-clean handkerchief as he kneeled at her feet. "A good girl like you shouldn't be living this sinful life. I'm a rich farmer, I'll make you happy, you'll see." He didn't seem aware I was in the room; he certainly wasn't concerned about my sinful ways. "Tell me your name at least."

"Marian." She caught my eye, and I offered her the smallest of smiles.

"Marian," he said. "Marian with the face of an angel. Marry me, Marian."

She walked over to the staircase and held out her hand to him. "Why don't you come upstairs with me?"

"You're not a sinful girl. I can tell that about you. Don't you want to get married? Don't you want a better life?"

She beckoned to him again.

He pounded the floor in frustration. "I'm. Not. Moving. Until. You. Agree. To. Marry. Me." He gave the floor a double pounding when he finished.

"She said no." The trick was to speak from your chest, to make sure your eyes and your mouth were telling the same story. I learned this from Fay, who had never needed a man for security at her place. "Either take what she's offering or leave."

He stayed on the ground for another minute and then lumbered to his feet, wincing as he straightened his legs. I would think of him unexpectedly, months later, when I too would struggle to stand with my new stomach.

"You could have us both," Rose said, gesturing to me. "Same price."

In that moment I decided we had enough money. I could work in a laundry again. Rose could teach art. We could grow our own vegetables and make our own clothes. Anything would be better than pretending the things Rose and I did together were for the pleasure of paying men.

"I wouldn't dream of defiling you," the man said to Rose. His eyes flicked over to me. He seemed genuinely surprised to see me there. "You then."

Sorry, Rose mouthed to me. She tried to reassure me with

her eyes. As we climbed the stairs to my room, the piano started up.

Enjoy the Spring of Love and Youth,
To some good angel leave the rest;
For Time will teach thee soon the truth,
There are no birds in last year's nest!

"Leave it on," he said as I went to unbutton my dress. He untied his shoes silently; his socks were a startling white.

"She's such a beautiful girl," he said as he climbed on top of me. He smelled of corned beef. I tried not to stare at his watering eye, although my own eyes kept seeking it out. Had someone scratched it? Maybe he was born that way. I tried to feel sorry for him. I imagined his eye was a window to the ocean; behind it lay sand, water, palm trees. The red was the light from the setting sun. "Marian," he said with a strangled cry. I wondered what he would do if he knew Marian was my middle name. He suddenly circled my neck with one of his hands, the calluses on his palms rough against my throat.

"Stop." But I didn't have a voice anymore.

"Marian." He squeezed my throat in time to the song she was now playing downstairs: *All things rejoice in youth and love, / The fulness of their first delight!*

His hand on my neck was hot and heavy, my throat an icy fire. The girls at Fay's still talked about the girl Emma from years ago, strangled in the house with her own stockings. Afterward, Fay shut down the house for a week and refused to reopen until the police arrested the man. I could feel my heart pounding wildly. I thought, *My heart is pounding wildly,* and then a blinding darkness came for me. When I finally woke—minutes? hours? I had no way to know—I was alone in the house. He had taken Rose. My money too. I found my empty stockings crumpled at the foot of the stairs.

I read about her wedding in the paper the next morning: "May Lead a Better Life: Wealthy Farmer from Carroll County Marries a Fallen Woman."* It said the bride wore her best outfit, a brown velveteen skirt trimmed round the edge with close vertical rows of braid. After her vows, the bride passed out cold. Once revived, they left on the eight o'clock train for Carroll County.

---

* Adapted from *The Louisville Courier-Journal,* November 14, 1888.

THE LOUISVILLE COURIER-JOURNAL

DEATHS AND FUNERALS

A male infant at the Home for Friendless Women died yesterday. Mrs. Edward Clarke, current Board president of the Home, said the boy had been sick with pneumonia and unfortunately succumbed to his illness late last night. The mother, a young friendless girl from Nashville, is suffering from hysteria and other nervous ailments and will recover at the asylum under the care of a physician. The funeral for the infant will be held tomorrow and will be a private affair.

"He that loveth his wife loveth himself."

———————————

"I was wondering if there is a painless way to insert a hairpin on a girl's wedding day."

I warily eyed the hairpins on Miss MacCorkle's dressing table. God, I was tired of these conversations.

"No."

"I never did find that tortoiseshell pin," she said.

"A good reason to avoid tantrums." I never understood why Miss MacCorkle let me talk to her the way I did.

"It's possible that after a long day, he will be too tired to care about my hair," she said hopefully.

"If he's too tired on the wedding night, he won't be the next day. Or the day after that."

"Leo is different from most men," Miss MacCorkle said.

"He's a man, isn't he? Better prepare a song to sing."

"Aloud?"

I gave her a look. This girl didn't understand the ways of the world at all. God help any child she brought into existence.

"The only songs I know are church hymns."

"Then make up one."

"I don't have much practice making up songs."

"For fuck's sake." Her mouth fell open in surprise, and I realized I had spoken aloud. "There's a song we would sing at Fay's, to send off a girl when she got married."

Miss Lucy had a baby.
She named him Tiny Tim.
She put him in the bathtub
To see if he could swim.

He drank up all the water.
He ate up all the soap.
He tried to eat the bathtub,
But it got stuck in his throat.

Miss Lucy called the doctor
The doctor called the nurse.
The nurse called the lady
With the alligator purse.

"Mumps," said the doctor.
"Measles," said the nurse.
"Not a damn thing," said the woman
With the alligator purse.

Miss Lucy hit the doctor.
Miss Lucy slapped the nurse.
Miss Lucy paid the woman
With her alligator purse.

Out ran the doctor.
Out ran the nurse.
Out ran the lady
With the alligator purse.

Miss MacCorkle was still laughing when I finished. I sometimes forgot how young she was. "Mrs. Clarke has an alligator
purse! She's terribly proud of that silly bag."

"I don't doubt it," I said, and I had to stop brushing her hair
because she was laughing so hard.

Minutes from the Meeting

"I don't understand the parasols girls are carrying these days," Mrs. Kesselman said. "The handles are the size of billiard balls. They practically have to use two hands." She held up her hands as if clutching an object as large as her head. "Do you have a parasol like that, Regina?"

"I assure you my parasols have perfectly ordinary handles," said Mrs. Shippen.

"There's such little regard for matching a parasol to one's complexion. I passed a redheaded girl on the street recently carrying a scarlet parasol, and the tints transmitted to the poor girl's face. Will this rain never end? One day of sun and now back to rain. The river will flood soon, mark my words."

"What progress have we made on finding a replacement for Lucy?" Mrs. Shippen asked.

"None. And the wedding will be upon us soon," Mrs. Clarke said. "Still a thousand small details to iron out. Her final dress fitting is this afternoon."

"Did she end up choosing . . . ?"

"Indeed."

"I hope it's more flattering than you feared."

"It isn't," Mrs. Clarke said. "When it comes to her replacement, I wouldn't mind an older girl. I think Lucy has been too free in what she shares with the girls. Greater care should be taken to prevent inmates from knowing what is said at meetings. It wouldn't surprise me to learn that the girls listen to these meetings with their ears pressed to the door."

"No need for that," I said to Annie. "Those old cows talk so loud it's impossible to tune them out."

We were in the dining room, tasked with polishing the silver in the house, which Mrs. Clarke displayed but rarely found reason to use. Remember to use an up-and-down motion, Mrs. Clarke had said to us before heading into the sitting room for the Board meeting, never a circular one. And be sure you turn the cloth to avoid depositing tarnish back on the other pieces. When she had turned to leave, I mock saluted her, which made Annie shake her head and smile.

"I had a thought recently," Mrs. Kesselman said, "about those two girls who left without permission last year. Going forward, I propose we mark such absences as expulsions."

"Why?" asked Mrs. Shippen.

"'Left without permission' makes it sound as if girls are allowed to wander in and out as they please, as if the Home were a fabric store."

"No one of any intelligence would mistake our Home and the good work we do for a fabric store."

"If our records give the impression that we are failing in our duties as the lady managers, then how long before a different group decides they should oversee the day-to-day operations of the Home?"

"You mean how long before us lady managers are replaced by managers," said Mrs. Shippen. "I understand your concern, but I don't believe that recording a lie is the best possible solution."

"We don't always deal in best possible solutions, Regina."

"I thought we also didn't deal in lies."

"What about the Davidson girl as mistress?" Mrs. Clarke suggested. "She's the right age. And the girls enjoyed that art lecture she gave a few months ago."

"I heard she has a new beau. Even if she were single, I would not be inclined to offer her the position. I never blamed Eliza for her behavior. The reverend—well, that's a different matter. Minnie became a very headstrong girl," said Mrs. Kesselman.

"Woman," said Mrs. Shippen.

"What now?"

"Minnie is close to my age, and I consider myself a woman, not a girl."

"Well," Mrs. Kesselman said.

"A great many fathers are overly indulgent with their daughters," Mrs. Clarke said. "I'll admit my own father was guilty of it. He used to let me get away with anything, and when it came to disciplining my brothers, he had a much firmer hand."

"Mr. Wrocklage wants to give a lecture on money and morals to the girls," Mrs. Kesselman said. "He suggested next month."

"We can't afford to pay lecturers at this time," said Mrs. Shippen. "All money is promised toward the new home."

"He said he would deliver it free of charge."

"The last time I saw Mr. Wrocklage, he informed me of his crusade to ban pernicious literature. He claimed the fallen of the city owe their first downward steps to a familiarity with vice through the reading of novels. And the daily paper, which apparently devotes too much time to crime and scandals."

"He sounds like my father," Mrs. Kesselman said. "He used to say I should spend more time reading biographies."

"And did you?" Mrs. Clarke asked.

"Good gracious, no. I always found biographies dull. War, war, and more war. Mr. Wrocklage means no harm."

"The man is a hysteric. I will not extend him an invitation to deliver a useful lecture on money only for him to change course and subject the poor women to a rant about the dangers of reading," Mrs. Shippen said. "If he wants a crusade, I would be happy to point him in the direction of more timely causes."

"To be fair, I do agree with him to some extent—the newspaper prints the most salacious stories. I suspect they do it simply to boost sales," said Mrs. Clarke.

"We would do well to remember that Mr. Wrocklage is a devout and rather wealthy man who, with a small push, might be induced to pledge a large sum of money toward the Home," said Mrs. Kesselman.

"Let him pledge money as a subscriber and then we can discuss lectures," said Mrs. Shippen. "But not until I have a check in my hands. Now, other thoughts on a replacement for Lucy?"

"What about Elizabeth Lister?" said Mrs. Kesselman. "She called off her engagement recently."

"To the Purcell boy?" Mrs. Clarke asked.

"I heard she recently learned about some nocturnal visits he's paid to the place over on Hancock Street. Daytime visits too."

"Is that Lizzie Morgan's?"

"No, Celia Fuller's."

"And how long before some poor girl from Madame Fuller's shows up here?" asked Mrs. Clarke.

"We should ask Samuel Purcell to be a subscriber then," Mrs. Shippen said. "A repentance subscription, if you will."

"Wasn't your girl Nell at Madame Fuller's?" Mrs. Clarke asked.

"No, she was at Mollie Taylor's," said Mrs. Kesselman. "Or was it Mollie McDonald's? It wasn't Mollie Burns, I know that."

"It makes you wonder if there isn't a connection between a girl's name and her character," said Mrs. Clarke. "All these Mollies choosing the same degrading path."

"As you might recall, Ed's first wife was named Molly," Mrs. Shippen said.

"She spelled her name *M-O-L-L-Y*," said Mrs. Kesselman.

"It might be too soon to worry about this, but what will we do with the girls in the fall and winter when they can no longer work in the garden?" Mrs. Clarke asked. "I fear they will not have enough to keep them busy."

"Preparing their own meals, attending church services twice a week, caring for the children in the Home, sewing curtains every night," Mrs. Shippen said, ticking off items on her hand. "They seem quite busy to me, garden or no garden."

"Thank God there's one reasonable woman running this place," I said to Annie. "I can't bear to think of the complaining from Mary Ann if they gave us more chores."

"The garden keeps them busy in the morning, which establishes an industrious tone for the day," Mrs. Clarke said. "Who knows what slovenly habits they might embrace without a rigid workload."

"What about baking? We're short several dozen cakes and pies for Saturday's lecture at the church," Mrs. Kesselman said. "They're in desperate need of ginger cakes."

"I have a recipe for ginger cakes—I'll have Annie write it down for you before you leave. It's simply a pint of New Orleans molasses, half a pint of lard, half a pint of buttermilk, two tablespoons of soda, two teaspoons extract of ginger. Heat the milk boiling hot, pour along with the molasses into a bowl with the soda and ginger. Stir in flour until stiff, then work in the lard, knead well, roll out, cut in cakes, and bake," Mrs. Clarke said.

"Even Nell would be hard-pressed to mess that up," Mrs. Kesselman said.

"What if, instead of taking on more chores, the women attended science lectures at the Masonic temple?" said Mrs.

Shippen. "Professor Richards has been delivering a morning lecture series on chemistry. Yesterday's was on the wonders of oxygen, and everyone was on the edge of their seats. He had to stay an additional half hour to answer all the questions."

"Lectures will not bring in additional money, which, as you reminded us earlier, we desperately need," Mrs. Kesselman said. "Besides, they had that art lecture from Minnie recently."

"That was months ago."

"I was thinking the girls could take in laundry, in addition to the sewing they are currently doing," said Mrs. Clarke. "Speaking of wonders, you wouldn't believe Belle's efficiency with the laundry. No stain is safe around her."

"Never be good at a bad job," Annie said to me.

"She ought to come to my house," said Mrs. Kesselman, "teach Nell a thing or two. I can't trust her with my better things. Anything nicer than flannel, I send out."

"If you don't grow up with quality clothing . . ." Mrs. Clarke said.

"They often learn the easiest way to do things, not the best. She tried to take a hot iron to my silk stockings the other day."

"Surely they do these things deliberately," said Mrs. Clarke, "as a jealous sabotage."

"It's not insidious, as far as I can tell. More of a *sow's ear, silk purse* situation," Mrs. Kesselman said.

"If the girls are to take on more laundry, and Belle will be the one managing the operation, we should buy her a new outfit," said Mrs. Shippen, "to show our appreciation for her hard work."

"I've never met a girl who doesn't enjoy a new dress," Mrs. Kesselman said.

"I've never met a woman who doesn't enjoy feeling appreciated," said Mrs. Shippen.

"Of course we would need to add the new articles gradually

to her wardrobe, to not incite resentfulness in the other girls," Mrs. Kesselman said.

"'A sound heart *is* the life of the flesh: but envy the rottenness of the bones,'" Mrs. Clarke said.

"Let's adjourn for today," said Mrs. Shippen.

"I wrote down the ingredients for ginger cakes," Annie called to Mrs. Kesselman as she walked by the sitting room.

Mrs. Kesselman took the paper from her and smiled broadly. "Annie dear, you're a mind reader."

Annie waited until Mrs. Kesselman was out of earshot before saying, "My mother used to say that if I'd been born earlier, I'd have been burned at the stake as a witch."

"That's a rotten thing for a mother to tell her daughter," I said.

"She was a very unhappy woman."

"So was mine," I said, "but in a different way, I think."

Annie looked over at me. "We've seen bad things, you and me. We have that in common."

"Some would say I've done bad things too."

"You had your reasons." She looked down at the platter in her hands. "I was a good mother to Tabitha," she said, "before they took her away. I was nothing like my mother."

I felt a chill despite the warm sun pouring in through the bay windows. "Who took her?" I knew, of course. But sometimes words need to be said out loud to give them power.

"The Board said I was too old to be a mother. And then one day they came into my room and said they'd found a better family for her." When she looked at me, her eyes were wide with unshed tears. "It's my fault Hattie wasn't allowed to give up Joseph for adoption. I threatened to go to the newspaper after they took Tabitha, to tell everyone they were stealing babies. After that, they started making the girls keep their children."

I thought of how avidly Annie read the letters Tabitha sent

her once a month. In the last letter Tabitha had included a picture she'd drawn of a young girl feeding a carrot to a cross-eyed beast. What's that terrifying monster the girl is feeding? Mary Ann asked, and Annie had laughed before saying, It's a horse, not a monster.

"I went to the newspaper anyway," she said, "but no one believed me."

"I believe you. And I don't blame you for Joseph's death. I blame them."

"That's why I think you'll make a good mother, Belle," she said, and we finished polishing the silver in silence.

"Boisterous talking and laughing . . . are all evidences of ill-breeding in ladies."

―――――――――――

"Black-eyed peas was the right decision," Annie said a few nights later as she handed out the Jumbo bags. She had embroidered mine with my initials and a rose. "Since you took such an interest in the rose garden last spring," she said.

Caroline teared up when she saw the wedding bell on hers. "Oh, it's beautiful, Annie." As she spoke, she pulled a long strip of dead skin off her inflamed cheeks. She was trying powdered Borax on her face again, and the new skin underneath was just as freckled, poor thing.

Mary Ann's bean bag was covered with lace, her initials in red.

Waiting for my turn, I imagined my bags easily alighting on the board again and again. A perfect score. We were all bad, though—terrible, really—and once we made our peace with that, we had a fantastic time.

Toward the end of the game, Mrs. Goss peered over the fence. "What are you girls up to with all that shrieking?"

"Bean bags," Annie said. Her cheeks were flushed, and with the setting sun lighting up her hair, she little resembled the haggard woman the newspaper had described. "Do you want to join us?"

"Doesn't look like a game for an old lady like me," she said. "How's young Tabitha?"

"She's learning to draw animals. She's very talented."

That night, I laid my Jumbo bag on my stomach and thought that it had been a nice day, the kind of day where the weather matches your mood.

I would leave this house with a baby and a job, and as far as life went, maybe that was the best you could expect. "When you're old enough, I'll teach you how to play," I told the baby. "I'll teach you how to play, Jennie," I said aloud in the darkness. "I'll teach you how to play, Frances. Matilda. Daisy. Marie. *Marie.*" That sounded like the name of a girl who was headstrong and smart. I didn't have any boy names in mind, even though Mrs. Clarke told me, based on how wide my hips were, that she thought I was having a boy. I had a hard time imagining my body growing something with a penis, to be honest. What would be the point in learning such a thing ahead of time anyway?

"The Bride Passed Out Cold: Part 2"

"What do you think?" Caroline asked. She twirled, and her wedding dress halfheartedly fanned around her. The dress, similar in color and fit to the sacks of flour in the pantry, was a donation from the Trinity Methodist Church women. Her freckled wrists protruded from the too-short sleeves. Pert beige diamonds were embroidered on the collar, while a faded cream band gripped her stomach.

"It reminds me of something my grandmother wore at her wedding," Mary Ann said. Her daughter had arrived the night before. Mary Ann said labor was no more painful than a bad toothache. Honestly, she said, I don't understand the screaming and carrying on some girls do.

Mrs. Clarke said that a baby did not need four names. Even so, Mary Ann insisted that her daughter's name be recorded as Pearl Margaret Katherine Sheehan.

"It's the nicest dress I ever owned," Caroline said, "even if it makes breathing a little difficult."

"Shallow breaths," I suggested.

"Tighten your corset," said Mary Ann. "I'd let you borrow my dragonfly hairpin, the one with the blue stone, but I can't have you running off to Florida with it. I'd like to give it to Pearl Margaret when she's old enough to wear it. And when she finally has hair." Mary Ann stroked her daughter's bald head.

"How about you wear this instead." I handed her the tortoiseshell pin, and Caroline's eyes filled with tears.

"Belle, that's too nice a gift."

"Where did you get that?" Mary Ann asked suspiciously.

"You have to promise me something," I said to Caroline as I slid the pin into her hair. "If he gets rough with you, you leave. Don't let him apologize or swear it will never happen again. Because if it happens once, it will happen again."

"I promise," Caroline said.

"I hope he's handsome," Mary Ann said. "Wouldn't it be dreadful to realize you've been corresponding all this time with Quasimodo?"

"What's a Quasimodo?" asked Caroline.

A flash of lightning suddenly lit up the room and thunder followed close behind. All day it had been doing this dance of light and noise without the release of rain.

"I heard it's good luck if it rains on your wedding day," Caroline said.

Mary Ann opened her mouth to argue but, at a look from me, quickly clamped it shut.

During her wedding, right after Caroline promised to love her husband, Fred, in sickness and in health, she fainted. She swayed, sank gracefully to her knees, and ended up flat on her back.

The look on her new husband's face as she was falling. *Not again,* the look said. Fred was no Dr. Shippen, but he wasn't Quasimodo either.

"It's her dress," I said as he and I knelt beside her. His hands shook as he awkwardly patted Caroline's hand while I fanned her face.

When she opened her eyes, he smiled in relief. "I thought you were dead," he said, not bothering to wipe the tears from his eyes.

She smiled up at him from her spot on the floor. What a trusting face she had.

"You certainly gave new meaning to the words *fallen woman*," I whispered as I helped her to her feet.

When they left for Jacksonville, I said something akin to a prayer.

Dear God, please let him be good to her.

> "Diligent hands will rule,
> but laziness ends in forced labor."

"Since you will be heading up the laundry project, we would like to present you with a new article of clothing." Mrs. Clarke handed me a pale pink handkerchief, the initials B.S. embroidered on the bottom left. "We don't want to create rivalries with the other girls, so best to keep that hidden in your room. There's more where that came from, if your efficiency with the laundry continues."

So much for a new dress, I thought.

"Thank you. Although may I ask what the *S* stands for?"

"For Sewell, of course."

"Sewell?"

"Your last name." Mrs. Clarke said this as if prompting a child to remember her manners.

"My last name is Queeney, ma'am."

"Oh." Her look of surprise made me laugh out loud, and after a moment she laughed too. "I wonder why I thought it was Sewell."

"The mind is a mystery," I said.

"We appreciate your hard work, Belle."

"Thank you."

"Do not let any unwholesome
talk come out of your mouths."

———————

Mary Ann and I sat on one couch, Rachel, Helen, and Christie on the other. Annie paced anxiously in the back of the room. Heading up the new laundry project was no small task. Mrs. Clarke had apparently convinced all of Louisville to bring their dirty laundry to the Home for me to wash. At this point, I surely deserved more than a measly handkerchief with the wrong initials. After a day spent in the basement, I was not in the mood for one of Mrs. Clarke's lectures.

"Do you like Pearl Margaret's dress?" Mary Ann held up her daughter, whose white dress was an explosion of ruffles and lace. Pearl Margaret blinked solemnly at me and then sneezed. "My cousin Effie sent it."

"Pretty," I said.

Mary Ann grimaced and moved away from me. "You stink, Belle."

I thought of telling her it was the smell of honest work, but I was too tired to argue, even with Mary Ann. My corset felt as if it were strangling me with every breath.

Mrs. Clarke gazed out at us. Her face said, *I am disappointed in you girls.* Yet there was a brightness to her eyes that also telegraphed that this disappointment, though inevitable, was not unwelcome.

"I have heard a report of improper language in the Home. I'm offering you girls the opportunity to confess."

The only sound was the noise of Annie's boots nervously tapping behind me.

"I don't enjoy these conversations any more than you do," Mrs. Clarke said.

The tapping grew louder.

"I'm a patient woman. I can wait all day."

I was ready to unleash a stream of foul words, if it meant we could retire to our rooms before dinner, when Rachel suddenly spoke up.

"I was lacing up my boots yesterday, and when one of the laces broke, I said *damn*." I had never heard Rachel speak in a voice louder than a whisper. We all leaned forward to hear her better. "I said it because I didn't have a spare one handy, but it was wrong to say it, and I'm sorry. I didn't think anyone heard me."

I thought of what I'd said earlier that day in the garden, when I'd discovered that hornworms had invaded the Roma tomatoes. *Damn! Damn, damn, damn!* And not in Rachel's quiet whisper either.

"Thank you, Rachel, for your honesty," Mrs. Clarke said. "I believe there is more to be uncovered."

Helen crossed and uncrossed her legs. She tucked a braid firmly behind her ear and cleared her throat. "I said *damn it* yesterday, when I was looking for Patrick's blue sweater."

"You said this in front of your child?"

Helen's braids knocked against her back as she shook her head. "No, ma'am. He was in the nursery, and I was in my room."

"Refrain from that language in the future. Anyone else have something they'd like to share?"

"Last week I said a word I would rather not repeat," Christie said. "What happened was I gave Auggie prunes with her breakfast, and I discovered, just as I was leaving for work, that they had disagreed with her digestion. When I was changing her, some—" She cleared her throat. "That is, part of what was in her diaper ended up on me and the floor and all over her back, and I had to change my own clothing and clean the floor, which I knew was going to make me late for work. I said an ugly word as I was cleaning up the you-know-what."

"I would have cleaned it up for you," Annie said. "Blood and excrement don't bother me."

"I appreciate your reluctance to speak the word again," Mrs. Clarke said to Christie. "Although if you would like to work in the medical profession, you will have to learn how to say the proper names for such fluids."

All this talk about blood and excrement was making me queasy. I took a deep breath, slowly released it.

"I don't recall using improper language, Mrs. Clarke. It's possible I said something vulgar while dreaming," Annie said. "I sometimes have the most startling dreams."

"I'm not concerned about utterances during sleep. While these admissions are upsetting, they are not the reason I called everyone in here. I recently found a poem in Miss MacCorkle's room, one she claims she learned from an inmate."

Something was happening to my stomach: a rumbling and a painful grinding.

"I'm too busy with Pearl Margaret these days to write poetry," Mary Ann said.

"It was more of a limerick," said Mrs. Clarke.

Saliva pooled uncomfortably in my mouth.

"It started with 'Miss Lucy had a baby.' There was also mention of a woman with an alligator purse."

I swallowed and shuddered. Sweat broke out on my arms.

"Please stand if you acknowledge the rules about foul language and agree to abide by them." Around me the other girls stood.

"Stand up, Belle," Mary Ann hissed.

I opened my mouth to speak and a rush of hot sickness rose up instead and splattered onto the rug.

⚜

"There's sewage in the basement," Dr. Shippen said. For once his shirt was crisply ironed. "Was she down there today?"

"She was doing laundry today," Mrs. Clarke said.

"All week actually," Annie said. "Belle's head of the laundry project."

"It might be yellow fever." Mary Ann stood in the hallway outside my bedroom, a blanket wrapped around her mouth and nose. "A letter from Caroline arrived yesterday, and I don't think the envelope was properly treated with sulfur at the post office."

Everything had been wrung out of me. What else was there to release? I sat up and dribbled spit into the bowl in my lap. My stomach made a loud, drawn-out gurgling noise, and everyone looked over in alarm.

"And the baby?" Mrs. Clarke asked.

My hands tightly clutched the bowl as I waited for his answer.

"The baby should be fine," Dr. Shippen said. "Really, Mrs. Clarke. This situation with the sewage is untenable. You really can't have her down there all day in her condition."

I collapsed on the bed in relief, my hands atop my stomach, which rolled and roiled. *I found the ocean after all, Rose.*

"For though I be absent in the flesh,
yet am I with you in spirit."

Miss MacCorkle took the glass bottle out of my hands and sniffed its contents, wrinkling her nose in disgust. "It smells worse than the stockyards."

I shook a healthy amount of the diluted onion juice onto her scalp. "It's a special hair tonic. The more your eyes burn, the better it's working."

She squeezed her eyes shut and covered her nose and mouth with a handkerchief.

The smell made my own eyes water, and I blinked back tears.

"I need you to clean Hattie's room today," she said, her voice muffled from the handkerchief. "A new girl is joining us tomorrow. Such a tragic story."

I wondered if Miss MacCorkle would find her own story tragic if presented to her: *The poor girl is balding and engaged to a man who once proposed marriage to a prostitute. And you would not believe the way her future mother-in-law belittles her.*

"She was at Madame Sewell's too. Maybe you knew her— Agnes?"

I shook my head.

"Does the spot look bigger to you today? When Mrs. Clarke was here yesterday, we had a rather heated exchange, and afterward, I brushed my hair rather fiercely."

"You shouldn't take out your anger with Mrs. Clarke on your hair. You'll undo all my hard work."

"We started talking about the article she wrote for the newspaper, and I said to her, 'If women could vote, Prohibition would pass tomorrow, and wouldn't that be a victory? And the amendment to grant licenses to houses of prostitution?'" She snapped her fingers. "'Voted down immediately.' She vehemently disagreed, claiming it would cause strife in families, and that a person must be always willing to back up a vote at the ballot with a bullet, and was I suddenly volunteering for military duty? Then she left in a huff."

"She didn't like you speaking your mind."

"Leo ignores the advice she gives him. Did I tell you he gave me a kitten yesterday? She has the sweetest striped face. I named her Zebra. After our argument yesterday, Mrs. Clarke said I couldn't keep a kitten in the house; she said cats spread diphtheria."

"An old wives' tale," I said dismissively.

"I didn't put her outside. I was afraid she would be snatched up by an eagle or a hawk."

"No hawks in Kentucky this time of year."

"Annie said she'd take care of her for me. She said she once hid a cat for several months and no one ever found out."

I pictured a striped cat kneading its striped paws on Annie's quilt, and the idea made me smile.

"I don't enjoy arguing with Mrs. Clarke," Miss MacCorkle said. "I should have made it clear to her yesterday that I don't think all women should be allowed to vote. Those who broke the law, for example. It would be unfair to give those women the same privileges as those who follow the rules. Actions should have consequences."

"Don't they always?"

"Mrs. Clarke said if we can't trust all women to make good choices, no one should vote. I've never understood the idea behind collective punishment."

"Someone like you should be allowed to vote, but not someone like me, I'm guessing?" I asked dryly.

"I would have no problem with you voting, since I know you. You know how most people are. They'll likely be unable to look past your mistakes." She removed the handkerchief from her nose and mouth. "How long before you can rinse out this foul-smelling stuff?"

There was no need for the onion juice to sit on her hair, but I said, "Another half hour at least."

"Maybe I should write an editorial like Mrs. Clarke."

I thought of all my letters to the paper that had gone unanswered. "Writing to the newspaper is a waste of time. Besides, you'll never vote on the issue of suffrage. If men had their way, they'd encourage women like you and Mrs. Clarke to argue with each other about suffrage. That way, they can keep doing what they're doing, which is nothing, while claiming you nattering hens are too divided on the issue."

"If my mother were still alive, she'd probably agree with Mrs. Clarke."

"If my mother were still alive, I would not be brushing your hair every morning."

"I started pulling out my hair after she died," Miss Mac-Corkle said. "Eyelashes too."

I already knew this, of course. "You wanted to feel something."

"I used to save the hair. Roll it into a ball and hide it under my bed. Sometimes I would paste it onto the heads of my paper dolls."

I felt an unexpected pang of tenderness for her. For me. Two motherless daughters.

"I don't do that anymore," she said. "Save the hair."

I nodded as if I believed her. Sometimes I really did feel sorry for this ridiculous girl.

"Do not carry gossip from one family to another."

———————————

The new girl whistled at the sight of the Pearline soap boxes. There was an easy familiarity in her words and her body, as if she had lived in the Home for months instead of hours. "It stinks of shit in here," she said.

"They have sewage problems."

I showed her the washtubs, the irons, the drying racks.

"Two irons," she said. "Fancy."

"The one for collars and cuffs works just fine on dresses as well. No need to heat up both."

"I just got the whole 'religion will not be thrust upon you' speech from Mrs. Clarke," Agnes said. "Then she gave me a Bible and told me to pray for forgiveness for my sinful ways."

"Prepare to be called a sinful woman for the next few months," I told her. "I hope you're not a Papist." This girl was surely going to chafe under the rules. I liked her already.

"I've been called worse," Agnes said cheerfully. "Although they'll have to tell me what's so sinful about wanting a roof over my head and food in my belly."

"From what I've gathered, good girls choose to slave away at a factory, and bad girls like us choose the better-paying, but sinful, brothel life."

Agnes let out a bark of laughter. "Thank God I'm too smart to be a good girl. You know," she said, "I had your old room at Fay's. The other girls still called it Belle's room."

"Were the gold curtains still up?"

"And the purple quilt," she said.

"You weren't there long," I said with a nod at her stomach.

"I had good luck my first month, convincing men to pull out. Then someone complained."

"Fay hates complaints. And complainers."

"I didn't open my own establishment . . ." Agnes drawled while looking down her nose.

It was a good impression and I laughed.

"One of the girls told me to use a lemon peel. And Charlotte gave me some of her Spanish pills, but all they did was turn my urine orange. I thought it was blood at first. I blame Fay."

"For your piss turning orange?"

"No, for the baby, you dummy. She should have had options for us. Ways we could protect ourselves from pregnancy."

"She says that's up to the girl."

"She's the boss, isn't she? Bosses should look out for their employees."

"I'd like whatever job you had to believe that. Who did Fay give my room to anyway? Charlotte was hoping for it when I left. She always said it was the biggest room. Except for Fay's, of course."

"The biggest room," Agnes scoffed. "Fay gave it to a new girl. Well, not a *new* girl. An old girl who came back. Someone named Rose."

Impossible, I thought.

"This girl was at Fay's last year, and then she married a farmer right before Christmas. Some of the girls said she was crazy to leave a rich husband, but I saw the way she was walking. Careful like." Agnes walked around the basement with an exaggerated limp. "I've walked that way enough times myself to know all the money in the world doesn't mean a thing if a man gets to thinking you're the reason he's unhappy."

How could Agnes not hear my heart pounding away? I heard it in my ears and felt it in my fingers. Surely even the baby could hear it.

"Do you know her full name? This Rose?" Amazing to hear my voice, how normal it sounded.

"Rose Walker, I think."

Rose Marie Walzer, she said her first day at Fay's. My friends just call me Rose.

"Do not conform to the pattern of this world."

———————————

Miss MacCorkle shook her head. "Mrs. Clarke wouldn't like it, and I've been trying to stay on her good side. The wedding is less than a week away."

"I won't be gone long. Please." I held my hands in front of my face. When I remembered this was what the farmer had done while begging Rose to marry him, I quickly put my hands down.

"You know how she is about you girls leaving the Home. I can't risk another argument."

"We don't have to tell her I left. It will only be for a few hours, she'll never know. I'm caught up on my chores today."

"What if she stops by unexpectedly?" She was wavering.

"Tell her I'm resting. Tell her whatever she wants to hear. She never found out about Zebra, did she?"

This was the wrong thing to say. "No," she said. "You agreed to stay here during your confinement, and if I let you visit a friend, then I'd have to let all the girls. Rules are rules." She held the hairbrush out to me. "Mrs. Clarke would have a fit to end all fits if she learned I gave you permission to leave. To return to Madame Sewell's, of all places."

"I'm not returning. I need to check on my friend. She was in Carroll County for months and months, and now she's back."

"There's nothing of interest in Carroll County," Miss Mac-Corkle said. "I'm not surprised she returned. Rules are rules." I could tell from her small smile that she liked the feel of those words in her mouth. She waved the hairbrush at me, and I finally took it from her.

Soon after she arrived at Fay's, I found Rose sitting in the backyard. I sat beside her and watched as she sketched the birds splashing about in the fountain.

I thought I saw a bowerbird, she said.

I don't know anything about birds.

She told me that bowerbirds build nests several feet tall, and they use a stick gripped in their beak as a paintbrush, smearing the juice of berries on the outside of their bowers to decorate them.

Why do they do this?

To attract a mate, of course.

She told me that when she was twelve, she and her uncle found a bower while on a hike. This particular one was all blue—blue flowers, blue scraps of ribbons, even blue pebbles. They walked around it, studied it from all sides. When they peered inside, they saw two rooms, a wall of sticks separating them. Her uncle asked her why she thought the male bird had constructed two rooms in his bower. She thought a minute and said, It's so the female can be alone while she decides if she wants to stay. If she wants to leave, she can fly away, and he won't be able to stop her.

Is that really why they do that? I asked her.

She shrugged. There's no way to know for sure. We can't exactly ask the bird what he was up to now, can we? She showed me the picture she had drawn. What do you think? Is it a good likeness?

Her eyes were so light compared to her dark hair. I spent a long time studying the picture that day, to avoid looking at her too directly.

It's beautiful, I said when I finally looked up from her drawing.

You can love someone long before you touch them, long before you know if they love you back. It's innocent—selfless, really—to love someone this way. How differently the world looks when you allow yourself this sort of love.

I laid a hand protectively over my stomach before turning to Miss MacCorkle. "You should have played with that doll. Your mother would have forgiven you."

Once on the sidewalk outside the Home, I realized I still had her hairbrush clutched tightly in my hand. I reared back and tossed it onto the Goss property.

Ten points.

"Eye for eye, tooth for tooth, . . .
wound for wound."

"You're having a girl for sure," Fay said. "I'm good at predicting these things." She shook her head in amazement. "I can't believe how fat you got. Use the back stairs so you don't scare off customers."

Rose was sitting in bed, staring at a book in her lap. I held on to the doorframe for support, since my legs were suddenly shaking uncontrollably. "You're very thin," I said.

"Not you," she said.

I lowered myself onto the bed beside her. "Are you hurt?"

"It doesn't matter now." She placed her hand on my stomach, and I placed my hand on top of hers. Her cuticles were ragged and bloodied.

"It matters to me," I said.

"I walked in on him, that day, with his hands . . ." She wrapped her own shaking hands around her throat. "I tried to pull him off you, but he was so big, and he said he'd kill you unless I married him." Tears ran down her face in a continuous stream. "I'm sorry," she said. "I'm so sorry, Bells."

"You have nothing to be sorry about, silly girl. I tried to find you. I sent letters to the newspaper before I was sent to the Home."

"They let you leave? Fay said they don't allow visitors at that place."

"Since when do I let someone tell me what I can and can't do?"

Her hair was too long and her nails too short, but my god, her smile hadn't changed a bit.

"Were you miserable there?" she asked.

"I didn't starve, did I? I'll have you know that you're speaking to the former head of the laundry."

"What does it feel like?" She gave my stomach a tentative pat.

Like falling in love, I thought.

"Terrible at first, better now."

"I bet it's like seeing a bower bird and a yellow-rumped warbler and a ruby-crowned kinglet all on the same day," Rose said.

"If she's a girl, we'll name her Ruby," I said.

"Kinglet for a boy," she said. "We'll call him King."

"God help us," I said, "two women raising a King."

"We'll figure it out," she said, and I nodded and squeezed her hand, hard.

She took back her hand and gave me the book in her lap. It was the Bible. "I brought you a present."

"I've read from that book nearly every day since you left. Did you know Mary Magdalen is mentioned fourteen times?"

"You haven't read this version," she said. "Go on, open it up."

A stack of bills fluttered onto the bed until we were sitting in an ocean of green, a green even purer than her eyes.

"He was a wealthy man after all, Bells."

PART III

Minnie

THE LOUISVILLE COURIER-JOURNAL
SEPTEMBER 26, 1901

The Home for Friendless Women will celebrate its silver anniversary today, and the Board of Managers will keep open house from 4:00 till 9:00 p.m. They will gladly welcome all friends of the Home, both old and new. Some cards have been sent out, but all may not have been reached, so we extend an invitation through the press. The cards contain a modest request for a quarter.

"If you build it, they will sin."

Two presidents shot in her lifetime, first Lincoln and now McKinley, dead at the hands of a madman, the most recent one an anarchist. Minnie had been seven when Lincoln died on that Good Friday, and she remembered her father's sermon that Easter, the adults around her openly weeping while she struggled to sit still, her blue-and-white-checked dress itchy where it met bare skin. For weeks after Lincoln's death, black fabric waved outside churches and homes. Even the saloons were shrouded in mourning.

Poor Mrs. Lincoln, her mother had said. First two sons and now her husband. It was one of the few times Minnie recalled seeing her mother cry. Later people would say Mrs. Lincoln's refusal to attend her husband's funeral was improper. Was there a proper way to grieve? Apparently, yes.

Thirty-six years later it was Minnie who cried after reading that President McKinley's last words had been: "It is God's way. His will be done—not ours." Likely her father would say something similar on his deathbed. Such a shocking way to die, shot by a stranger. An intimate death rendered impersonal. The country offered up thoughts and prayers, and then, as before, collective grieving gave way to business as usual, for a dead president did not halt the days of the living for long. Another day of meetings, the Home's silver anniversary party in two days, and the boys' birthday dinner tonight, and Minnie foolishly promising to make her famous chocolate cake because, as she told her husband, Roland, you only turn six once.

"Chocolate cake! Chocolate cake!" Mark chanted at breakfast, and Lucas joined in a minute later, a pattern she imagined her sons would repeat their whole lives. The boys ate their toast and drank their juice and no one spilled it today, a miracle that was truly cause for celebration, and they were off to school.

"Don't play in the streets after school," she called after them. "Come home straightaway." From the living room window, she watched them disappear up the street. Her sturdy towheaded boys, full of newly acquired opinions and bluster. Their light hair, so unlike her own, served as a daily reminder they were hers and not hers. This didn't make her sad. Twins at thirty-seven had made her more practical than sentimental.

"Why don't I pick up a chocolate cake at the bakery run by your ladies?" Roland asked after the boys left. *Your ladies* was his term for the women who left the Home. She found it endearing, since the Board's president, Mrs. Kesselman, always used the less appealing *former inmates.*

"I don't mind making them a cake. It's nice to prepare food they enjoy as opposed to always nagging them to eat food they don't."

"Don't forget the paintings from the art gallery are arriving this afternoon."

She stared at him blankly.

"The Caperton house," he prompted.

She'd forgotten. "There's the tea after the lecture. No matter," she said when she saw his face. "I'll be there. I'll find the time."

❧❧

As a child, Minnie was often admonished to think of those less fortunate. When she was very young, she heard the words *those less fortunate* as the name of a girl, Lessa Fortunate. When

Minnie balked at liver and onions for supper—Think of Lessa Fortunate. When Minnie wanted to know why they spent the week before Christmas baking cookies and pies only to give them away—Lessa Fortunate. And whenever she heard the name Lessa Fortunate, she always pictured a pregnant girl from the Home. All her life she had been told to pray for those poor girls, and even as a child, Minnie understood that she was being asked to pray for them because they were not like her. We cannot be charitable to our equals, her mother often said. Minnie didn't need to know the meaning of the word *charitable* to understand that she, though younger and smaller, was better off than the Lessa Fortunates of the world.

If there was a time her life hadn't been intertwined with the Home for Friendless Women, she couldn't recall it. Her mother was the Board president for years. The idea for the Home had been her father's, after he claimed a woman entered his church one Sunday and asked why the good Christians of the city did not build a shelter for sinners like her. A compelling if not entirely believable tale, Minnie always thought. Still, her father was able to convince his congregation and a group of like-minded ministers to help him raise funds.

This is a time for action rather than words, he exhorted his congregation week after week. Society should seek to reform, not scorn these fallen women. We will teach them home industries and to be self-sustaining so that they might leave their path of sin forever.

In a few short years, there was enough money, $2,300 in fact, to purchase the Home. A shelter for sinners. Redemption and salvation for all.

The Home became as familiar to Minnie as her own home. She spent Christmas Eve and Easter there, she attended meetings and luncheons with her mother and Sunday school lessons and lectures with her father. She donated her old dresses and quilts to the girls, she helped bake cookies for fundraisers, and, after a vigorous campaign led by her mother years ago, she even joined the Board herself. Still, the women remained as abstract to Minnie as Lessa Fortunate. She felt for them, especially the young ones. She pitied them, worried for them. She also believed they had done something bad or—wasn't this the same?—had allowed something bad to happen to them.

After Paris, Minnie didn't believe that. Not one word. But the residue of all those years, of who deserved what, was hard to purge.

ဢ☄

Even though the women had lived in the house on Kentucky Street for nearly twelve years now, Minnie still thought of it as the new Home. The gray brick and narrow windows of the old place had been replaced with cheerful red brick and large east-facing windows. The new Home boasted a green door instead of the bloodred one Minnie remembered. Even the scowling gargoyle that once guarded the porch was gone. Walking up to the Home now, Minnie was nearly run over by Victoria and Ella, who were carrying a rolled-up carpet out the front hallway.

"Are you here for an art lesson?" Ella asked hopefully. "I've been working on the basic forms, and spheres are giving me fits. I've grown to hate lemons and apples."

Minnie laughed. "Keep at it! Next week we'll experiment with shading and light, and before you know it, you'll be churning out sketches at a dizzying rate. Here, turn it this way," she said, helping them maneuver the rug onto the front porch.

"Matron found me a harp and I've been practicing every day," Victoria said. "After chores of course," she added. "It's been a while since I've played for a large crowd, but I don't think I'll sound *too* bad."

"She's being modest," Ella said. "She plays like an angel."

"I'm glad we learned of your talents with the harp. A live concert will add a nice touch to the party." Minnie didn't add that Mrs. Kesselman had vehemently opposed the idea, and it had taken a vigorous persuasion campaign to convince her it would be charming, rather than unseemly, for Victoria to play at the silver anniversary party.

"Girls, be sure to beat both sides," Elsa Mae called from the doorway as the women draped the rug over the front porch railing.

"It's always struck me as rather silly to clean before a big party," Minnie said. "You have to do it all over again after everyone leaves." She lowered her voice. "But don't tell Elsa Mae I said that."

She saw the girls exchange a conspiratorial look, Ella mouthing *Elsa Mae* as if it were a funny, even scandalous word.

They think I'm ridiculous, Minnie thought, and she was both embarrassed and comforted by the notion. Wouldn't she find herself a little ridiculous if she lived here?

Inside was a swirl of activity: Nancy was cleaning the woodwork in the hallways, Daisy was using a whisk broom to dust the back of a mirror, and Birdie was rubbing a white mixture onto the front of the glass cabinets, and bustling among the chaos was Elsa Mae. The matron of the Home was a foot shorter than Minnie and substantially wider, yet she moved with the quickness of a much younger, slimmer woman. Minnie had never met anyone as organized and efficient as Elsa Mae, as if the woman had been patiently waiting her whole life to step into her current position. Maybe she had, since the week after her husband died of consumption, she arrived at the Home with the newspaper in hand and announced they could stop their search for a new matron because she was willing to do the job for less than the offered salary. She said that living in a house full of pregnant women and crying babies sounded marvelous after spending the last year caring for a sick husband. Within days, Elsa Mae could rattle off the name and hometown of every girl in the home, along with their birthdays, favorite foods, and allergies. She kept detailed lists: where the girls took jobs, how long they stayed in the Home, marriages, funerals, et cetera. If it happened on Elsa Mae's watch, it was dutifully recorded.

Not long after she joined the Board as treasurer, Elsa Mae had taken Minnie on a tour of the new Home, and Minnie had marveled aloud at how different the Home was from its predecessor: the larger bedrooms, the chapel (Named after your dear father! said Elsa Mae), the in-house infirmary, the nursery, the spacious laundry room with stone floors, each room more light-filled than the next. It had the unmistakable smell of the original Home, though. Underneath the vinegar and Borax, the sparkling floors and windows, lurked the deeper tang of milk and sweat. The animal scent of motherhood, an unwelcome reminder of what pregnancy did to a woman, how unnatural this very natural thing was when it was your own body daily transforming.

Elsa Mae waved her over. "Mrs. Morton, as you might recall, I'm in the process of reorganizing the contents of the library." She was always reorganizing something.

"The record books from the first part of the Home's history are missing. Now it's possible the first matron of the Home did not keep records—an irresponsible and careless thing to do, but I'm not here to judge."

Minnie made a noise of assent.

"I'm not discounting the possibility they were lost during the move. At the risk of sounding critical, it's clear the move here was rather haphazard. Just yesterday I found a box in the corner of the basement full of bean bags. You'll never guess how the box was labeled."

"Dried beans?"

"'Wedding present.' For all we know, the missing record

books could be tucked away in a box labeled 'baby quilts.' I had a stroke of luck yesterday when I found a box of record books that predate the move. All I'm missing are the years 1877 and 1878. Might your father know where those books are?"

"It's possible, although recordkeeping was Mother's domain. And the chances of her remembering are next to impossible."

"Such an unfortunate disease." Elsa Mae gave Minnie's arm a motherly pat that Minnie found touching, since they were the same age. She led Minnie over to a series of portraits on the wall. "I had the girls move your mother's portrait into the living room so we can honor her contributions during the party. It's a great likeness," she said about the portrait Minnie herself had painted years ago.

The eyes were all wrong, she saw now, much too wide and innocent for someone her mother's age. She'd never been very great at mouths either; her mother's lips were unnaturally fleshy. But she had managed to capture something of her mother. She could see it best in the slight tilt of her head, how her mother always seemed on the verge of asking for a point of clarification.

"Such a handsome woman, your mother," Elsa Mae said, and Minnie realized with a jolt of surprise that, yes, her mother had been rather pretty.

"Mrs. Williams and Mrs. Kesselman are waiting for you in the kitchen." Elsa Mae lowered her voice. "Mrs. Williams brought cookies." In a more normal voice, she added, "Oh, and please tell Mark and Lucas happy birthday from me."

"I will."

What a memory this woman had.

☙❧

"It's more than the frowsy hair and slovenly dress," Mrs. Kesselman was saying when Minnie entered the kitchen. "I truly believe the bicycle is making young women downright cruel. Just yesterday I saw a girl nearly collide with a delivery boy, and you wouldn't believe what she shouted at him as she pedaled away." She handed Minnie a tray of cookies. "Ruthie wants to serve these at the party." Mrs. Kesselman punctuated this with a dark look.

After her son, Edward, left for college, Ruthie took up baking, which she said brought her unadulterated joy. Unfortunately, eating her unusual desserts rarely brought such joy to others. Over the years Minnie had been forced to sample her friend's candied asparagus chip cookies, vinegar pie, and something Ruthie called "grasshopper bread," the thought of which still made Minnie's stomach churn.

"What's in these?" Minnie sniffed the cookie. It smelled safe enough. "Didn't we finalize the menu last week, strawberry cakes and orange tarts?" She said a prayer the cookie was not a relative of grasshopper bread and took a small bite.

"Bicycles would help the girls get to the bakery," Ruthie said to Mrs. Kesselman. "And most doctors agree that bicycle riding is beneficial, not injurious, for girls."

"I've never heard a woman use such coarse language. The near collision was her fault, not his."

"The only people opposed to bicycle riding are those who have never tried it and therefore don't have the facts to speak authoritatively about it."

"Cheeky girl." Nearly a term of affection by now, coming from the much older Mrs. Kesselman. Minnie and Ruthie were both married women in their forties, but to Mrs. Kesselman they would always be girls. Cheeky ones, at that.

"I don't think one foulmouthed bicycling girl should keep us from buying a few bicycles for the Home. Minnie, what do you think?" Ruthie asked.

"I think bicycles are a brilliant idea. It would allow the girls to take jobs farther from the Home." She gestured to the cookie in her hand. "These are delicious."

Ruthie beamed. "Guess what's *not* in them?"

"Asparagus?"

"Now who's being cheeky?" Ruthie said. "Eggs and butter. I can easily make a few dozen before the party."

"Leave the recipe with Elsa Mae, and the girls at the bakery can make them," Mrs. Kesselman said.

"They've already done so much to get the house ready for the party. I'll make them myself."

"They're not here on vacation, Ruthie. These girls need the hard work."

This time it was Ruthie who appealed to Minnie with a look.

Mrs. Kesselman was fond of quoting from the Home's initial charter, that theirs was a charitable home designed to "restrain, instruct, protect, and care for friendless women, in order to restore them to virtue and usefulness." She always emphasized *restrain* and *usefulness* in her recitation, which made Minnie think of a wild horse that needed breaking in.

An apt analogy, yes, Mrs. Kesselman had said.

The first year Minnie joined the Board, she and Ruthie often butted heads with Mrs. Kesselman, and they sought diplomatic, and later not so diplomatic, ways to convey to Mrs. Kesselman that it was time to make a few changes at the Home, that protection and care of the women was also part of the Home's mission. However, Geraldine Kesselman had been a widow for more years than she'd been married and was unaccustomed to dissenting opinions. It made Minnie wonder what sort of man Mr. Kesselman had been.

Timid and soft-spoken, Ruthie had ventured during their diplomatic phase.

When the younger women made a point of learning the

inmates' names: A waste of time, Mrs. Kesselman had said dismissively.

When Ruthie suggested the inmates be allowed to relax on Saturday afternoons after sewing and working all week long: You'll turn this industrious home into a den of bone-idle sloths.

And those were minor dustups compared with the near brawl over the bakery.

A condition of admittance to the Home was that the women promise to embrace the dual saviors of Jesus Christ and hard work, and Minnie soon discovered that the only acceptable work in Mrs. Kesselman's view was domestic work, preferably performed at her home, *where a girl's return to virtue can be carefully supervised*. It was practically a rite of passage for a girl to work at Mrs. Kesselman's before leaving the Home.

When Minnie and Ruthie proposed the Board buy the empty storefront at Fourth and Broadway and convert it into a bakery to be managed by the women: What on earth do these girls know about running a bakery?

Think of all the useful skills they'll learn, managing their own business, Ruthie had said. Maybe they'll teach me a thing or two about baking.

Surely that is reason enough to open the bakery, Minnie had said privately to Mrs. Kesselman.

We don't have the money for such an undertaking—to which Minnie countered that thanks to Roland's generous donation they had more than enough money to purchase the building as well as baking equipment and supplies.

By this point, Minnie and Ruthie were in agreement that Mr. Kesselman must have been a long-suffering fool.

After one particularly fraught meeting, Minnie told Roland she feared all these arguments about what constituted appropriate work—How is managing a bakery not respectable women's work?—were liable to send her, much like Mr. Kesselman, to an early grave.

The next day Roland sent a letter to the Board that began, *In order that the women might be restored to virtue and usefulness through hard work, I humbly request that my donation be put toward the purchase of a business that the women might manage themselves,* and so the Broadway Bakery was (grudgingly) purchased, with the condition that the women work at the bakery and as a domestic servant before leaving the Home. Minnie and Ruthie (grudgingly) became more adept at picking their battles with Mrs. Kesselman, instinctively trading off whose turn it was to tangle with her. Last meeting it had been Ruthie, after Mrs. Kesselman lamented that women's colleges were encouraging bluestockingism.

"We mustn't cosset these girls," Mrs. Kesselman said now. She ran a hand across the kitchen table, as if checking for crumbs; like everything else in the home, the table was spotless.

"The bakery girls are already tasked with making the cakes and tarts, and everyone else has been cleaning since Monday," Minnie said. "Hard work is beneficial; exhaustion serves no one."

"At least send me home with the recipe," Mrs. Kesselman said. "Ida can make several dozen. She's become a better cook, although she still can't properly wash a dish to save her life."

"How does one improperly wash a dish?" asked Ruthie.

"Exactly," Mrs. Kesselman said.

"Did I tell you Mrs. Caperton is having a dishwasher installed?" Minnie asked.

Mrs. Kesselman shook her head. "Splashing water on dishes doesn't clean them. The whole thing is unhygienic."

"She's getting the kind in restaurants and hotels. It uses water pressure."

"Next you'll be suggesting we buy one for the Home. I'd like to be on the record opposing such a frivolous purchase."

"Duly noted," Minnie said.

"I had a thought about the strawberry cakes," Ruthie said.

"What if we served salad instead? There's a growing tendency to substitute a green salad with cheese in place of heavier milk and egg desserts."

"A growing tendency among whom?" Mrs. Kesselman asked. "Rabbits?"

"Eggless and butterless cookies are one thing, but a salad instead of a cake would befuddle the poor guests. People expect cake at a silver anniversary party," Minnie said.

"Befuddled and hungry guests don't make generous donations," Mrs. Kesselman said, "which, I need not remind you both, we are in desperate need of these days. That odious woman struck again."

"Again? How many is that now?" Minnie asked.

"The Cains make nine. They gave her five dollars."

A woman claiming to be associated with the Home was soliciting funds from their subscribers. In the last six months, she had managed to swindle money from nine of their wealthiest patrons, and the Board still had no idea who she was or how to stop her. Dark hair, fancy dress, said Mrs. Hoover about the impostor. Blond woman with a pleasing manner, said Mr. Berry. A redheaded woman with dark eyes, the Todds said. The amount of money handed over to this woman was staggering: three dollars, five dollars, even seven dollars from Mr. and Mrs. Todd.

"She must be incredibly charming," Minnie said. "I would consider it a victory if we coaxed a single dollar out of the Cains."

From the next room they heard a loud crash and a yelp, followed by a curse.

"Precisely what the girl on the bicycle said," Mrs. Kesselman said. "I tell you, it's an epidemic among young women these days."

"I don't know what else we can do," Minnie said. "Last week

Elsa Mae sent letters to all subscribers warning them to only give money to one of us. We ran that announcement in the paper as well. How is she still able to convince people to open their purses?"

"She's an experienced liar," Ruthie said. "She told the Todds the money was to replenish the bakery's pantry after an outbreak of weevils."

Weevils! You had to admire the woman's nerve.

"She told the Cains the money was to purchase new cradles. According to her, we recently discovered the majority of our cribs were unsafe," Mrs. Kesselman said.

"Maybe she's someone the Home turned away years ago, and she's been carrying a grudge ever since," Ruthie said.

"We rarely turn women away," Mrs. Kesselman said. "We took in that Jewess years ago. Other homes said no. Not us."

"We've turned away our fair share of girls," Minnie said. "The name Mabel Smith comes to mind."

"Oh, not her again," Mrs. Kesselman said.

Last month a dark-haired woman named Mabel Smith from Madame Fuller's had applied for admission to the Home. She was several months pregnant and proclaimed a desire to be a Christian. The Board voted unanimously to admit her, but the day she was set to move in, Mrs. Kesselman abruptly changed her mind, claiming she'd received a tip that Mabel Smith was part colored. Minnie had to inform Mabel she needed to find somewhere else to stay. Minnie suggested the Catholic Home for the Poor over on Tenth and Magazine, which had recently added an addition for colored people. How am I supposed to prove I'm not colored? Mabel kept asking.

"Last week, I stopped by the Home for the Poor to check on Mabel, but the sister who answered the door said they didn't have an inmate by that name."

"Precisely why she's not here. I could tell she was untrustworthy, someone liable to be a pernicious influence on the others. And that is the last I want to hear about Mabel Smith."

Under the table Ruthie gave Minnie's hand a sympathetic squeeze. "Might this impostor be an unhappy former inmate?" Ruthie asked.

"Unhappy? These women are given a safe and comfortable home to reside in during their confinement. They're fed and clothed, and all they are asked to do in return is some light sewing and cooking. Tell me how that could make a woman so unhappy she'd willfully steal money from us."

"It's fair to say more is asked of the women than light sewing and cooking," Minnie said. "They work, they care for their children. In fact, many of these girls work from sunrise to sundown."

"Agreed. It would behoove us to look through the admission books," Ruthie said. "It's possible a—"

"*Ungrateful* women, I've certainly seen my share," Mrs. Kesselman said. "Tell me how being saved from the dregs of society could make a former inmate so desperately unhappy she'd target our Home, although as I've told you too many times, I've long believed people place too much emphasis on securing happiness these days. The surest way to be unhappy all your days is to dedicate yourself to a pursuit of happiness."

"When I came in earlier, Elsa Mae asked after the early record books for the Home," Minnie said. "If we find those early books, we could compile a list of all the women who have stayed here since the Home's opening and see if any of them match the description of the woman."

"She's either a dark-haired woman, a redhead, or a blond woman," Ruthie said. "That should narrow it down."

"If there's one thing the subscribers agree upon, it's that the woman is young," Mrs. Kesselman said. "The women who lived here when the Home first opened would not currently be described as young in appearance. And as I told Elsa Mae earlier, the early books were likely lost in the move."

"I'll check with Father," Minnie said. "He might know where the books are."

"Your father has more important things to worry about these days than record books from twenty-three, twenty-four years ago," Mrs. Kesselman said. "I still remember the inspiring sermons he used to deliver when the Home first opened, before we even had a chapel in the Home, and he would take time out of his day to drop by and instruct the girls. You'd be hard-pressed to find a former inmate who doesn't remember his erudite lectures with fondness. That reminds me, I've been meaning to visit your parents, meet their new girl."

"Svetlana has been a godsend. I don't think Father could manage without her."

"I have nothing against Slavic women, but they are often so lugubrious and superstitious. Unnaturally large-boned too."

By these standards, her mother's nurse would not be considered Slavic. In fact, Minnie had thought while visiting her parents that if she suddenly fell ill, she'd prefer Roland hire someone less pretty and good-natured than Svetlana.

"It's such a shame that neither of your mothers can attend tomorrow's party." Minnie was surprised to see Mrs. Kesselman's eyes suddenly fill with tears.

"Oh, Mrs. Kesselman," Minnie said. "If you start crying, I will too."

"Me too," Ruthie said. "All week I've been thinking how much Mother would enjoy knowing the Home was celebrating its silver anniversary."

"So many people fought the idea of this very Home. 'If you build it, they will sin,' we were told. But your mothers believed in this Home's mission, and here we are twenty-five years later, going strong. We proved all those naysayers wrong, didn't we?"

"A number of former girls have said they will attend," Ruthie said. "It's always encouraging to see the joyful lives most women lead after their time here."

Minnie heard the clock in the hallway chime eleven. "That's my cue to leave," she said. "There's a lecture and tea at the Women's Club."

"Minnie, don't forget to prepare a little speech encouraging donations and subscriptions," Mrs. Kesselman said.

"I jotted down a few words the other night. And I plan to set a basket by the front door for donations, in case some are moved to donate more than a quarter after my rousing speech. Who knows—maybe I'll discover I'm as skilled an orator as the impostor."

"An unattended basket of money?" Mrs. Kesselman shook her head. "The things you girls suggest. You really can't be so trusting around this crowd."

THE LOUISVILLE COURIER-JOURNAL

KENTUCKY CLUBWOMEN
TO ACT ON RACE QUESTION

At the state meeting next month, delegates from around Kentucky will bring up the much-discussed question of admitting clubs of Negro women in the General Federation. Perhaps the following resolutions, drafted by the Women's Club of Louisville, will voice the opinion of the entire state federation:

Whereas, We hold the opinion that the question of admission of clubs of colored women in the General Federation is one of vital importance.

Whereas, We of the South have the best means of judging the Negro race as a whole, and the result of unprejudiced observation leads to the conclusion that they are not fitted to add to the working power of the General Federation.

Whereas, We also believe that such forcing of the race development would be highly injurious to them, and that they should be encouraged and helped to make an original and independent intellectual and educational development.

Whereas, For these reasons we believe that admission of clubs of colored women would be an unwise step, harmful both to said clubs and to the interest of the General Federation.

*Resolved, That the delegates from the Women's Club of Louisville to the State Federation be instructed to protest against the admission of clubs of colored women to the General Federation.**

---

* June 4, 1901.

Lady Anarchists, Lady Artists

"We have a problem," Mrs. Jewell said when Minnie arrived at the Women's Club. Her tone of voice made clear she had not forgiven Minnie for their argument last week. "A rather serious one. The lecture starts in thirty minutes, and there's no sign of this Abby Remond. Likely she'll be a no-show like that flibbertigibbet Irene Snodgrass."

"To be fair, Miss Snodgrass was a no-show because a carriage ran over her foot."

Mrs. Jewell stared at her without blinking. "It reflected very poorly on us, Minnie."

"She'll be here," Minnie said. "These artsy types are often late."

"I hope you did your research on this one, unlike that Enid shrew."

Years ago, Minnie asked the sculptor Enid Yandell to give a talk to the club. She presumed Miss Yandell would discuss her contribution to the Woman's Building at the World's Columbian Exposition, and instead, Miss Yandell chose to rehash the very public rejection of her proposed Confederate monument to the Lost Cause. Much like anarchists, Lost Causers were everywhere for a spell. Minnie once came across a group decorating Confederate graves at a nearby cemetery, weeping and carrying on while a choir belted out the national anthem.

Laughable, really, although that day Minnie had been alarmed at the size of the crowd; they seemed to blanket the entire cemetery. All that pageantry and pomp for the losing side? People were peculiar, as Roland liked to say.

My husband lost his life in the war, Mrs. Jewell had said frostily to Miss Yandell after her talk, fighting for America and righteousness. Frankly, I wish all monuments meant to commemorate traitors were rejected and destroyed.

This from the same woman currently waging a war to keep Negro women out of their club.

We are called the Women's Club, Minnie had said to Mrs. Jewell at last week's meeting. Shouldn't we embrace hardworking women, regardless of their race, so that we might find strength in numbers? We don't want to go on the record opposing equality of opportunity.

In case you forgot, Mrs. Jewell had said, my husband fought in the war to end slavery. How dare you suggest I oppose equality. Then she burst into tears and everyone rushed to comfort the wailing Mrs. Jewell, whose carrying on was not all that different from the Lost Causers.

No, people weren't just peculiar. They were often hypocritically self-righteous.

"For all we know," Mrs. Jewell said, "Abby Remond could be a lady anarchist, in cahoots with that man who shot poor Mr. McKinley."

"She's not an anarchist, Mrs. Jewell." Although who could be sure of these things anymore? Just this morning she read about a woman anarchist shot in the street, in the middle of the day, by her former lover. She wasn't expected to recover, and now the whole world knew her as a woman who penned anarchist literature and—God rest her soul—erotic poems. Hopefully Mrs. Jewell hadn't read that article.

"I won't be able to stay for the luncheon today," Minnie said.

Mrs. Jewell looked at Minnie as if the younger woman had just confessed to wearing trousers under her skirt.

"Roland needs my help at the Caperton house."

Mrs. Jewell's face changed instantly, as Minnie knew it would. "You should have said so," she chided. "Before he died in the war, Mr. Jewell was fond of saying, 'An excellent wife is the crown of her husband, but she who brings shame is like rottenness in his bones.' And now it's suddenly old-fashioned—outdated even!—for a wife to submit to her husband." Mrs. Jewell shook her head. "The world has changed so much that if Mr. Jewell were alive today, he'd be aghast."

Minnie saw, in that moment, how easy it would be to start an argument with Mrs. Jewell today. The older woman's posture made clear she was still miffed about last week's meeting. All she had to do was laugh and say, *Old-fashioned to submit to husbands?* If it were truly passé to submit to your husband, Minnie would stay for the luncheon she helped organize, rather than running off to help Roland. And Roland was one of the good ones.

Minnie arranged her face into a polite smile. "Roland often says, 'Change is the law of life.' Now let's find you a seat up front while we wait for Mrs. Remond to arrive."

ରୁ୧ଓ

Even though her artistic life was mostly confined to art lessons at the Home these days, Minnie still secretly thought of herself as an artsy type. She'd even sold a few paintings, mostly to friends and family. She'd been good but not great, which was true of any artist really. You had to practice to achieve greatness, you had to make time for your art. And if you made time for your art, what were you neglecting? Her mother had called her desire to be an artist "incurable vanity." So a modicum of support didn't hurt either. She told Roland that someday, when she had all the time in the world for such an undertaking, she would write a book called *Things You Shouldn't Say to Women Artists*.

Chapter 1: "Why don't you focus on embroidery instead?"

When she and Roland first met, she shyly showed him dozens of her paintings, and he quizzed her about color choices and brushstrokes and where did her inspiration come from, and if he wasn't genuinely curious, he did an admirable job faking it. She was lucky; most men were not like Roland. Her friend Marie's husband, Felix, for example. Minnie and Marie met in Paris while copying sketches at the Louvre for the director-general of the French museums, a rather dreary undertaking that sounded glamorous to everyone back home in Kentucky. Marie's husband was an artist and had grave, immutable opinions: real art was created in a studio, never outdoors; real art favored line over color; real art required control, not spontaneity. In a pique, he once tossed one of Marie's paintings out the second-story window of their home after learning she painted it outdoors. Such a shame, because no one could capture the transformation of white clothing in sunlight quite like Marie. In her hands, a woman's white dress in the sun became golden blue and pink. White is never just white, Marie liked to say.

Back in Kentucky, Minnie sent Marie several letters. No answer. Easy to imagine those too had been tossed out a window.

Chapter 2: "Aren't there enough lady artists in the world?"

Luckily Abby Remond seemed safe enough, neither an anarchist nor a Lost Cause supporter, but a graduate of the Fine Arts School of Boston and later the Pratt Institute, where she taught drawing for three years until her marriage to the architect Mr. Dwight Remond. Since then her focus had been the architectural side of design (*Et tu, Abby?*) and creating Mother Goose prints for schoolrooms and nurseries.

Wouldn't it be lovely to sit outside at a café, similar to the ones she remembered from Paris, and talk with a fellow artist? She could ask Abby what she liked to paint before she married and suddenly had to dedicate her time and talent to her husband. Or maybe they could talk about Rosa Bonheur, whose death had made Minnie cry even more than McKinley's. Miss Bonheur, with her short hair and cigarettes and animal paintings. Now *she* was an artist.

Five minutes before the lecture was to begin, Abby arrived. "So sorry," she said. "I got lost on the way here." She was younger than Minnie expected, easily a decade her junior. Petite with enormous blue eyes, the word *dainty* clung to her. Windblown hair, pink cheeks from her bicycle ride. The lack of corset was noticeable. More and more Minnie found herself baffled by the fashion of younger women. After twins, a corset was a necessary evil. But, oh, to be twenty years younger, zooming here and there on a bicycle. What freedom of the body. How different the world must appear from up high. You'd feel you owned the whole city. A few weeks ago, Ruthie's son, Edward, attempted to teach Minnie and his mother how to ride a bicycle, but Minnie could never shake the feeling she was one fall away from a broken arm.

Minnie led the young woman to the stage. "It's my pleasure

to introduce Mrs. Abby Remond, whose lecture today, 'The Art of the Ordinary,' should be of great interest, even to those of you who claim you don't have an artistic bone in your body."

"She's talking about me," Mrs. Jewell stage-whispered.

"Now don't sell yourself short, Mrs. Jewell," Minnie said. "After all, we have Mrs. Jewell to thank for the floral decorations on the table." She paused for the clubwomen to clap enthusiastically, an olive branch for last week's meeting. "After the lecture, Mrs. Remond's Mother Goose prints will be for sale. It's never too early to be thinking about Christmas presents. Let's offer a warm club welcome to Mrs. Abby Remond."

"Thank you, Mrs. Morton," Abby said. "I'm here today to dispel the myth that art is only created in a studio. For me, art is everywhere: in the blades of grass, the way the sun colors the sky magenta on a warm summer night, the soap bubbles dancing across a dinner plate . . ."

Minnie was reminded of all the sermons she listened to as a child, except her father had been waxing about God, not art. Last spring he retired from the church after her mother fell ill. It happened slowly enough: a forgotten word here, a passing bout of confusion, and then one day she got lost walking home from the church, a path she had trod for nearly thirty years. Senile dementia, the doctor said. Over the past few years, Minnie had watched her mother fade into someone much gentler and kinder than the woman she had always been. Sometimes Minnie felt guilty that her mother's mental decline signaled a calmer phase of their relationship.

The dementia had certainly made her mother a more forgiving person. Take the Slavic woman who now lived with them. Despite the substantial age difference, Mrs. Davidson thought she and Svetlana were childhood friends. Minnie's mother happily ate the dumplings Svetlana prepared, and she even allowed this divorced woman to help dress her. This from the person who once claimed Slavic women were hard-hearted, that dumplings were food for the poverty-stricken, and that a divorced woman was no better than a hired girl let go without references.

". . . a colorful parasol on an overcast day, a basket of ripe strawberries, a woman absorbed in her ironing . . ."

Minnie suspected that Abby started cataloging the art of the ordinary after she traded her art career for a husband, when even a simple walk through the park likely filled her with longing. Minnie had experienced something similar after her own marriage, although what had caught her eye and occupied her thoughts had not been art but babies.

Babies—on every street corner.

Babies—in every shop.

Babies—sleeping, wailing, babbling away in their carriages.

For years Minnie had no desire to be a mother, something she often voiced aloud, much to her mother's chagrin. Her friends with children were hardly an advertisement for health or happiness. From a young age, growing up in the shadow of the Home, she saw how exhausting motherhood was. Pregnancy was no picnic either. *No thank you,* she always thought.

After she and Roland married, she saw the distinction between having a child and having his child, and suddenly she wanted the one thing she had always disparaged. Yet the months ticked by, and she remained stubbornly, decidedly, not pregnant.

Her mother: You used to say you didn't want children. I'm not saying it's your fault for waiting until you're nearly forty, but . . .

Her father: Poor Minnie.

Roland's mother: Poor Roland.

Roland: We've been trying for a year now. Maybe it's time to discuss adoption.

During one particularly tearful supper, she told Roland she'd counted fifteen baby carriages that day, and Roland's suggestion that she walk by the riverfront, where she was unlikely to encounter a parade of baby carriages, only made her cry harder. Still, she heeded his advice, and a few months later she was pregnant with the boys. (Roland had been right, of course—no one else was foolish enough to walk by the riverfront and brave the smell of the nearby stockyards.)

Abby held up one of her Mother Goose prints, this one featuring two pigs—

This pig went to market,
That pig stayed home,
This pig had roast meat,
That pig had none,
This pig went to the barn door,
And cried "wee wee wee" for more.

—and the women clapped again. One of the pigs wore a striped bib, a knife and fork clutched in his small hooves.

"She's very pretty," Mrs. Jewell whispered approvingly to Minnie.

"Yes, she's quite talented," Minnie whispered back. An art teacher in Paris once declared, Everyone has talent at twenty-five. Minnie saw now he'd been lamenting his own impending middle age, his studio full of fresh-faced artists, eager to learn at his knee so they could surpass him. Youth wasted on the young and all that.

Progress, not perfection, one of the suffragists said. She couldn't remember which one. Lucy Stone probably. And if neither progress nor perfection occurred in your lifetime, what then, Mrs. Stone? What if the girls who followed you were confident enough to ride bicycles and leave their corsets at home, but they too couldn't escape the downward pull of their sex, abandoning promising careers in order to advance their husband's? The lucky ones found time to make art to hang on the walls of nurseries before they were expected to fill up their own nursery. After all the lectures and the club meetings and the marches she'd attended over the years, somehow all that had changed was fashion. Minnie was suddenly grateful for the Caperton appointment; no time to talk art and life with Abby. The girl was so young she'd probably never even heard of Rosa Bonheur. How depressing.

Chapter 3: "You don't need art to be happy— pretend your iron is a paintbrush."

Before she left, Minnie bought the pig print. It was more than she would normally spend on a print for the boys' room, but it was good to support a fellow artist, and she shouldn't be so hard on Abby. What did she expect from these young women anyway? Everything and nothing. The world changed, but never at the speed you desired. *Wee wee wee,* you cried all the way home.

"Very thought provoking, thank you so much." Minnie gave Abby's arm a motherly squeeze on her way out. Such thin arms on the girl.

Well, life would toughen her up soon enough.

THE LOUISVILLE COURIER-JOURNAL

WOMEN BACHELORS

It is a little curious to note that so many of our heroines have never cared to write the title "Mrs." before their names. Rosa Bonheur, over seventy, is one of these women bachelors. It is said she had fewer offers of marriage than the others. Miss Bonheur has too much of the masculine element about her to encourage suitors, and her extreme matter-of-factness makes it difficult to approach her sentimentally. Very many artists have fallen in love with Rosa Bonheur from her work. Crowned heads have bent before her, and more than once, princes of the blood, becoming acquainted with her, have told her of their very great adoration for herself and her genius. But this strange woman persists in neutralizing her personality before that of the animals she portrays and points to them saying, "Could anyone do less with these for models?" If you ask a notable woman why she has not married, she will respond flippantly. Press her closer, and she will show embarrassment. And then you get the truth, which is that women of great intellect invariably love men of small brains, men whom they pity at first and then eventually marry. When a woman remains single, it is because she is ashamed to ally herself with such men, men who cannot support themselves and who could never mold the opinion of the world.*

* Adapted from *The Louisville Courier-Journal,* September 2, 1894.

Millionaires Row

Halfway down the block and Minnie regretted her impulsive purchase. The twins had no interest in nursery rhymes and pigs in bibs; they delighted in playing soldier, transforming tree branches into rifles. Terrifying, really, their newfound interest in war games, their constant staging of death—I killed you! Now you're dead! She couldn't help worrying they were acting out their future fates. Roland said she might as well complain about snow in the winter—You mustn't coddle them, Min. Roland believed that peace occasionally had to be purchased by war, and wouldn't she rather have sons with the moral courage to fight for what they believed was right and true?

Of course not. Like every mother since the beginning of time, she would prefer a living coward for a son instead of a brave corpse.

Minnie found herself thinking about the copy she made of Rembrandt's *Bathsheba at Her Bath* the summer she was in Paris. Where was it now? Doubtful the director-general kept it. During her classes at the Louvre, she struggled with the woman's dreamy expression. A servant woman carefully washed her feet while Bathsheba held a letter from the king. *What could the king possibly want with me?* she seemed to be thinking. Only a man would paint Bathsheba this way. A woman Bathsheba's age knew exactly why a powerful man summoned another man's wife to his castle. Minnie couldn't figure out how to capture the before of Bathsheba's life—before her husband was killed, before she was raped by the king, before she became queen—so familiar was everyone with the calamity that followed.

You made her look bilious, the director-general complained when Minnie finally presented her reproduction.

My work here is being applauded and encouraged, she wrote to her parents.

I suspect she was bilious, Roland said when he heard this story. Loyal Roland.

∽✺∾

At least it was a pleasant day for a walk to the Caperton house. Last year Roland's architectural firm had won a bid to design a home for Samuel Caperton, who made his fortune in the leather tanning business. The Capertons wanted "elegant simplicity inside" (Minnie's job) and "impressive ornamentation outside" (Roland's job).

In other words, they want their new money to look old, Roland said. As someone who gave away his inheritance a decade ago, Roland didn't think much of people with money, old or new. Roland's family had been appalled at his decision to donate the bulk of his inheritance to the Home for Friendless Women: his father decried his selfishness, his mother begged him to think of his future heirs, and his sister, Sarah, threatened to never speak to him again.

As the treasurer for the Home, Minnie had been sent to collect the check from Roland. She presumed the anonymous donor would be older—a balding and unappealing man who expected an appreciative audience to his generosity and who had no qualms addressing his comments to her breasts rather than her face. Instead, she got Roland, who had a full head of sandy hair and whose brown eyes did not stray from hers as he explained it was his grandfather's fortune, and that giving it away brought only relief, with a tinge of guilt. Not at the thought of his heirs ending up penniless, because, he was quick to add, he had no children. It doesn't strike me as all that generous to donate another man's money, he had said. But I hope it can do some good.

She told him that most men who donated to the Home did so out of a sense of guilt as well, although their guilt often had very different origins. She thought about him as she walked home that day, his check clutched tightly in her hands. Surely she'd been a teenager the last time sustained eye contact with a man made her blush so fiercely. But she'd never seen such expressive and attentive eyes on a man. Beautiful eyes, really. They made her think of the coffee she drank in Paris, the darkness softened by a splash of cream.

Not that she would ever tell Roland he had beautiful eyes. Roland wasn't like most men, but he was still a man, after all.

☙❧

Minnie cut through the park and passed the statue of the man on horseback. So many sculptures of men in this city. Wouldn't it be nice, revolutionary even, to sculpt the mother or wife of one of these great men, those invisible women who sacrificed so their sons, husbands, and brothers might achieve greatness? Imagine the predictable chorus if a sculpture of a woman were to suddenly appear in public: *Who's this shrew? What did this flibbertigibbet ever do?* Et cetera, et cetera.

She kicked a few leaves on the path before her as she walked. There was a time when it had been revolutionary to walk alone as a woman, and now it wasn't. What was revolutionary now? Riding a bicycle without a corset, she supposed. At age twenty, she and Ruthie traveled by train to hear Lucy Stone give a speech. Her mother was furious when she learned about the trip. She thought women like Mrs. Stone wanted to destroy the fabric of society with their demands for suffrage. And her father, well, he was more hurt than angry: You don't trust me to vote on your behalf, he had said sadly.

So much time she wasted as a young person, quarreling with her parents. She regretted that now. But she didn't regret hearing that speech. All these years later, she could still quote the ending of it, and the words would come to her unexpectedly: while giving the boys a bath, preparing a meal for an elderly neighbor, walking to a meeting. Stone had said that women *are part of the eternal order . . . Now all we need is to continue to speak the truth fearlessly, and we shall add to our number those who will turn the scale to the side of equal and full justice in all things.*

After the speech, as they traveled back to Louisville, Minnie had gazed out the window, and everything—the farmhouses and the fields, even the cows calmly eating—brought unexpected tears to her eyes. *Full justice in all things.* She felt the power and weight of those five words deep inside her, and she was certain in that moment that her life would be nothing like her mother's, all the doors closed to Mrs. Eliza Davidson would swing open for Miss Minnie Davidson.

Well, she was very young then.

She turned onto Third Street. Mr. Caperton had taken to calling his new street Millionaires Row. I haven't heard anyone else calling it that, Roland had recently grumbled to Minnie. But if the Caperton job was a success, Roland's firm would be asked to build more houses on this block, and Roland would finally prove to his family he didn't need their money to succeed.

She found Roland in the Capertons' dining room, surveying a row of landscape paintings lined up against the wall. All around were the sounds of a house coming together: hammering, sawing, muffled voices. Two men walked past carrying planks of fresh-smelling pine, one of them whistling a tune she didn't recognize. From upstairs she heard a crash followed by a loud curse.

"The problem is, these all look the same to me." Roland's voice echoed in the mostly bare room.

She laughed. "They're of different scenes. They can't possibly look the same to you."

"They all feature water. Luckily I have your artistic talent to guide me."

She pointed at the middle painting, horses grazing by a fast-moving river. "That one will match the rug I bought." She said this even though she preferred the painting on the left, of the haystacks. Years ago she'd painted something similar, although hers had been less about the haystacks and more about how the rising sun colored the haystacks. This painting, in contrast, was strictly about the haystacks. *A haystack is never just a haystack,* she imagined Marie saying.

"What a pity," said Roland. "I prefer the haystacks. It reminds me of that painting your parents have in their front room."

"Mother hates that one. She only displayed it because Father insisted."

Chapter 4: "You used to paint the most realistic landscapes."

———————

"What if you painted something for them instead?" Roland said.

"For my parents?" Minnie was trying to remember when she made the haystack painting. Twenty years ago? No, closer to twenty-five. Before Paris, for sure. After the boys were born, she moved her paints and brushes into the basement. A temporary relocation, she assured herself at the time. *Ha.*

"No, for the Capertons," Roland said. "You miss painting; they need art on their walls. Two birds, one nest." He gently nudged her with his elbow, and she smiled despite herself.

"You know that's not the expression, right?"

"Someone once told me she didn't like the visual image of two birds getting stoned to death."

"That person sounds overly sentimental," Minnie said.

"She's also adept at changing the subject when she doesn't want to discuss something."

"I'll think about it." She didn't add that if she were to unearth her art supplies, it would not be for the pretentious Capertons.

Roland nodded at the parcel in her hands. "Did you bring me something?"

"The lady lecturer was selling them." She showed him the print. "The Capertons would never agree to hang this in their nursery."

"Not unless you told them it was priceless," Roland said. "I do like that pig in the bib, though."

"I'll give it to Elsa Mae at the silver anniversary party."

Minnie thought, not for the first time, how much she disliked the Caperton house. How cold and unwelcoming it was. Everything from the walnut paneling in the dining room to the limestone out front was designed to eclipse their neighbors, to highlight their Very Important status. No amount of haystack paintings or brightly colored rugs could hide that the Capertons didn't want a home. They simply wanted a container for their expensive things. It struck her as an exhausting way to live, always needing more and better than your neighbors. No, she didn't like the idea of something she created hanging on the walls of such a place.

A gentle breeze blew in through the open windows behind them, and goose bumps suddenly appeared on her arms.

"Someone's walking across your grave," Roland said.

"Full justice in all things."

_____

After she left the Caperton house, she contemplated going home. She could be smart and start in on the boys' birthday dinner. But it was so nice outside, and when was the last time she'd allowed herself to do something she wanted to do, as opposed to something she had to do? And so she found herself heading toward Ruthie's house. She passed a harried-looking woman pushing a carriage, a dark-haired baby fast asleep inside. She had been that mother not so long ago, hadn't she? Breakfast, dishes, laundry, supper, and a collapse into bed for a few hours of sleep before waking the next morning to do it all over again. Enough time had passed that she felt almost nostalgic for the hazy exhaustion of those days. She supposed that meant someday she would look back on the boys' obsession with war with a similar wistfulness.

"I'm stopping by unannounced," she said when Ruthie opened the door. "Don't tell Professor Hill."

The esteemed professor Thomas Hill had authored the etiquette book they had both been forced to read as young girls. Don't wear that, don't sit like that, don't say that. Don't, don't, don't. What relief Minnie had felt when the doctor announced she'd delivered boys. Fewer rules for them, at least when it came to performing respectability.

"I'm glad you stopped by," Ruthie said. "I want to show you the dress I bought for the silver anniversary party."

A minute later Ruthie returned with a dark-gray-and-emerald-green gown with wide brocade buttons. "Be honest with me, Min." She held the dress under her chin. "When I showed it to Eddie's girlfriend, Libby, she said it was perfectly suited for someone my age." Ruthie made a face. "When did I become 'someone my age'?"

"Who on earth are Eddie and Libby?"

Ruthie laughed. "That's what Edward wants to be called now. And his girlfriend is no longer Elizabeth, she's Libby."

"This is what I have to look forward to—Mark and Lucas suddenly changing their names and questioning my fashion sense. And I like it. It's not frumpy, if that's what you're worried about, not with those bold buttons."

"Thank goodness." Ruthie draped the dress on the back of the couch and sat down. "I don't have time to shop for a new dress. And I haven't even offered you tea. What an uncouth hostess I am. Professor Hill would chastise us both today."

"Your house is awfully quiet—is Edward out?"

"You just missed him. He and Libby are golfing today. I think he wanted to escape after I showed Libby some of his baby pictures."

Minnie picked up a small gray photo album on the table beside her. Inside was Ruthie's careful print. *Edward, age 2* below a photo of Edward looking at two ducks nearby. His expression was one of delighted terror. She turned the page. *Edward, age 2.5. Edward, age 3.* "I meant to make an album for the boys, but I never got around to it." Minnie carefully tied the navy ribbon around the book before placing it back on the table. "Golfing sounds fun, doesn't it? I don't remember that being an option when we were their age."

"Their generation is so active," Ruthie said. "They can't sit still to save their lives."

"Their generation is so lucky," Minnie said, with more feeling than she intended. She didn't begrudge these girls their freedoms, not really. She'd just been feeling so tired all day. Tired of endless meetings and art lectures given by people barely out of college, tired of decorating the homes of other people. But mostly she was tired of calling herself an artist and never painting. Someday when the boys were older she would have more time, and what would be her excuse then?

"The boys turn six today," Minnie said now. "Somehow it seems they were born both yesterday and twenty years ago." She'd been lucky with the boys; after finally getting pregnant, she'd had few complaints. An easy labor too, although it had taken her a while to accept that motherhood had left a permanent mark on her body: softer stomach, pouchy breasts, wider hips. Considering some women paid with their lives, a softer body was not the worst pregnancy could do to you.

"Six is a funny age, isn't it?" Ruthie asked. "They're so full of questions. When Edward was around that age he once asked me if his name had always been Edward, or if his first mother had given him a different name."

Minnie thought of all the babies Ruthie miscarried before she and her husband adopted Edward from the Home of the Innocents. How many times had Ruthie been pregnant—five? Six? After the last and final one, the doctor said she wasn't strong enough to carry a child. I'm a barren woman, Ruthie had said. I'm not a real woman anymore. She grew so thin her hair began falling out.

God, those had been grim days.

"What a question," Minnie said. "I wouldn't know how to answer that."

"I told him that he was baptized with the name Edward Daniel Williams, so that was his real name. Although he likely did have a different name. How strange that would be, to have two names."

"We have two names," Minnie said, "as married women."

"But we know our name before marriage and we know our name after marriage. Imagine not knowing the very first name you were given or the person who gave you that name."

People often commented on the strong resemblance between Ruthie and Edward: the same light brown hair, the same pale green eyes, even the same open smile. He takes after his mother, strangers would say about him when he was younger.

"I find myself thinking about the woman who gave birth to him this time of year," Ruthie said. "Surely she thinks about him too, what his name is now, what he looks like. Mother used to tell me not to think about her."

Ruthie's mother had been a thin, perpetually anxious woman, made more anxious by the salacious rumors constantly swirling around her husband. A month after his wife died, Mr. Norris married a former inmate of the Home, a woman younger than his own daughter, before moving to Tennessee. Ruthie once said it was akin to losing two parents in the same year.

"How could you not think about her?" Minnie asked. "If she hadn't abandoned him, then you wouldn't be his mother."

"We're connected, this woman and me. She's both a stranger and part of someone I love. I've always had the sense that if I passed her on the street, I would recognize her. That I would somehow know her. I'm sure that sounds mad."

"Not to me it doesn't."

"I used to be so fearful, when Edward was a baby, that she would return and ask for him back. If I met her today, I would tell her that Edward is a handsome and generous man. That I'm thankful every day he's my son. I think it would comfort her to know that she gave him a better life when she left him outside the children's home all those years ago."

Not long after the twins were born, one of Minnie's neighbors died unexpectedly, leaving behind two small boys. Minnie saw the brothers at the park a few months after their mother's death. She sat on a nearby park bench, her own babies asleep in their carriage, and she blinked back tears as she watched the boys laughing and running. Their mother was dead, but on that day, they were very much alive. Happy even. Minnie remembered thinking that their mother would be comforted to see them enjoying a nice summer day. But she would be sad too, at the realization that a dead mother did not halt the days of the living for long.

"She must have been desperate, to leave him on Christmas Day."

"I used to wonder why she never applied for admission to the Home," Ruthie said. "She would have been provided a place to stay, given a job, earned money. It's clear the Home wasn't very good at outreach back then."

"There's also the possibility she applied and was turned away," Minnie said. "The woman caring for my mother right now is a divorced Slavic woman. And a Catholic. Twenty years ago, that same woman would never have been granted refuge in the Home."

"Imagine Mrs. Kesselman's objections if we asked to admit a Catholic Slavic woman today," Ruthie said.

"It would rival the Mabel Smith incident," Minnie said. "God, I still feel so guilty about her."

"What could we have done any differently? Mrs. Kesselman has the final say when it comes to admissions. I keep hoping she'll retire soon, although she doesn't seem to age, does she?"

"No, she's like a vampire," Minnie said grimly.

"If we're still on the Board in twenty years, we'll likely be the ones thwarting the efforts of the younger women. 'Those ideas are outrageous and ill-conceived,' we'll say."

"Oh god, what a dreadful thought. I like to think we'll be more than happy to pass the torch to this generation of golfing, corsetless women."

"Imagine if we could tell our younger selves, the girls who attended the Lucy Stone rally," Ruthie said, "that one day they would serve on the same Board as their mothers."

"It's funny you mention that—I was thinking of that rally earlier today. We were so hopeful that day, weren't we? It was easy to believe the world might bend to our will after all."

"We're not the same people who went to that rally," Ruthie said.

"You're right," Minnie said. "Now I'm old and gray." She was only half joking. For years her hair was reddish gold, and then one day it was reddish gray, and soon it would simply be gray. There were worse things than gray hair, of course. That didn't mean she wanted those either.

"What would you do differently? If you could go back and do it all over again?"

"Everything," Minnie said. "Nothing at all. If I told myself not to join the Board, I wouldn't have met Roland. And without Roland, I wouldn't be the boys' mother." She didn't add that she would tell herself to be more serious about her art, or to tell the director-general of course she made Bathsheba look bilious on purpose, because no woman in her right mind would look dreamily curious at such a summons.

"I would tell myself not to worry so much about motherhood, that things would work out in the end," Ruthie said. "I would say, 'Someday a baby boy in yellow-and-white-striped booties will show up in your life, and you will discover there is more than one way to become a mother.'"

Minnie had a sudden memory of seeing a baby boy in yellow-and-white-striped booties. Whose baby? Not Mark or Lucas. She'd been worried she wouldn't be able to tell the boys apart, and for a brief spell, she dressed Mark in green and Lucas in white. A silly concern in hindsight—even as infants, their personalities had been different enough there was no mistaking them.

"Would you listen?" Minnie asked. "Likely I would treat an older version of myself like I did my mother, ignoring all the pronouncements and decrees. On the way over here, I passed an exhausted-looking mother, and I found myself thinking that someday I'll be nostalgic for all of this. When I'm really and truly old, I worry I'll wonder what it was all for, all the protests, all the meetings. *Full justice in all things.* How young we were. So young and foolish." She could feel the threat of tears behind her eyes, and she pinched the fleshy part of her hand, between thumb and pointer, to hold them back.

Ruthie looked at her in concern. "Are you all right, Min?"

"Ignore me." Minnie forced a laugh. "I'm in a mood today. It must be the boys' birthday. Truly, I'm fine." How often she'd said that over the years, I'm fine, it's fine. She could almost believe it was true. "I should go home, make the chocolate cake I promised." When she stood up, she realized she had been sitting on a photograph of a baby. "Who is this? Surely not Edward."

"You sound like Libby," Ruthie said. "She couldn't believe that dark-haired baby was her Eddie. I told her that no matter how I combed that boy's hair, it would always stick straight up in the air."

"I remember him as a blond baby." Minnie picked up the photograph and studied it. Something unpleasant tugged at her, stronger this time. Nothing worse than a baby with cold feet, someone had said, and the baby kicked his legs, as if showing off his new striped booties. Where had that happened?

"By the time you returned from Paris, his hair had already lightened. As a new mother I thought there might be something wrong with him, that his hair changed so dramatically. The doctor assured me it's perfectly normal for a baby to have dark curly hair that turns lighter and straightens out. Isn't it silly what young mothers fret over?"

His sister will covet those curls someday, Minnie had said

about the baby boy at that long-ago Christmas party at the old Home. How soft his curls were when she brushed her hand across his head. She shivered, thought of Roland saying, Someone's walking across your grave.

"How old will Edward be this Christmas?"

"Twenty-four. I can hardly believe it myself."

Your father has more important things to worry about these days than record books from twenty-three, twenty-four years ago, Mrs. Kesselman had said.

It's clear to me the girl can't care for two, Minnie's mother had said about the twins. Also: Especially the boy. Wouldn't Ruthie be a wonderful mother to him?

"How lucky that the Home of the Innocents knew to contact you when they found a baby outside." As a young girl, Minnie once tugged at a loose thread on her stockings during one of her father's sermons, and she watched in surprised horror as it unraveled from her calf to her thigh in seconds. Why was she tugging on the threads of Ruthie's story today? What did she think was going to happen? She felt defenseless in her sudden desire to speak what had gone unsaid all these years. Buried, yes, although not very deeply.

Ruthie looked over at her in surprise. "Didn't I ever tell you? Your mother brought him to us. She's the one who found him in a basket outside the Home of the Innocents. The sisters offered to take him in, but your mother told them she knew the perfect family for him. She personally delivered him to us on Christmas Day, in a basket tied with a green bow."

Minnie remembered a quiet woman with plaited hair and a green ribbon around her throat. They're no trouble to me, she had said about her twins.

Minnie thought of the girl with the short hair. How brightly her hair glowed that night as she stood in front of the Christmas tree, the baby in her arms. Minnie had never seen a woman with hair so short. More important, she had never seen someone speak that way to her mother. They can't take this one now, the girl had said, and then all hell broke loose.

Only now, more than twenty years too late, did Minnie understand. They can't take this one now. Except they had. My god.

What did you do, Mother?

THE LOUISVILLE COURIER-JOURNAL

HAPPY MOTHERHOOD

Motherhood ought always to bring happiness. But it is often the beginning of life-long unhappiness. As a preparation for motherhood, and as a preventive of the ills so often following maternity, Dr. Pierce's Favorite Prescription has been hailed as a "God-send to women." It heals diseases peculiar to women, tones up the system, makes motherhood practically painless, and establishes the sound health which insures healthy children.

"During the past year I found myself pregnant and in rapidly failing health," writes Mrs. W. J. Kidder of Hill Dale Farm, Enosburg, Vt. "I suffered dreadfully from bloating and urinary difficulty. I was growing perceptibly weaker each day and suffered much sharp pain at times. I felt that something must be done. I took twelve bottles of Dr. Pierce's Favorite Prescription and also followed his advice. I began to improve immediately, my health became excellent, and I could do all my own work (we live on a good-sized farm). I had a short easy confinement and have a healthy baby boy."

Dr. Pierce's great work *The People's Common Sense Medical Adviser* (paperbound copy) is sent *free* on receipt of 21 one-cent stamps to pay cost of mailing only. Address Dr. R. V. Pierce, Buffalo, N.Y.*

---

* August 20, 1901.

"Be thankful for your regrets."

———————————

In Paris, her wardrobe was an old-fashioned bookcase with glass doors and silk curtains. *When one lives in small quarters, one is forced to be orderly,* Minnie wrote to her mother, who appreciated such sentiments. This was her way of apologizing for the things she had said before she left, things like *That girl's death is on your hands* and *When I'm a mother, I hope I'm nothing like you.* Minnie sent home sketches that made her Parisian apartment look cozy rather than cramped. She didn't tell her mother that some nights she took down the curtains in her bedroom so the moon could shine in. Sunlight, moonlight, light as it filtered through trees, light as it reflected off water. How could the light here be so different? Impossible to capture, but she tried, daily.

There was no one to talk to about what she had seen that night. Not her own mother. Not Ruthie, who had her own troubles that Christmas. What was there to say? You could say, *There was so much blood.* You could say, *I didn't know a person would do such a thing to herself.* But words would never capture how differently blood flowed compared with water. A red swollen darkness Minnie had never encountered, and one she tried and failed repeatedly in Paris to re-create with her paints.

In her letters to her daughter, Mrs. Eliza Davidson offered a running commentary on the French artist Rosa Bonheur: *You can see such regret in Rosa's latest painting, but of course marriage*

is no longer an option for someone her age. Your father says hello and
wonders if you are remembering to read your Bible. Rosa's father
allowed her to cut off her hair and dress in trousers, so you should be
thankful your father cares about your soul. Move those silk curtains
away from the window or the sun will bleach them.

This was her mother's way of apologizing for the things she
had said, things like *You don't have the faintest clue how the world*
actually works and *You're an ungrateful and selfish daughter.*

If Minnie had regrets, it was not about marriage.

One afternoon Minnie made a collage out of these letters
and secured it to her easel: *Marriage cuts the soul. Be thankful for*
your regrets.

André found Minnie's reaction to these letters amusing.
He was an artist too, and he was fond of making broad pronouncements about Americans, especially American women.
American women, he liked to say, argue too much with their
mothers. He was working on a series of paintings featuring
the women from Shakespeare, and Minnie was his favorite
model. So many paintings of half-clothed women already in
the world—hadn't she sketched a fair number at the Louvre?
And André was eager to add his own interpretation. A person might start to believe the only way to learn about line and
color, balance and contrast, was by painting the female body.
Sometimes Minnie could sketch these Venuses from the past
with a practiced, jaded eye. Other times it was more difficult,
like pretending the emperor was wearing clothes.

The third time she posed for one of André's paintings, he
told her his name, in French, meant "manly."

That particular day she was Ophelia, beautifully drowned,
and when he said this, she started laughing so hard the gauzy
fabric draped across her shoulders fell to the ground. When she
went to pick it back up, he shook his head.

Leave it, he said.

She did.

"Bombs away!"

————————

Minnie stood by the kitchen sink, the dinner dishes floating in the rapidly cooling water. She'd pulled out the good china to celebrate the boys' birthday. White with a blue hawthorn border, the plates were a wedding gift from her mother. Minnie had preferred the set with the dark blue border and band of gold, but her mother said gold borders were unlikely to be in style in a few years. Had she genuinely preferred the dark blue plates, or had she trained herself to desire that which her mother opposed? Impossible to know at this point, so tightly braided were the two.

Out the window she spied the family dog on the back porch, watching the boys play. Weren't dogs supposed to jump about and bark? Not this one. He'd shown up at their house a few years ago, matted yellow fur, bloodied ears. Roland had patiently washed him in the backyard. Careful, he might bite! she called from the porch. Soon the dog was hanging around. Let's call him Bandit, Roland suggested, and the boys helped Roland build a doghouse. Lucas even donated one of his blankets to keep Bandit warm. He has a fur coat, she said in exasperation. She was the only one who found Bandit's silent presence unnerving. This summer she'd look out the window to see squirrels a few feet away from Bandit, chomping into her newly ripened tomatoes, while Bandit calmly, silently watched.

"Bombs away!" Roland shouted from the backyard, and the

boys screamed and chased after their new toy, a giant cucumber balloon that wriggled about as if alive when thrown up in the air. She'd bought it at the new toy store downtown. In the front window of the store had been a detailed dollhouse with a second-floor piazza decorated with tiny flowering plants in pots, a library with a telephone, and even a hallway with a miniature hat rack. While Minnie was paying for the balloon, a young woman came into the store to buy the dollhouse. She didn't seem old enough to be married, much less have children old enough to play with such a toy. I hope your daughter enjoys it, Minnie had said unprompted to the young woman. I spent hours playing with my dollhouse as a child. And the woman had laughed and said it wasn't for her daughter but for the children at the Home of the Innocents, and Minnie told her that she had a friend who made a donation there every Christmas, and she'd left the store feeling that the world was generally full of decent people.

All the familiar objects in her kitchen—the flour sifter with the green handle from her grandmother, the rolling pin from Roland's mother, the skillets and the ladle and the pots and the pans: what she would have said made hers a home rather than a house—were suddenly unfamiliar. Even the dishes lolling about in the sink were suspect. Why did she have all these things?

Next week the dishwasher arrived at the Caperton house, and it would be her job to explain to Mrs. Caperton, who would then explain to a servant, how to operate the fancy new machine. Minnie had been good at arithmetic when she was in school, better than most of the boys, but those same boys had grown up to be engineers and architects who designed fancy machines and expensive houses, and she, who once went an entire year without missing a single problem on a single test, had grown up to be a wife and mother tasked with explaining to other wives and mothers how to operate their fancy machines in their even fancier houses. She had grown up to manage the finances of the same Home her mother once managed, and her skills were used to secure money to purchase bakeries and cradles, baby blankets and new furniture.

Money for this, not for that.

What she wouldn't give to solve a simple arithmetic problem right now.

Q: *On Monday, Maud sold 3/7 of her pears; on Tuesday, she sold 16 more than 1/2 of the remainder and had 20 pears left. How many pears had Maud at first?* Q: *A piece of cloth measured 12 2/3 yd. before sponging and 11 5/6 yd. after sponging. How much did the cloth shrink?* If you did it correctly, you could always learn how many pears Maud had on Monday, how much your cloth shrank after sponging.

Q: *A girl had 2 babies. The next day a woman took 1 away. Who is the boy's mother?*

Andrew, Augustus, Arnold, Benjamin, Charles, Calvin, David, Daniel, Donald. She had a feeling she would know the baby's name when she stumbled upon it.

On the kitchen counter were the remaining slices of cake. Not her best effort, although the boys hadn't cared. After making such a fuss about baking the cake herself, she had no memory of making it. It was lopsided and crumbly, so she must have iced it while it was still warm. Who told her that—never ice a still-warm cake? Who knew. It was something she learned long ago. Mark wanted to feed a slice to Bandit, but Roland told him dogs didn't like cake. In Paris, Minnie had once watched a woman at an outdoor café slip food to the small dog in her lap. *I've seen it all,* she thought that day.

If she could only remember the baby's name, the way she remembered that woman feeding her dog.

Franklin, Gregory, Henry, Harold, Isaac, John, Matthew.

Earlier when Roland handed her a slice of cake, she lied

and said she was full. Impossible to swallow past the tightness radiating from her stomach up to her throat. This morning she had talked, swallowed food, washed dishes. This morning the objects in her kitchen had not confused her. From her spot by the sink, she watched Mark suddenly snatch the balloon out of Lucas's arms, and then the boys dropped to the ground, wrestling for control of the balloon. Roland stepped between them and took the balloon. He said something she couldn't hear, and the boys stood up. Lucas thrust out his hand and Mark did the same, and their grudging handshake quickly became silly, their small arms pumping wildly, and when Roland threw the balloon again, they raced after it, their anger forgotten.

A baby found outside an orphanage on Christmas Day. How convenient. That Christmas she'd been focused on her upcoming trip to Paris, focused on herself. What happened at the Home that Christmas made her even more anxious to flee her parents' house. When she returned that fall, though, and Ruthie suddenly had a baby? What was her excuse for not understanding then?

Years ago Minnie learned about a man leading a double life. Two different wives, six children total, one family in town and the other across the river in Jeffersontown. For months everyone wanted to talk about this man, and once at a dinner party Minnie declared, You'll never convince me the women didn't suspect his dishonesty; women instinctively know these things. To which another guest countered, Yes, but knowing something and taking action aren't the same, aren't they?

Nathaniel, Patrick, Phillip, Richard, Robert, Samuel, Sebastian.

A few months before she and Roland married, she told him she was thinking of keeping her maiden name. That's what Lucy Stone did, she said. Someone like Marie's husband, Felix, might have erupted in anger. Roland said it was her decision, and later, when she read that Lucy Stone was not allowed to vote in Massachusetts, after the legislature approved suffrage, because she hadn't taken her husband's last name, Minnie had changed hers, and she didn't regret it. Truly she didn't.

Timothy, Theodore, Thaddeus, Victor, Walter, William.
William. Yes.

She was willing to push, she saw, but rarely to a place of personal discomfort.

As if a spell had suddenly broken, she plunged her hands into the sink and washed the dishes, handling them as carefully as if they were a newborn baby.

Dear Board of Managers,

I saw your notice in the paper about the silver anniversary party. Years ago my wife stayed in your Home, and I thought you might want to know, as you are celebrating the accomplishments of former inmates, that she has done very well since her time at the Home for Friendless Women. She owns her own dress shop, Belle's Boutique, which is, I can proudly report, one of the most successful businesses in our Nashville neighborhood. She is a loving wife as well as a wonderful mother to our son, King. I am enclosing this small sum of money as a thank-you for helping her years ago.

All my best,
R. Marie Walzer

Portrait of a Woman

––––––––––

After bath time, a fight broke out between Mark and Lucas about who could sleep with the balloon.

"No one," Minnie said, "will sleep with the balloon. Balloons don't belong in the bed."

While she was hiding the balloon downstairs, the boys got into a different fight over possession of an imaginary Bandit-shaped balloon, and she told them if they didn't stop arguing, she would throw away both the imaginary and the real balloon.

"We're pretending," Mark said. "You can't be cross with us for using our *imagination*."

"You can sleep with the Bandit balloon," Lucas said magnanimously to his brother, and Mark made a big show of making room in his bed for the imaginary balloon, even pretending to tuck it under his quilt.

She read the boys their favorite book, about a group of friends who tour Europe in a hot-air balloon with their uncle Robert. Mark was asleep before she reached the second page of the story. Lucas, however, remained wide awake until the end.

"Our uncle Robert would never take us on a balloon ride," Lucas said.

"No," Minnie agreed, thinking about the uptight man who married Roland's sister, Sarah. "He's not the type to take children on a balloon tour of Europe."

"Maybe when we're older," Lucas said.

"Ever the optimist, you are," she said.

"Mark and I will always have the same birthday," Lucas said. "That's fine, because Mark is my favorite brother."

She smoothed his hair back from his forehead. "Silly goose. He's your only brother."

"If I had another brother, Mark would still be my favorite."

As an only child, she hadn't been prepared for the bond between the boys, how they often acted as one mind with four legs and four arms. As babies they slept in the same crib, facing each other. As toddlers they babbled away to each other in their own language. They'll never learn to speak properly if you allow them to speak nonsense to each other, her mother had said.

Mark had a clockwise whorl in his hair, Lucas a counterclockwise one. Once she was in the kitchen with Lucas, and Mark fell upstairs and scraped his knee on the bed, and before he even started crying, Lucas pointed at his own knee and cried out, It hurts! Impossible to imagine the one without the other.

How young the boys were, how old they thought they were. Someday they would smell like men—sweaty, busy, important men. Tonight, even after a bath, they smelled of chocolate cake and grass.

You won't break them. Babies are sturdier than they look, her mother said when she saw how gingerly Minnie held her newborn twins.

It was her heart that wasn't so sturdy. No one told her that happened when you became a mother. Likely she wouldn't have believed them anyway. She'd made a painting soon after she discovered she was pregnant in which she sought to capture herself from every angle: above, below, straight on, from behind, from the side, from the inside. A woman as she saw herself and as seen by the world. *Portrait of a Woman*, she titled it. She turned herself into a series of overlapping shapes, and in her reduction and subsequent transformation, she became more than a body, she became something powerful, something substantial.

When had she stopped seeing herself this way, as a force to be reckoned with?

Menstrual Derangements

Such a thin line between a high-spirited girl and a rebellious one, the line a result of chance, opportunity, timing. Money too. High-spirited girls succeed; rebellious girls fall. At fourteen Minnie felt faint at the presence of blood down there, and then, at age twenty, she was faint at its absence. All the things a person learns to accept and expect from the body. Dr. John Hooper's Female Pills for nervousness and headaches contained six pills, but it took only three to dislodge the obstruction when she returned from Paris.

Pill one—nothing.

Pill two—nothing.

Pill three—vomiting and cramps, the cramps a dizzying comfort since they were accompanied by a violent rush of blood.

Her life was on hold for those three days while she waited to see if the pills would work: she ate supper and went to church and brushed her hair before bed, and amazingly, no one could tell how weighted with meaning these mundane actions suddenly were. Was she a mother? She prayed with a vengeance during those three days. *Please, God. Please. Please. Please.*

She kept the remaining three pills as a reminder. A talisman. God only knew what was in them. Best not to know. The last time Roland saw the green bottle in their bathroom, he asked if the pills helped with headaches, and she said, Oh yes. Worth every penny.

The Impostors

So far they have claimed to be raising money to build a gymnasium for the Home for Newsboys and Waifs (a well-equipped attraction to keep the little urchins off the street), to purchase cradles for the Home for Friendless Women (these convert into a swinging crib, which can be operated with a foot pedal), and to buy special typewriters for the Kentucky Home for the Blind (the blind are frequently taken for imbeciles, yet nothing could be further from the truth—some of these girls can type as fast as you or me). Even though Sophia and Kate are tempted to keep all the money, they always mail half—a tithing—to Sister Frances at the Home of the Innocents. Sister Frances, who all these years has kept the yellow-and-white-striped-booties Sophia was wearing the day she was left in a basket outside the Home. My Christmas miracle, Sister Frances said. A few months later, Kate was brought to the Home in similar yellow-and-white-striped booties. My Saint Valentine's miracle, Sister Frances said, even though Kate arrived a few days after Valentine's Day.

"Old habits are hard to break," Kate says with a sigh.

When Sophia and Kate were young, they decided the yellow-and-white booties were evidence they were not abandoned orphans but long-lost princesses whose parents would someday arrive at the Home to claim them. No matter they looked nothing alike. They entertained themselves with stories about what was waiting for them in their castle: New clothes. New toys. All the candy they could possibly eat.

Books in every room, said Kate, who by age ten had read every book in the Home, including the Bible, cover to cover.

Sophia and Kate visit the Home every Sunday, and the children keep an eye out for their arrival, their faces pressed to the window. They know they can count on the young women to bring them something exciting: a new train set, a shiny ribbon, cinnamon candies. You'll spoil them rotten, Sister Frances always gently chides the young women.

Even though it's only September, Sophia has already bought a Christmas gift for the girls, a cunning little dollhouse with porches and a small front lawn and, in the library, a tiny imitation rug with an animal head. There's even a hat rack in the front hall, complete with miniature hats.

They have big plans for all the money they're saving. Sophia plans to travel, once Sister Frances is gone. She will take a boat across the ocean, eat foods with foreign-sounding names, and she will fall in love. Her future husband will find her clever and beautiful and will never feel sorry for her. God, she can't stand for people to feel sorry for her. Kate's plans involve medical school, which will also wait until Sister Frances is gone since she's under the impression Kate is studying to be a schoolteacher.

They joke about using the money to open their own home.

The Home for Motherless Women.

The Home for Long-Lost Princesses.

The Home for All Women.

"A place for everything
and everything in its place."

————————

Her parents were seated at the breakfast table when Minnie arrived the following morning. She'd hardly slept, flopping from her back to her side all night, until finally sunlight thrust its way through the bedroom window, and she could slip out of bed without arousing suspicion.

You're up early, Roland mumbled sleepily, and she said she needed to collect something from her mother before the party—how easily the lie slipped from her mouth—and he was asleep again by the time she was dressed and quietly closing the door behind her.

Her mother pointed at the newspaper on the table. "Whatever happened to that man?" She addressed the question to no one in particular, looking from Minnie to her husband. "The one who went to the theater that day?" Even with her hair combed and her clothes straight, a sense of dishevelment clung to her. It was her eyes that betrayed her, alighting in confusion on the people near her. They were similar to the eyes Minnie had given her mother years ago in the painting, too wide and blank.

"You're thinking of John Wilkes Booth," Minnie's father said. "He died not long after shooting President Lincoln."

"Yes." She nodded vigorously. McKinley's assassination had prompted her to continually revisit Lincoln's death. "Booth, yes. That was a sad day." She rubbed the surface of the paper and studied the ink on her fingers.

"Mrs. Davidson, no," Svetlana said, appearing out of nowhere, as Minnie's mother went to put her ink-stained fingers in her mouth. "Use your handkerchief."

"My *what*?"

Svetlana handed her one and mimed wiping her fingers on it, and Mrs. Davidson obediently followed.

"I made that for you when I was learning to embroider," Minnie said.

"And who are you?"

"I'm your daughter, Minnie."

"Are you Minnie too?" she asked Svetlana, who shook her head.

"When I struggled with embroidery," Minnie said, "you would tell me, 'Whatsover thy hand findeth to do, do it with thy might; for there is no work, nor device, nor knowledge, nor wisdom, in the grave, whither thou goest.'" Nothing held its original shape anymore, not even Ecclesiastes. "You used to say Ecclesiastes asked the most of us, but it also gave us the gift of accepting God's will."

"Who said that?" Minnie's mother asked.

"You did," Minnie's father said. "You used to say all sorts of wise things, Eliza."

Once during a game of hide-and-seek with her cousins, Minnie hid in her parents' bed. She pulled the comforter over her head and lay there, still and silent. The sheets smelled different in their bed, deep and dark, not the smell of her own bed at all. She thought of how her mother looked at her father when he was delivering a sermon, the noises she heard from their bedroom most nights. What a shock she'd had, years later, when she recognized that same smell, those same sounds, in her own marriage bed.

"Isn't that something," her mother said. Her laugh was free and easy, so like the boys' laughter as they played with their cucumber balloon. Minnie wondered if this was what her mother had been like as a little girl. What she knew of her mother's childhood would not fill half a page. Raised by an aunt and uncle, and then sent to a girls' home, and then marriage and motherhood. Everything else was a mystery. You mustn't pry, her father told her. She doesn't like to revisit the past.

Minnie didn't want to revisit the past either, and yet she was hurtling toward it, and there was no stopping the inevitable collision.

"What brings you by so early, Min?" her father asked.

"The matron of the Home is reorganizing the library ahead of the silver anniversary party, and she can't find the first record books. I thought I might look around the house, see if Mother kept them here for some reason." *For some reason.* She studied her father's face to watch his reaction, but his face didn't change.

"That doesn't sound like her, to be honest." He slathered butter onto his toast, and even though she hadn't eaten since lunchtime yesterday, she realized she wasn't hungry. Maybe she would never eat again. Maybe she would stay in her bed for a week, like Ruthie did after her final miscarriage, and then it would be someone else's job to find the books and attend the party and right the wrongs of the world. She remembered that when Ruthie finally left her bed, she walked like a much older woman.

"'A place for everything and everything in its place,'" her father said, quoting one his wife's favorite sayings. "Although this senile dementia was likely affecting her long before we noticed, she managed to hide it from us. Such a smart woman."

"Stubborn too," Minnie said.

"Now, Minnie—"

"I know, I know," she said. "Be patient with her." How many times had her father said that to both her and her mother? Patience hadn't been in either of their natures.

"Mother, do you remember where the books from the Home are? The ones from the first two years it was open, 1877 and 1878?"

Her mother tapped the paper, now upside down in front of her. "Whatever happened to that man?"

∞

After her parents and Svetlana left for a walk—Svetlana says daily exercise is good for the body and mind, Mr. Davidson said, patting his soft stomach—Minnie started in on the bookshelves in her father's study. The room where her father retreated to write his sermons had been off-limits to her as a child. Even now she felt like a trespasser, although if the lack of dust was any indication, this room was regularly cleaned by Svetlana. The books in here were organized by color, her father's preferred method. She knew she was not going to find the book carefully arranged on the shelf behind her father's desk, but she felt the need to be thorough. Methodical. Conscientious. She pulled out each one, starting with the green books on the left and working her way over to the red ones.

How did you know you wouldn't be happy unless you gave the money away? she once asked Roland, and he thought a long moment before answering. She used to think he was weighing his words carefully, but no, that was just his way. It was the right thing to do, he said. You recognize the truth by its sound.

She moved from room to room, opening drawers and cabinets. Not in the study, not in the living room. She had a moment of euphoria when she found a weathered book wedged behind the silver urn in the dining room sideboard, but it turned out to be an old recipe book from her grandmother. Her mother used to complain that her mother-in-law's cooking always featured lard—lard in gingerbread, lard in green beans, lard in custard pies. Minnie had never minded Granny's cooking.

"Still at it?" her father asked when they returned. "It's getting cold out there. If I didn't know better, I'd say it might snow tonight. Wouldn't that be something, Eliza, snow in September?"

Her mother looked at Minnie, kneeling on the floor by the sideboard. "What's that girl doing down there?"

"She's looking for some old books."

"I know her," Mrs. Davidson said. "We were at the girls' home together." She lowered her voice. "An uppity girl, we didn't get along."

After her parents left the room, Minnie noticed Svetlana had stayed behind. The woman suddenly kneeled beside her, and Minnie looked over in surprise; Svetlana's face was so close she could smell her violet perfume. "I think I know where your missing books are," she whispered.

☙❧

The attic stank of mothballs and the chloride of lime solution her mother used to clean the floors. While Svetlana rummaged among boxes in the corner, Minnie opened one of the windows and breathed in the cold outside air. God, she despised the smell of mothballs. As punishment for talking back, Minnie was once made to clean the attic; she'd purposely neglected to add fresh mothballs to her trunks, and the following year she'd found a dead moth sitting atop her favorite gown and best cape. A job half done is as good as none, her mother said unsympathetically about the ruined garments.

"I found this box when I was cleaning out my room," Svetlana said. "Your room," she corrected. She handed Minnie the box. "I moved it up here."

"Thank you," Minnie said.

"I wasn't trying to hide it."

"You did fine," Minnie said. She waited until Svetlana was gone before opening the box.

At the top was her old diary, a gift from her father when she turned seventeen. He wanted her to record her favorite Bible verses, but she'd used the pages to transcribe dinner party menus and potential beaus. After she lost it, she told her mother it was a sign she shouldn't marry. She'd wanted to upset her mother and she'd succeeded. The cover was soft, no longer the deep purple she remembered. She continued to dig through the box, nearly slicing open her hand on a pair of rusty shears. An empty liquor bottle unpleasantly grimy to the touch. Why on earth had her mother saved this odd menagerie? At the bottom, she found it; she immediately recognized the faded red leather book with its cracked cover. It was the same book that she remembered seeing on her mother's desk or tucked under her arm when she left for Board meetings. A place for everything and everything in its place. The book sighed in defeat when Minnie opened it. Inside was her mother's tidy, tiny handwriting. You know the truth by its sound.

The entry she was looking for was between an announcement about an upcoming lecture at the Home on the curiosities of ancient Egyptian art and a discussion about the matron's salary (*Some of the ladies feel the amount disproportionate to our means*).

January 3, 1878: *Two women have been sent to City Hospital, one to Insane Asylum, one expelled.*

There was only the one asylum in town, whose official name was the Central Kentucky Asylum for the Insane, although most called it Lakeland Asylum or even just Lakeland. Every few years the hospital managed to make headlines, most recently for dumping raw sewage into Goose Creek. As Minnie dimly recalled, the commissioners had been indicted on charges of infecting the water supply.

A few years ago, Roland's firm put in a bid to build the new addition at Lakeland, and after his team toured the facility, he told Minnie that he hoped they didn't get the job because he never wanted to return to Lakeland. The smell, he said. No matter how many times Minnie washed the shirt he wore that day, he claimed he could still detect it. She didn't argue with him because she knew what it was for your clothes to carry a memory. She hadn't been near the girl when she cut herself, and she never found a single drop on her clothes, but she'd also felt her dress was indelibly tainted. Poisoned by the blood of another.

The girl with the braids and the ribbon around her throat had gone to bed a mother to twins, and the next morning she had been sent away for refusing to give up one of her children. She had been hauled away to a place that Roland, years later, would say smelled worse than death: the smell of those barely living, the body reluctantly carrying on as the mind wandered far, far away. And she had been sent there by Minnie's mother.

And what about the baby girl? What had happened to her?

If the twins' mother were here before her, Minnie would say, *I know where your son is.* She would say, *His mother loves him very much, and I'm so sorry for what my mother did.*

How little she'd allowed herself to think about that Christmas Eve. It was easy, surprisingly so, to take a memory and seal it away, not unlike a ball gown in a trunk. If you really practiced, you could forget a little more each year until what remained didn't seem real or trustworthy. She'd invited moths inside the memory, encouraged them to eat to their hearts' content, and now that she was ready to open the trunk, expose what was left to the light, it was too late, all that remained were flimsy scraps.

Before leaving for Paris, she'd passively accepted her mother's hug, her own arms limp at her sides. And then she was on a ship carrying her far away from the Home. Away from the blood and the babies. Away from her mother. In Paris she tried to focus on the light, rather than the darkness back home.

"'Ask, and it shall be given you; seek, and ye shall find,'" her father said cheerfully when he spied the box in her arms.

The people Minnie passed on the street looked up at the sky in wonder, as if they had never heard of the idea of snow, much less seen it.

"Life is but a Dream"

———————

She never learned to swim. People didn't do that sort of thing when she was a child, not where she grew up at least. But she has a feeling she would have liked floating in the water, she has a feeling she would have been good at it, that her arms and her legs would move effortlessly, instinctively. *Row, row, row your boat.* She found pills in the girl's room, hidden inside a box of old rags, and she didn't say a word. Not one word. And now the words are there and gone, *gently down the stream.* How far she has floated from everyone—all those girls from the orphans' home are waving from the shore. *Merrily, merrily, merrily, merrily.* If they're surprised at how good she is at floating away, at leaving them behind so she might become Mrs. Eliza Davidson, they keep it to themselves. They don't say a word to her now. Not one word. Whatever happened to that man? No one will tell her, no one knows.

"Give her time."

"Cora's the one who came up with our new advertising campaign. 'Give her time'! You've seen it, I'm sure. With the child carrying a grandfather clock?" Matthew Pyle pretended to stagger under the weight of an enormous clock, and Minnie laughed politely. Even though Matthew was the heir to a minor fortune, he often dressed quite strangely, with too-short pants or mismatched socks. He does all that to make a point, Roland once said, who knew a thing or two about such matters. For tonight's party, Matthew was wearing his suspenders on the outside of his clothing, which even Minnie found startling. But the man generously donated to the Home every year, so Minnie supposed he could arrive wearing a dress and corset and no one would say a word.

"'Give her time, and almost every soap-using woman will come around to the use of Pearline,'" Cora Pyle recited. "'There's ease, economy, quickness, health, and safety in Pearline washing and cleaning.' I told Matthew that a product that claims to make a woman's life easy and is good for her health will practically sell itself." Cora looked like she would be right at home in a Rubens painting, with her blond hair and fleshy arms. Unlike her husband's clothing, her silver-and-gold dress was clearly expensive and wildly impractical for the sudden cold weather, the folds of silk carefully encasing her curves.

Behind the Pyles, Minnie could see Victoria playing the

harp. Even with her substantial bump, her arms moved gracefully over the strings, her eyes closed in concentration. Minnie's
mother had forced piano lessons on her, and worse than the
mind-numbing scales was the humiliation of being trotted out
like a show pony to play for visitors. She would pound ungrace-
fully on the piano, as if to prove that artistic talent could be
cultivated, but passion couldn't be faked. Minnie wondered
where Victoria had learned to play; she'd never thought to ask.
A small crowd had gathered to listen, and Minnie was happy
that, for tonight at least, Victoria was allowed to forget where
she was and be transported somewhere else through the beauty
of her playing.

"The Home is so appreciative of the soap you send every
year," Minnie said to the Pyles.

"It's important to give back," Cora said. "Matthew and I
both believe that."

Such a round, youthful face on her. Minnie remembered
that she had been practically a child herself when she was in
the Home. She had a sudden memory of sitting beside her
on the old sofa and how tightly Cora had gripped her hand as
the short-haired girl lay on the floor, bleeding.

"This house is so much grander than the old one. One of
the girls gave us a tour, and I couldn't believe the size of the
bedrooms. Easily twice as big as the one I had."

"Were you happy at the old Home?" Minnie didn't dare ask
what she really wanted to know.

"Well," Cora said in surprise, "is anyone happy during
pregnancy?"

"No," Minnie said, and Matthew chuckled uncomfortably.

"It's a shame our daughter, Grace, couldn't join us. She's
busy planning her wedding these days." Cora practically radi-
ated pride. "A big society wedding. We expect a lengthy write-
up in the newspaper."

"Grace could have had her pick of anyone in the state, you

know," Matthew said. "Clever too. In fact she came up with the 'Doing stunts' campaign: 'You can stand on your head, for instance. Almost everyone could do it, if it were necessary or desirable. But standing on the feet is more natural and more sensible—and easier. So with soap and Pearline.'"

"I've seen that one," Minnie said. "My boys always try to imitate it."

"It's a family business, you know," he said, pleased.

"Speaking of businesses, I was speaking with one of the girls earlier, and she told me she works at a bakery. That sounds divine compared to working for Mrs. Kesselman." Cora lowered her voice. "Once after I cleaned her kitchen, she suggested I walk around with a damp cloth to catch any dust before it fell."

"Unbelievable," Minnie said. "Also, entirely believable."

"I should be thankful to Mrs. Kesselman, then," Matthew said. "If she hadn't fired you, you might not have applied to work for the Pearline company."

"I was a good stenographer," Cora said. "Better than I was at sewing, that's for sure. I feel sorry for anyone who had their curtains mended by me. My stitches were never as neat and tidy as the other girls'."

"Do you stay in touch with the other girls?" Minnie asked. She was breathless at her own brazenness.

"You still correspond regularly with Sarah," Matthew said to his wife, "and Margaret."

"Do you remember Maggie?" Cora asked Minnie. "She has that . . ." She gestured vaguely at her cheek. "Anyway, she married a Pyle boy too. Matthew's cousin David. They live across the river, in Indiana."

"He's an eccentric fellow," Mr. Pyle said, giving his suspenders a little snap, "but nice enough."

"They had another child recently. A complete surprise. Maggie thought she was dying at first," Cora said.

"Anna Matilda Pyle," Mr. Pyle said. "But they call her Maddy. Why you give a child one name and then call them by another is beyond me." Across the room Minnie saw Mrs. Kesselman blanch when Matthew punctuated this last statement with another loud snap of his suspenders.

"She's a terribly anxious mother," Cora said. "I tried to convince her to attend tonight, but Maggie was worried Maddy might catch a chill. I told her the new Home isn't nearly as drafty as the old Home."

"Her fear of drafts is unrivaled," Matthew said. At a look from his wife, his face softened. "But understandable, I suppose."

"She lost her eldest daughter to pneumonia a few years ago," Cora said.

"I'm so sorry," Minnie said. "I didn't know." There was so much she didn't know.

Minnie wanted to ask Cora if the twins' mother had been a good sewer or a worrier. She wanted to ask Cora for her name and if she knew how long she'd been in the asylum and what had happened to her daughter. She wanted Cora to tell her everything she knew even though she didn't know what she would do with the information.

Instead she told the Pyles they should be sure to try some of the baked goods from the bakery and hugged them both before moving easily through the crowd, greeting guests and smiling as if there really was a reason to celebrate the Home on this snowy evening.

☙❧

"I noticed someone put a basket by the front door," Mrs. Kesselman said to Minnie, "for donations." She bit into a white cookie, and powdered sugar promptly dusted the front of her gray dress. "The bakery girls call these snowball cookies. Fitting name for a dessert tonight, isn't it? I'm glad to see this weather has not kept people at home—we've had a larger crowd than expected." She brushed at the sugar on her dress. "Still, I asked Edward to keep an eye on the money basket. A man standing guard is a powerful deterrent to thievery."

Minnie looked over and spotted Ruthie's son in the hallway. The last time she saw him had been just a few weeks ago, when he tried to teach her and Ruthie how to ride a bicycle. Afterward she told Ruthie she hoped that Mark and Lucas grew up to be as kind and patient as Edward. She watched as he yawned and rocked back on his heels, casting a longing glance at the grandfather clock. It was clear he did not want to spend his night guarding a money basket at a silver anniversary party, yet he was there because his mother had asked for his help and he was a good boy.

A good man, Minnie corrected herself.

"He goes by Eddie now," she said.

Mrs. Kesselman laughed. "I can ask people to call me the queen of the Nile. That doesn't mean it's my name. His name is Edward, and that's what I'll call him."

"I believe his name is William." Minnie felt the same jolt of surprise she'd felt six years earlier, when her water broke during her daily walk by the river. What had been abstract that morning was suddenly, painfully real.

"William?" Mrs. Kesselman didn't look guilty so much as confused. Minnie suddenly realized that this had been a common practice, taking children from their mothers, sending away girls who disagreed with them. It had not happened once. "What are you going on about?"

"He had a twin and his mother named him William. Before my mother gave him to Ruthie, his name was William."

"Your mother found Edward outside the Home of the Innocents, and she brought him to Ruthie, who had been trying, and failing, to have her own children for years."

"I found the old books."

This time Mrs. Kesselman didn't look confused. She didn't look guilty either. Minnie felt a surge of anger, so pure it revealed itself in the sudden tightness across her shoulders and back.

"You should think carefully about who would be hurt the most by your discovery of these books. Because it's not you."

"Don't lecture me as if I were one of your wayward girls improperly washing a dish. Because that is all I have been thinking about. As a mother. As someone on this Board. As one of Ruthie's oldest friends."

Mrs. Kesselman sighed, set down her plate on the table. Minnie dimly noticed that the punch was dangerously low, as were the tarts. Ruthie's cookies were mostly untouched. Something was terribly wrong with her, she thought, that she could still notice these things.

"We cannot be charitable to our equals, which means we are forced to make decisions that, from the outside at least, appear difficult and messy. Look around you, Minnie," Mrs. Kesselman said, suddenly serious. "Look at all these women who have returned to celebrate the Home. They are not here to eat snowball cookies or hear that girl play the harp. These women went from friendless, wayward girls to decent Christians. When they were scared and alone, we gave them a place to stay. We gave them a new life. They are here tonight to give thanks and give back. Because when they had nowhere else to go, there was the Home."

"What about the Mabel Smiths of the world we turned away? What about the women whose children were taken from them? What kind of life did they receive?"

"Again with Mabel Smith! You're permitting one rejected inmate to overshadow all the good we've done. Cora Pyle was fourteen years old when she showed up here, and now she's the heiress to a fortune. That woman over there came here from Madame Sewell's, or maybe it was Madame Mollie's, I can't remember, and now she lives in Florida with her husband and their five children. That girl over there is married to a dentist in New York City. We found husbands for these women, we helped them secure jobs, we gave them a new chance at life. When everyone else gave up on them, we believed they were capable of repentance."

"I'm starting to believe that we are the ones who should be seeking repentance." She'd nearly forgotten how anger traveled in her body, migrating from her neck and shoulders down to her hands and feet, until her whole body thrummed with it. "For the things we have done and the things we have failed to do."

"We provided a Christian home for sinners."

"At a cost!" Minnie said, her voice rising. A few guests turned and looked over at them. "Our help came at a great cost."

"All help comes at a great cost, Minnie." Mrs. Kesselman briskly wiped her hands on a napkin. "I'll ask one of the girls to bring out more punch and tarts."

☙❧

The cold air was welcome after the warmth inside, and Minnie breathed deeply as her eyes adjusted to the darkness. She walked away from the house before turning around to study it. How cheerful the Home looked right now, with the snow falling, the lamps casting a cozy light on the guests as they moved from room to room, talking, eating, drinking. She'd been giving the girls in the Home art lessons for several months now. Eventually her plan was to have them paint the house with watercolors. In her mind's eye she pictured the women walking the perimeter of the house, sketchbooks and pencils in hand as she instructed them to take note of the parallel lines and horizontals to help with their proportions. *A light touch with the pencils,* she'd remind them, since watercolors were so translucent. She'd started with watercolors herself, and even now, she liked how they forced her to slow down, to notice the play of light. With watercolors, it was easy to darken an object, but you had to be careful with shadows, for if you lost the light, you were in trouble.

Earlier in the evening, Elsa Mae had unwrapped the pig print and laughed in delight. Her laugh sounded the way it was written in children's books: *ha ha ha.* Look at that pig with the bib! she had said. Oh, Minnie, aren't you a dear.

How different the Home would look if she were a friendless girl who had exhausted all other options—a girl with no money to buy pills, a girl without relatives to take her in for nine months, a girl whose stomach grew and tightened a little every day. She imagined lifting her hand to knock on the dark green door, the weighty pause. Was this truly the only option? The knock, quick and decisive, before she could change her mind. The fear of being turned away, the fear of being admitted.

That summer after Paris, while she waited to see if the pills would work, she had imagined all manner of terrible scenarios. What if she were forced to marry an older parishioner from the church, someone chosen by her parents? Or sent to live with her father's dour sisters in Tennessee, where her condition could be hidden? She'd imagined her life forever altered, yet she never imagined herself as an inmate in the Home.

Across the street, just outside the glow of the gas lamp, stood a woman. Minnie watched her watching the Home, and after a moment, she crossed the street to stand beside her. The woman's hair was wet with snow, as if she had been there awhile. Her lavender scarf was wrapped tightly around her neck.

"I didn't think I would come," the woman said. Minnie took

in her graying hair, her calm manner. "But I was too curious to stay away when I received the invitation for the silver anniversary party. I even imagined giving a speech, and yet here I stand, not quite able to go inside."

"When did you stay at the Home?"

"I was at the old Home, when it first opened. I heard this new place has a chapel."

"It does." Minnie didn't add that it was named after her father.

"We were allowed out of the house once a week, for Sunday services. I could probably still recite Psalm 25, I read it so often while waiting for services to start."

Minnie remembered watching the women file in on Sundays, their stomachs preceding them as they slid, one by one, into their pew at the back of the church. Why do they sit at the back? she once asked her mother.

Because they have sinned, her mother had said.

"You weren't an inmate here," the woman said. She had a plain, proud face. "Current or former Board member?"

"Current. I'm the treasurer."

"Is the Home still in financial trouble?"

"It's better now. The girls work at a bakery over on Fourth Street. Broadway Bakery. It's very popular in the neighborhood. They run it themselves." She spoke quickly, too quickly. She had a sudden fear the woman would vanish, and she didn't want that, not yet. "It brings in more money than sewing."

"I never minded all the sewing. I found it comforting after a long day. Some nights I still dream about the girls in the Home, and in my dreams we are always sewing curtains. I was expelled from the Home"—she said *expelled* with a practiced flatness—"on Christmas Day."

Two women have been sent to City Hospital, one to Insane Asylum, one expelled.

The woman looked at her, and something in her expression made Minnie suddenly fearful the woman knew her to be Mrs. Eliza Davidson's daughter.

"Do you have children?" the woman asked.

"Two boys. You?"

"I had a daughter. She's twenty-three now."

"What's her name?"

"I named her Kate, after my friend. I don't know what they called her at the Home of the Innocents. At the hospital they said I shouldn't hold her, that it would make things harder, but I did. It was the right thing to do. She had the tiniest ears, like shells."

"I'm sorry." Minnie was sorry she'd spoken at all, the words too hollow, uttered decades too late.

"It was my decision," the woman said. "Now I'm a wife and a nurse, and I found I needed to see if this place really existed or if I somehow imagined it all."

They stood there in the cold, both staring straight ahead at the Home, as if waiting for a train or a carriage to take them somewhere else.

"They sent my friend Kate to the asylum the same day I was expelled. I tried to find her, after I gave birth. I even visited the asylum, years ago, but they said there was no one named Kate staying there."

Kate, Minnie thought. *Her name was Kate.*

"We don't do that now," she said helplessly, "send women to the asylum."

"Sometimes I can almost convince myself Kate was released and reunited with her children. She was a worrier. An optimist too. She always found a way to see the goodness in others, even when they failed her." Her voice made clear that she believed herself to be one of those who had failed Kate. "I hope that whoever ended up with her children baptized them. That mattered to her. It mattered to her a great deal."

Minnie told her, without saying a word, that Kate's son was loved and cherished. Baptized too. She had been there that day, standing beside an exhausted and happy Ruthie. For Edward's baptism, she bought him a sterling silver rattle, and when she had her own children, years later, she'd laughingly apologized to Ruthie for buying such an impractical, frivolous gift.

"I didn't catch your name." It seemed important she know this much at least.

"My name is Ruth." She cocked her head to the side, in a way that might have seemed flirtatious on someone younger. "You don't remember me, do you, Minnie?" The woman turned back to the house. "I recognized you straightaway. I was quite envious of you, when I lived here. I thought you had so many freedoms."

There was a time Minnie would have laughed at this. Free? Her? Yet the way Ruth's words landed, uncomfortably heavy in her stomach, she knew they weren't untrue.

"You were there that night. That Christmas Eve."

Minnie did remember her now. How calmly Ruth had stepped forward to offer her unborn baby. I don't want this child, she had said. Months later, those same words would run through Minnie's head, when she returned from Paris.

"I used to think your mother and Mrs. Kesselman enjoyed being cruel. That the cruelty was the point."

"Do you still think that?"

"No," Ruth said. "Now I think they simply treated us the way the world treated them."

The front door opened and a woman stepped onto the porch. For an impossible moment, Minnie thought she was seeing the blond girl, the same glow of the lights behind her. As if the past, now unburied, would insist on repeating itself moment by moment. Minnie blinked, and the figure became Ruthie.

"I always wondered why they called it a home," Ruth said. "I remember thinking, on those nights we sewed curtains, that it was a passing-through place, a stop on my way somewhere else. But it was never my home. It was never really a Home for Friendless Women."

"Minnie?" Ruthie stepped off the porch and stood across the street from them. "Mrs. Kesselman sent me out to find you. She wants you to give your speech soon."

Her father had said, in that long-ago sermon about the Home, Let us not love in word or talk but in deed and in truth. Lucy Stone had said, All we need is to continue to speak the truth fearlessly. Roland had said, You know the truth by its sound. She was so accustomed to hearing the thoughts of others in her head, she'd lost the ability to hear her own. What if speaking the truth hurt someone you loved? Minnie closed her eyes, felt the September snow gently kiss her cheeks.

It would be easy to go inside and give the speech she had prepared, to speak of all the good the Home had accomplished over the years, and the night would end with a basket full of generous donations. All help comes at a cost. When she was younger, she had thought the world would change in great and impossible ways; when it didn't, she had allowed herself to change instead, in small and then not-so-small ways.

"Minnie?" Ruthie called again. "Are you coming back inside?"

She'd always thought of anger as unhelpful, an emotion best ignored and suppressed. But what if anger, when channeled into something bigger than yourself, became a hopeful, guiding force? *I didn't make Bathsheba look bilious,* she should have told her art teacher in Paris. *I made her look angry, the way I feel every time I look at this painting.*

She turned to Ruth. "I know what happened to your friend's son." Her voice was hoarse. May God, but mostly Ruthie, forgive her someday. "I'd like to help you find out what happened to Kate. To her daughter."

Ruth looked at her, eyebrows lifted in surprise. Minnie hoped it was surprise and not incredulity. She'd forgotten what it was like to truly surprise someone. To surprise yourself.

Ruth studied her with an intensity that would have made Minnie blush, had the gaze been from a man. "Yes," she said finally. "I'd like to learn the truth as well."

Minnie nodded, and the two women crossed the street together as the snow fell carelessly around them.

THE NASHVILLE BANNER

DECEMBER 21, 1889

The residence of Dr. William Munro, on W. Mary Street, was destroyed by fire yesterday around three o'clock in the afternoon. The house occupied by the doctor, his wife, and three children was a large three-story frame and was completely enveloped by flames. Dr. Munro was the only occupant in the house at the time of the fire and perished. In the death of Dr. William Munro, the city lost one of its finest physicians. In his thirty years of practice, he never refused a call, no matter the circumstances. The origin of the fire is unknown, but two women who recently moved in next door to the doctor noted that he often enjoyed smoking cigars. "It's a nasty habit," said his neighbor Belle Queeney. "I've been saying for a while it would only lead to trouble for the good doctor."

Acknowledgments

I would never have learned about the real-life Home if not for my 2017 internship at the Filson Historical Society. Special thanks to Simona Bertacco for encouraging me to apply for the internship and to Filson curator Jim Holmberg for offhandedly mentioning the Home one day and inadvertently sending me on this journey.

Big thanks to Root Literary, including Holly Root and Melanie Figueroa, who remained cheerful and persistent advocates for this book even after the rejections started rolling in. Thank you to the Vintage team, especially Ellie Pritchett, who read multiple drafts with a clear, thoughtful eye and helped me locate the heart of the story (especially in Belle's and Minnie's sections), and Nancy Tan, who is an astonishingly good copyeditor—any mistakes in this book are mine and mine alone.

Several people read early drafts and offered valuable feedback, including Pamela Beattie, Deborah Lutz, Karen Mann, Kiki Petrosino, Susan Ryan, and Nancy Theriot. Emily Denton read a very early draft of the book and helped me select an author photo that didn't scream "wan and moody." Julia Forman offered helpful, and hilarious, feedback on this book, as she does on all my work. It's possible I write books just so she can read them. Xoxo, Julia. David Dominé didn't read an early draft but said "I told you so" when he heard it would be published—thanks, Big D!

I'm grateful for my family, including my mom, who called me a writer long before I called myself one, and my dad, who did not live to see this book's publication but who I know would have celebrated it. Thanks to Brooks and Kimmy, very supportive siblings who are definitely not characters in this book. Special thanks to my sister-in-law Cynthia, who read every section of this book within hours (!) of receiving it.

Aaron Morris encouraged me, years ago, to take myself seriously as a writer and pursue my MFA, and I'm thankful for his support.

I learned so much about writing, and myself, from my time at the Naslund-Mann Graduate School of Writing. Thank you to Kathleen Driskell and all my workshop leaders, mentors, and fellow students.

I feel compelled to write about motherhood because of my kids—being their mom is a joyful privilege.

And finally, thanks to Jason Hill, who lived with these characters and this Home alongside me while I wrote this book. Thank you for reading every single draft and for encouraging me to tell this story the way I wanted to. Everything good in this book, and in my life, is yours.